EARLY PRAISE FOR
ALL HER LOVED ONES, ENCODED

Keefe has delivered a haunting depiction of a near
future America, where living virtually is both a debili-
tating strain on a failing society and the new American
dream. At its root, though, this novel is all heart, the
story of one family's struggle to survive in an ever-
changing and collapsing world.

— WILLY VLAUTIN, AUTHOR OF *THE
NIGHT ALWAYS COMES*

In *All Her Loved Ones, Encoded*, Michael Keefe gives
us a beautifully interwoven story connecting one
woman's quest to save her family with the struggles of
the generations that came before her. A prescient,
captivating novel.

— ETHAN CHATAGNIER, AUTHOR
OF *SINGER DISTANCE*

Equally brutal and tender, Michael Keefe's *All Her
Loved Ones, Encoded* is smart, unflinching, and full of
grace.

— LARA MESSERSMITH-GLAVIN,
AUTHOR OF *SPIRIT THINGS*

ALL HER LOVED ONES, ENCODED

MICHAEL KEEFE

RUNNING WILD

For Liz, my champion

CHAPTER ONE

FEBRUARY, 2057

K iana leans the shovel against the hard wall of earth. She rubs her forearms, the tense muscles vibrating beneath her skin. The vegetable garden spreads out before her, its yield shrinking every year. Next to that is the clutch of thorny vines where her beloved strawberries once grew. Javi, her dying husband, used to pick them for her. Now Kiana is digging his grave.

Her throat tightens, breath shaking in her chest. But she can't lose herself to grieving yet. She scoops another shovel-full of dirt onto the mound above. And another, and another. It's waist-deep now, the grave. Deep enough, probably. She can't stand to think about Javi as a body, as a thing whose dimensions must be accounted for.

Low angles of sunlight filter through the brown-gray smog. The evening sky casts an eerie glow on the pale yellow house that she and Javi rent. Kiana has lived on this land—the former Seabreeze Organic Farm—for the past fifteen years, since she first moved to Costa Perdida to work at the desalination plant. She's watched the desert move in quickly from the east. Sage-

1

brush and cactus: that's mostly what grows on the old farm these days. The pond, where she used to sit and read, is now a neon-green puddle of toxic algal bloom. Most of the mammals in the area have either fled or gone extinct.

A rare winter chill bites at Kiana's skin. She squints into the west, where the sun dips behind the oak tree in front of their house. A memory jabs her between the ribs. Their daughter, Anza, playing in that tree with a couple of other kids from the area, the three of them laughing bright and loud. Kiana watched them from the kitchen window, while scooping baked pasta into bowls. A moment later, she called in Anza for dinner, and the other kids scampered off. That's it. That shard of memory, over the last three years, remains stuck inside her. One of the last normal moments. A week later, spectral fever escaped the quarantines in Southeast Asia and swept like a sandstorm across California, the Americas, the world. Half a generation of children, wiped out in less than a year.

Including Anza.

Kiana shoves the memory back down, into a dark corner of her heart. Another thought she can't bear right now.

She grips the edge of the grave, the dirt cool beneath her fingertips, and heaves herself up, aboveground. She finds herself lying at eye level with a small brown lizard. It watches her skeptically for a moment then darts away. As Kiana stands and dusts off her jeans, she remembers a similar encounter with a scorpion from a few years back. While rock climbing in a nearby arroyo, she came face-to-face with the sand-colored arachnid, sunning itself on a granite ledge. Its venomous tail curled, aimed between her eyes. She swung away, slipped, and nearly died from avoiding its sting.

Walking away from the grave, Kiana passes the solar panels and the gray water cisterns behind their house, where a generator softly rumbles. When she opens the kitchen door, César ambles over to greet her, wagging his golden tail. Kiana scratches the dog on the head, and he follows her down the hall, to the bedroom.

Javi lies flat beneath a thin blanket, a nasal cannula strapped to his head. Even after only an hour away from him, her husband looks frailer, more ashen. The transformation— the depletion—shocks Kiana every time. A fist to the heart.

She sits at Javi's bedside. The cannula is connected by a rubber tube to a ventilator—a boxy plastic machine perched atop a rolling stand. The ventilator hums its endless *om*, exhales its steady mechanical breaths. Kiana bought it used on the black market, from a weaselly guy who smacked his lips when he talked. The ventilator barely worked. Kiana had to repair it herself. Now it tirelessly pumps oxygen into Javi's cancer-ridden lungs, keeping his beautiful brain alive while his body wastes away.

The brain that she will soon upload to Level Up. If she is able.

When Kiana first created her avatar during freshman year of college, she never could have imagined that a video game would play such a crucial role in her life. Back then, Level Up was just another program that simulated real life, limited to flat-screen graphics and standard audio. Gradually, virtual sense technology improved to the point where taste, smell, and touch could be encoded and transmitted. The multi-sensory internet was born.

Kiana remembers her excitement when Level Up adopted the new tech. She quickly incorporated layers of sensual experience to the online worlds she'd created. The cold snap of a wet breeze on her cheek in 1960s Berlin, the murky green scent of a freshly cut lawn in 1990s Los Angeles. Even the simple pleasure of sipping a sweetly bitter cup of Starbucks coffee as it might have tasted in the year 2000 seemed like a revelation.

But a dark side of Level Up emerged when the developers added consciousness uploading technology. Kiana knew plenty of people who, when faced with the choice of living their increasingly shitty real lives or permanently inhabiting their avatars in Level Up or similar programs, opted to digitize their minds and then off themselves. As a rash of suicides swept the planet throughout the 2040s, the daily news tracked the dwindling populations, the dwindling tax bases, the dwindling GDPs. Remembering that time, Kiana can still feel the anxiety buzzing in her chest. The era ended in 2050, when the government passed a law compelling service providers to cap internet transfer speeds. As intended, the newly throttled internet proved too slow to run the immersive version of Level Up, much less facilitate consciousness uploads. People marched in the streets, they vandalized the offices of service providers, some killed themselves in protest. But the government wouldn't budge. Now, only those corporate entities deemed essential—hospitals, banks, the military, utility companies—have access to unrestricted internet speeds. It's outrageous to Kiana, the degree to which a handful of people in power control everyone else's lives. And their deaths.

From the bedside table, Kiana grabs her tablet and her electromagnetic skull cap. The cap's electrode net communicates with the areas of her brain responsible for motor control, vision, and sound. The other senses, too, but she doesn't bother turning those on anymore. Despite its dangers, Kiana longs for the old days, when she could completely lose herself in her virtual worlds.

With a sigh, she launches Level Up. A series of chimes tinkle in her head, and a welcome room appears to surround her. Kiana's personal menu of virtual realms is spread across the pastel-yellow wall before her: *Germany 1945*, *Los Angeles 1991*, and so on. These historical locales are like pins stuck into her family tree. When she visits these places, Kiana feels connected to family members that her reclusive mother never allowed her to know. Throughout Kiana's adult life, whenever the anxieties of real life have brought her low, these virtual realms are where she goes to feel grounded again.

At this moment, like so many moments, the person Kiana misses fiercely is her daughter. Her virtual hand reaches toward the button labeled *Home*. Then she hesitates.

Before Anza died—and while she remained lucid—Kiana and Javi uploaded Anza's mind to Level Up. At first, they attempted to do it themselves, but their own throttled internet connection was totally inadequate. Though she knew that intellectually, Kiana had to run a sample test, to see for herself. The interface app on her tablet kept warning of "potential packet loss during transfer process." Packet loss? Fuck. This wasn't some email attachment. This was the contents of her child's brain. So, they paid half their life savings to a pirate group up in Point Nada, who encoded and uploaded Anza's mind. Now, she lives as an avatar in Kiana and Javi's virtual home. But Anza's presence is limited to a holographic image, to a digital replication of her voice. It's not the same. *She's* not the same. Kiana aches to hold her actual daughter in her arms, to drink in her scent. Even just to virtually feel her daughter's embrace—that would soften the harshest edge of Kiana's ache. Still, to have retained a facsimile is better than to have lost her completely.

Now she needs to find a way for Javi to permanently inhabit his avatar, just as Anza does. But she has few options. The FBI arrested the pirate group that encoded Anza, and Kiana hasn't been able to track down another. While prowling online chat groups, she's read that unregulated terminals could be obtained in order to gain full internet speed. Of course, purchasing or using such a device is a criminal offense.

Kiana stares at their own speed-capped terminal, which sits atop a small wooden desk shoved into the corner of the bedroom. A little plastic box, it doesn't look particularly formidable, but apparently fiber optic terminals are extremely difficult to hack. Alex Hemley, Kiana's de facto aunt, is a coder. When Kiana emailed her to enquire about this possibility, Alex confirmed what Kiana had gleaned from the message boards: what was once vulnerable technology thirty years ago is now practically unbreachable. Also, Alex warned, using an unregulated terminal at a residential address would be noticed "pretty quickly" by the service provider, who could remotely cripple the terminal's throughput and then be obliged to report the incident to the police.

Those are risks Kiana is willing to take. Tonight, she's scheduled to meet with a black-market vendor and purchase an unregulated terminal.

The needle-pricks of panic are poking at Kiana's chest. Her own damn brain, it won't stop worrying. She needs a distraction. On her tablet, she clicks *San Francisco 2008*.

Seconds later, her avatar is standing outside a virtual City Hall, a hazy blue sky above, the pulse of traffic at her back. She watches as two newlywed men in tailored suits emerge from the building's elaborate, gold-gilt doors. One of the men is Kiana's favorite great-grandfather, Frank Olsen. The other is Jonathan Perry. At 70, Frank's thin hair is completely white, but he's retained the athletic build evident in photos from his Air Force days. Seven years younger, Jonathan is slender and not yet entirely gray. The two had been life partners since 1983. That's when Frank came out to his then-wife, Ilse, prompting their divorce. Frank and Jonathan got hitched the week after same sex marriage became legal in California. How typical, Kiana thinks, for the justice system to lag so far behind morality.

Currently, this scene in her Level Up realm ends with Frank and Jonathan reaching the bottom step of City Hall. The other day, Kiana discovered a video clip online that a wedding guest must have taken. She switches to her web browser, loads the video, clicks play. As she watches, the smiling couple are ushered into the back of a town car. Two seconds after the car pull away from the curb, the video stops. She downloads the file to her tablet. Later, when she has more time, she'll integrate the images into Level Up and tinker with some world-building. Kiana thrives in the act of remaking the past, especially when the present and the future are so often hard to bear.

Javi's fingertips touch Kiana's arm, and she suspends the app.

Her husband's eyes blink halfway open, fall shut, stretch open again. His sleepy gaze finds hers, and the corners of his mouth rise into a faint smile.

Kiana squeezes his hand, then worries she's squeezing too hard. Until six months ago, such a thought never would have occurred to her.

"Hi, baby," she whispers, as if the force of her normal speaking voice might squeeze the life from his lungs.

Javi raises his thick eyebrows, forming the arches of question marks.

Kiana nods. "I'm meeting with the seller in about an hour." Another black market vendor, someone calling herself Nadine. She'll be wearing a red hoodie, according to her last email. They're to meet in the parking lot next to the pier, just south of town, near the desal plant. "A genuine unregulated terminal. Government approved and fully tested."

Javi half-smiles again. Then he tilts his head toward Kiana's tablet. "Can we?" he whispers. He wants to visit with Anza.

Kiana walks around the bed and climbs in alongside Javi. She eases her husband's cap over his head and powers it up.

Then she clicks open their joint profile and, this time, touches *Home*.

Kiana finds herself sitting beside Javi on their living room couch—a nice new couch that, unlike their real couch, isn't cloaked by a wool blanket to cover the gashes and stains in the fabric. In Level Up, the appliances never break, a garden full of vegetables grows outside, and the weather is perpetually mild. There are no scorpions, no rattlesnakes. Daily life is gentle and clean. Kiana's avatar wears a floral skirt and peach tank top, instead of dirty jeans, an old tee-shirt, and rugged sneakers. Otherwise, she and her virtual self are twins: petite frame, lean build, chin-length brown hair streaked with purple, hazel eyes, and the lightly golden skin tone that comes from her scrambled heritage of German, Native Hawaiian, Swedish, Japanese, Ukrainian, Scotch-Irish, Cajun. Virtual Kiana is reading a science magazine—a replica of an actual print magazine, from back when paper production was still legal.

Virtual Javier is watching a soccer match on TV. His avatar is a perfect replica of how he used to look: stocky and strong, his skin a vibrant brown, his black hair rumpled, his goatee neatly trimmed, his smile full of life. A wonderful illusion. If only an illusion could hold her in the night.

With a thought command, Kiana inhabits her avatar.

She sets the magazine on the coffee table and turns her attention to Anza, who sits cross-legged on the rug, bent over a sketchbook. Using a pink crayon, her daughter carefully outlines a nestled bunch of flower petals. The drawing has dimensionality, perspective. Her artistic abilities have grown tremendously over the last three years, since the upload. Is the progression normal or accelerated? Kiana isn't sure. How precisely do other dead girls draw?

"That's a pretty flower there."

Anza turns. Her narrow face is unblemished and pure, her

8

brown eyes clear and bright. Not for the first time, Kiana wonders: Do those eyes reflect a real life from within, or is their luminosity an artifact of the program? Where does her daughter end and the simulacrum begin?

"Thank you, Mama." Anza's voice has grown eerily even-keeled over the past three years. Again, program or girl?

In some ways, she seems like a normal ten-year-old. Her knowledge base has expanded in an age-appropriate way, as dictated by the software. And her avatar has steadily grown, her limbs stretching long and lean.

But Level Up has a strange effect on how children develop. From what Kiana's read, the technology for modeling the brain has yet to surpass the stage of capturing its electrophysiology—the signals between neurons. What's missing is the effect of the body's metabolism on how the mind matures. And then there's the environmental factor. In Level Up's default settings, phys-ical dangers are greatly reduced and even cruelty can be blocked, making for fewer challenges to overcome. Kiana wonders, has this pseudo world left their kid less kid-like?

Sometime last decade, a philosopher coined the term "Level Up inertia" to encapsulate the tendency for those who exist solely in the virtual realm to gradually shed their human essences. Because these uploaded minds are able to take every-thing for granted, they too often fall into mindless habits and routines. With no obstacles or moral dilemmas to face, their values and passions atrophy. They become automatons.

Kiana is constantly telling herself that she ought to devote more time to raising her daughter herself. She's become overly reliant on her avatar. Sometimes, Kiana will log in only to observe the parenting skills of virtual Kiana. Actually, it's uncanny how well digital Kiana has learned to mimic her flesh-and-blood self. Uncanny, and a bit unnerving. An existential conundrum, but a common conundrum these days. So many people, staring at themselves in the mirror ... or is the person in the mirror staring back at them?

From his seat on the couch, Javi leans forward. "What kind of flower is that?"

His voice is robust. Kiana drinks in the sonorous tones. In real life, his speech has become raspy, quiet, depleted.

"It's a rose, Papa," Anza says. "Like the ones in the front yard. See the pattern of petals?"

"Oh, sure." Javi says.

Kiana can hear the uncertainty in his words. Or maybe she's projecting, and he's just tired. For her, manipulating her avatar requires almost no effort. Not so for Javi—for the real Javi, the man lying beside her in bed.

Anza stares at her father, her eyebrows crimped with worry. Her lips form a pout. "Papa, you seem tired."

"Un poquito. Just sleepy is all."

"Silly Papa," Anza says. "It's not your bedtime yet." Then she turns back to her intricate drawing of the rose.

Kiana pauses again and peeks over at the real Javi, whose eyelids are fluttering, struggling to stay open, failing. He emits little grunts as he focuses his dwindling energies on causing his avatar to interact with Anza's. With each grunt, Kiana worries that he's slipping one millimeter closer to the end. Is the experience worth the effort?

She checks the clock in the corner of her tablet's screen. 7:28. Half an hour until her meeting with Nadine at the pier. Half an hour until the terminal is in her hands. Then she can upload Javi to Level Up. Right now, she can't afford to think about what will happen after that.

Kiana logs out for the both of them, quits the game.

Javi quickly falls back asleep at her side. In the fading light of twilight, the hollows of his cheeks look deeper, his skin grayer. The ventilator hums away, causing his chest to barely rise and fall. But is he still—? Kiana's breath snags in her chest. She presses two fingers to the inside of Javi's wrist. The double-pulse of life is there—though not as strong as it once was, it's still going.

Kiana sets her tablet on the nightstand. Then she curls toward Javi and lays her head, gently, in the shallow where chest and shoulder meet. She tries to ignore the humming and clunking of the ventilator, tries to ignore the fact of death, so near. For just a moment, she'll pretend that life is normal and good. Then she'll do what needs to be done.

CHAPTER TWO

AUGUST, 2050

J avi crouched by the leafy little bush and plucked the biggest, reddest strawberry from its stem. Anza squatted beside him, jabbing a plastic spade at the ground. Dressed in green overalls and wide-brimmed straw hat, she was a three-year-old miniature farmer. Javi nibbled off the tip of the berry and held the rest out to her. She bit into the fruit and chewed. An uncertain frown fell above her wide brown eyes. Javi nodded in agreement. "A little on the tart side, hija?"

"Yeah, tart," she said, between open-mouthed chews.

Not enough acidity in the soil. Or the hard ground beneath the bed no longer allowed for proper drainage. Javi was hardly an expert. He and Kiana weren't farmers, and Seabreeze had shuttered its business operations a decade ago. Their landlords had retired and moved far away. They didn't give a shit about shrinking crop yields. Javi didn't care too much about the berries, either. It was the vegetable garden that helped sustain his family.

But Kiana loved strawberry shortcake, and Javi liked to surprise his wife every now and again with a treat. So, he kept picking berries, plopping them into the small clay bowl at his feet.

With the back of his hand, he pushed the sweat from his forehead. The mid-morning sun was insane. After just fifteen minutes outdoors, the back of his shirt was already soaked.

In that time, Anza and her toy spade had barely carved a dent into the dirt. Her face had pinked from the effort, from the heat.

"What do you think? Should we go inside and cool off?"

"Okay." She dropped her plastic tool and tottered off toward the house.

Javi chuckled. How liberating it must feel, not to worry about cleaning up after yourself or standing around politely while others pulled themselves together. Then again, his daughter was too short to open the door. A sense of liberty only carried a little person so far.

Anza had stopped at the edge of the garden. She stood dwarfed by the pale green stalks of corn. "Come on, Papa!"

"Sí, sí. Ya voy." He gathered the spade and the bowl and joined his daughter. Together, they headed toward the yellow house.

In the coolish kitchen, he rinsed the berries. After a glance into the living room, where Anza had begun rearranging wooden alphabet blocks on the rug, he sliced up the ripe red fruits and tossed them in a bowl with a dusting of sugar. Now he'd let them sit in the fridge and sweeten up for dessert.

What next? He stood barefoot on the linoleum, thinking of the projects he should be doing while Kiana was at work at the desal plant. Weeding the garden, fixing the sagging fence. He stared into nothingness, his feet unwilling to drag his body back out into the summer air.

A framed photo on the wall snagged his spacey gaze. He, Kiana, Anza, and Ellen, in the backyard of Alex's house in the

Santa Cruz hills. Anza was still in diapers then, nearly two years ago. Was it on that same trip that Kiana's mom had announced she was dying? Bulbar Palsy. Her speech had deteriorated a lot since then. Soft foods only. Limited mobility. But Ellen kept hanging on. Probably for the sake of her family. Javi felt halfway guilty every time he drove his wife and daughter up to visit her. Were they prolonging her suffering? Or would she suffer more if they stopped visiting and allowed her to die? He shook his head. The argument was academic. Obviously, they would keep making the monthly drive to spend time with Ellen, for as long as she willed herself to stick around.

Javi joined his daughter in the living room. With her blocks, Anza had spelled out DOG. She looked up, grinning, and pointed to the word she'd made.

"Muy bien, hija." He hoped a little praise would distract her from her mission statement. Javi was still warming up to the idea of getting a dog. His mother had terrible allergies, so Javi hadn't grown up with pets.

As he stood there, restlessness built up in his blood. Inaction felt morally wrong. He ought to be doing *something*, right? Kiana was always telling him he needed to relax more. He contemplated the old, yellowing novel sitting on the coffee table. It took place in Northern Ireland during the previous century. Political strife, complicated love, and lots of rain. Three chapters in, and reading about the cool, damp weather was his favorite part. He put the novel back on the bookshelf.

Javi's father, a former professor of literature, would be disappointed in him. Having retired last year from the University of Tijuana, Javi's dad now lived alone in a house too large for a widower whose two adult kids had long ago fled to El Norte. Javi worried the old guy was going senile. He should give him a call. Or, better yet, check in with his sister in Boston, who talked to their father more regularly than he. But his sister complained about every little thing, and their conversations always wore Javi out.

No, what he needed was to escape—to clear his mind of unfinished tasks, fatal diseases, and the potential loneliness of old age.

"Hey, hija. Should we go cool off at the pretend beach?"

"La Playa!" Anza beamed her goofy smile and clapped her hands.

Javi took that as a yes. As he gathered his tablet and their electromagnetic caps, he wondered why he bothered to qualify the beach as "pretend." His child had never stepped onto a real beach. The entire California coastline was barricaded by a concrete seawall. The only beach that Anza knew existed in Level Up.

He sat on the living room couch, and Anza climbed up beside him. She pulled on her child-size skull cap over her unruly mop of deep brown hair. Javi tugged on his own cap, making sure that the raised rubber arrow in the front lined up with the bridge of his nose, otherwise the electrodes wouldn't properly align with the corresponding brain regions beneath. Then he straightened his daughter's wonky cap and logged into their family account.

Instantly, the living room disappeared, all of his senses overridden by incoming signals from Level Up. He and Anza stood in the welcome portal, the menu of their worlds projected before them. Javi reached out, selected Costa Perdida Beach.

A cooling breeze lifted off the ocean. Javi felt the relief on his skin even before the sight and sound of the waves that gently crashed upon the sand. Instead of shorts and a sweat-stained shirt, Javi wore only his red swimming trunks. Anza stood beside him in her pink one-piece decorated with unicorns and rainbows, which she herself designed. The beach was a communal space, and plenty of other avatars frolicked in the ocean or lay out on beach towels. Javi took his daughter's hand and they strolled down toward the water. The sand grew wetter and squishier between his toes. Because Level Up had yet to master the sensations of textures, the sand felt slightly synthetic compared to the real deal. But the soft, cool dampness still felt pretty damn amazing.

Javi tried to appreciate each of these virtual getaways as if it might be his last. And it really might be. Each day, the news chronicled the gathering of world leaders in The Hague, where they argued the fate of the internet. The European Union and the Alliance of the Americas called for a neutering of Level Up and similar programs. If users were no longer able to touch, taste, and smell their virtual surroundings, wouldn't they be more inclined to log out? To go back to work? To pay taxes, for god's sake? The Middle East Federation seemed skeptical, but Pan-Asia seemed likely to vote for the measure. Javi couldn't believe the global consortium of service providers would go for it. Nonetheless, more and more nervous pundits speculated that the regulation might soon be adopted.

Javi had no say in the matter, of course. Instead, he returned his focus to Anza at his side, to the spritzing of salt air against his bare chest, to the man trudging toward them across the beach. He looked familiar, but Javi couldn't quite place him yet. The man had a large canvas bag strapped to his chest and a trash picker in his hand. Every few steps, he snatched up a piece of debris invisible to Javi and dropped it into his bag. When the man looked up, Javi recognized the tanned and smiling face of Phil Cohen, a former chef at PastAlgae. He and Javi had worked together for several years. Until sixteen months ago, when, after his husband filed for divorce, Phil hanged himself from a beam in his garage.

The sight of dead people in Level Up always ran a shiver through Javi's gut. He forced himself to raise his arm and wave.

"Hey, Javi." Phil stopped before them. "How's life back in the real world?"

"Uh, good. Yeah." Javi couldn't tell whether he was smiling too much or not at all. It freaked him out that many permanent residents of Level Up regarded their everyday surroundings as *not* real. Even though they were right, it wasn't real. Was it? "Um, how are ... how about you, Phil?"

"Oh, can't complain, really." Phil raised his picker, like knight with his sword. "Keeping busy, you know?"

"Sure."

"I finally took up the trombone," Phil said. "But I guess it's one of those things that's more fun when you watch other people do it." His smile turned a little sad, his gaze shifting to the sea. "I gave haiku a try. Dabbled in some watercolors." He shrugged. "But none of that was truly fulfilling, you know? So I took up volunteer work." Once more, Phil's smile brightened.

"Hey, good for you, man." Javi had read a couple of pop psychology articles about people in Level Up. The general theory held that brains actually got bored of virtual perfection pretty quickly. At first, folks would travel the world, have lots of casual sex, maybe do some skydiving. Then, like so many retirees from days gone by, they'd start searching for meaningful activities to fill their idyllic days. Or they would succumb to Level Up inertia.

Phil lunged to the side and thrust his picker toward a patch of sand. "Got it!"

Anza erupted into laughter.

Phil chuckled along good-naturedly. "Man, that sucker almost got away from me."

"Yeah, close call." As Javi nodded at his dead acquaintance, the anxious itch in his blood returned. Was he messing with his daughter's sprouting mind by exposing her to these strange layers of reality? He also felt the constraints of the ticking clock.

It wasn't healthy to stay in Level Up too long, especially in conditions too different from one's actual surroundings outside the program. The body didn't enjoy being tricked. Following prolonged immersion, users frequently got headaches and colds. "Well, I promised my daughter here a swim in the ocean before we, uh, you know, log out."

"The water's perfect today," Phil said. "And I should be moving on, anyway. This beach won't clean itself!"

"Nope," Javi agreed.

They waved their goodbyes and parted ways.

As they continued their stroll toward the lapping waves, Anza tugged Javi's hand. She was grinning up at him.

"Yeah, hija?"

"Papa, that man, he was funny." She lunged as Phil had lunged. "Got it!" she yelled, then cackled with delight.

Javi smiled. Maybe it *was* funny. A land where dead people weren't exactly dead, and where litter both did and did not exist. Schrödinger's trash. A virtual farce. Kiana was right: he should lighten up. Enjoy this crazy ride while it lasted.

They stopped to face the ocean, and the mellow surf splashed their feet. Javi looked south, to where the pier stretched out into the ocean, unimpeded by any concrete seawall. A memory struck him: an outing with his sister and his parents, when he was just a couple of years older than Anza. They'd driven from Tijuana down to Rosarito Beach. Javi had stood beside his father just like this, and a similar wooden pier had jutted from the Baja shore. His sister was splashing in the waves. And his mother stood nearby, gazing out to sea. For her to have left the house—much less venture fifteen miles from the city—that must have been a rare good day for her.

Would Anza remember this day? Would Javi look back on it with fondness? The day he and his daughter went to the virtual beach.

A wave broke at their feet, spraying their legs with water. Anza hopped back and giggled, the sound as light and lovely as the salty mist that landed in Javi's beard.

He watched the next wave cresting, white froth capping the blue water's furl. Then the wave stuttered. The cool air warmed quickly and the ocean crackled like static. A moment later, enormous words in bold rent font filled the sky: UNKNOWN SERVER ERROR.

Javi's body jolted on his living room couch, as if wakened from a nightmare. He turned to Anza, afraid that he'd somehow left her behind, trapped in a faulty hunk of hardware. She looked up at him. Her lips trembled, and she burst into tears.

CHAPTER THREE

FEBRUARY, 2057

K iana sits in the driveway, her car idling. She hates to leave Javi's side, even for an hour. The end could arrive at any time. Best then, she supposes, not to linger.

As she turns the car around, her headlight beams land on the falling-down yurt near their house. Fifty years ago, back when Seabreeze was a thriving organic farm, Kiana's mother, Ellen, spent several of her teenage years living in that yurt with her mom, Kiana's Grandma Lindsay. Their landlords, the Wardell family, had lived in the yellow house then and are Kiana's landlords today. The Wardells have long since retired to climate-friendly Vermont. Everyone who can afford to leave the wasteland of California has done so by now.

Kiana bumps down the dirt driveway and turns onto the long gravel road that cuts through the sparse desert community where they live. A hazy indigo sky hangs above the black rolling hills that surround the parched valley. Only a handful of porch lights interrupt the twilit countryside. Dark shapes jut from the earth: solitary oaks, stands of eucalyptus, plenty of sagebrush, a few stray saguaros. When she turns westbound onto the paved two-lane highway, Costa Perdida glows faintly between the hills.

Even with the windows of her mom's hand-me-down Accord rolled up, the cold sneaks in through rattling gaps. The nearer Kiana gets to town, the damper the chill. She stops at the railroad crossing and zips up her hoodie. Across the street is the station for the local commuter train. That's the train she would ride to work each morning, if it were at all reliable. Fortunately, her work friend, Vanhi Briggs, is a procurement officer. Vanhi gives Kiana a good deal on the hydrogen fuel cells that the desalination plant produces from electrolyzed brine. Several years ago, she and Javi converted the old Honda's engine from biodiesel, which Kiana's mom had converted from gasoline before that.

A mile or so down the road, the cold deepens, and she turns on the heater. Nothing. She presses her palm to the vent, waits for a sign of warmth. Still nothing. Kiana meant to fix the damn thing last winter. This year, she hasn't had the energy. She can barely manage to make it through each day.

The weight of her thoughts sinks through her body. The silence is too heavy. She clicks on the radio.

"— to you live from Costa Perdida tonight, where a man now identified as Walter Brogan has been arrested for murder. According to a witness at the scene, Brogan shot and killed his wife and child. After exiting his 3rd Street home, he then fired shots at his next-door neighbor and a UPS android, before surrendering to police. We'll have more on this shocking story as it develops."

Kiana turns to a classical station. Harpsichord and gently plucked strings. That, she can tolerate.

This shocking story. The story is awful. Sickening, even. But Kiana isn't shocked. Everyone she knows feels pushed to the brink: by the scarcity of jobs, by the failing infrastructure, by environmental collapse. Kiana is well aware that she, herself, may have recently strayed beyond the brink. She just hasn't killed anyone in the process.

The road dips into a valley, the barren inland gradually yielding to fields of wildflowers, copses of trees. Then Kiana's headlights graze the stretch of hillside where last summer's wildfire stripped the woods bare, devouring two hundred homes along the way. Every year, larger swaths of the state succumb to flames, leaving the land black as night.

As she reaches the outskirts of town, a heavy bank of clouds rolls in, smothering the waning yellow moon. She remembers now: the forecast for Costa Perdida calls for intermittent storms. Just then, lightning zig-zags across the sky—as if, with a thought, Kiana commanded that bolt to strike.

In real life, her wishes never manifest a single goddamn thing.

Right now, she wishes Javi were sitting beside her in the passenger seat, healthy and happy. Instead, she's left him unattended and alone. Should she have called Makia? For the past two months, the neighbor girl has been looking after him while Kiana's at work. Makia Humetewa is twenty years old and makes Hopi overlay jewelry that she sells online. While not tending to Javi's bodily needs, she works her craft at the dining room table. Kiana's always finding snips of sterling silver wire on the placemats, or stepping on the backs of earrings. But Makia's a sweetheart, a terribly earnest girl. Kiana couldn't include her in illegal activities, like the procurement of an unregulated fiber optic terminal. Same with Gilberto Ferreira, the middle-aged nurse from Brazil. He visits the house twice a week to check on Javi and to advise Kiana on his changing palliative care needs: treating bedsores, setting up an IV, how much morphine to administer and when. Gilberto's never asked where the morphine comes from, and Kiana hasn't volunteered that information. Everyone uses the black market, but no one talks about it.

As she's crossing 12th Street, heavy drops of rain descend, splattering on the windshield. Kiana sets the wipers on high. By the time she hits downtown, the rain has turned to ice. She can't even see well enough to pull over. No headlights shine behind her, so Kiana slows to a stop in the middle of the street. 7:49, according to the dashboard clock. Time enough before she's due to meet up with Nadine. These hailstorms usually pass quickly. But she's impatient: anxious to get to the pier, anxious to get back to Javi. Kiana drums on the steering wheel, the sound drowned out by the fusillade of ice pellets bouncing off the beleaguered Honda.

Then, like the flipping of a switch, the hail abates. Kiana remembers when it used to drizzle on the Central Coast. Now, the storms are infrequent but severe. All anyone can do is wait them out and hope their lives aren't washed away. She shifts back into drive, crunches ahead.

Costa Perdida is deathly quiet tonight. Just a handful of busses and cars on the road, a few stray pedestrians on the sidewalks. Displaced people are huddled in doorways, zipped into sagging tents, crowded under slipshod shelters of plywood and cardboard. There are plenty of empty lots to choose from: spaces where homes and businesses collapsed during the earthquake of 2040 and were never rebuilt.

Just ahead, at the next intersection, the green sign for Pastalgae glows. That's where Javi works. No: worked. The company grows microalgae as the primary ingredient for an assortment of pastas. Among the few protein sources they can afford, microalgae spaghetti tastes way better than all the bug-based foods on the market. Javi's been at Pastalgae for eight years now, a supervisor for the past five. It's a small company, like a family. Kiana knows they're worried about him, too.

She soon comes to the stoplight at Beachfront Drive, where the seawall looms high. The occasional working streetlamp illuminates a swath of vibrant graffiti art on the concrete wall. It always reminds her of the Berlin Wall, so faithfully recreated by the cadre of Level Up historians dedicated to that historical period. Great-grandmother Ilse had once lived on the wrong side of that Wall. Of course, the monstrosity in Berlin was built to keep people in place, whereas the wall in front of Kiana is meant to keep the rising waters from devouring the land. Sometimes, she wishes the ocean would break through already. Wipe out her parasitic species. Then the world could reset itself.

The light changes to green, and Kiana turns south onto Beachfront. A commuter train approaches, rumbling along the tracks on the other side of the road. Its headlights are aimed up the coast, toward Point Nada, one town over. Through the windows of the train, a handful of cheerless faces blur past. No one wants to be out on a night like this.

Kiana sees it now: the dark outline of the old pier, rising above the seawall. It looks like a prehistoric creature that got caught wading out into the Pacific, its wooden limbs forever moored in salt water and sand.

A little further down the coast, an aura of artificial light rises above the seaside cliffs. The eerie glow comes from the desal plant. Not for the first time, Kiana considers another option for obtaining an unregulated terminal: she could attempt to steal the one connected to the mainframe at work. But the plant security droids would likely apprehend her. Even if she evaded the droids, her theft would be captured by any number of security cameras. She'd be walking away from any last semblance of her normal life. Her career would be over, obviously. She'd probably go to jail. She couldn't afford to lose the paycheck, a chunk of which she converts to cryptocurrency and pays to Level Up for hosting Anza's uploaded mind. Soon, that chunk will be twice as large. Thankfully, her landlords offer them cheap rent, and she and Javi still manage to grow some of their own food. Kiana will get by. She has to. She will keep her family virtually alive for as long as she possibly can. She will pay the monthly fees until all her money is gone—or until Level Up shuts down its servers. And when it's Kiana's turn to die? There won't be anyone to subsidize a virtual afterlife for her. Her body will go into the ground, and her encoded loved ones will vanish into the digital void.

Nervous energy balloons in her chest as she nears the pier. Her heart feels like it's smashed against her ribcage. She hates meeting strangers like this, making shady deals. But what choice does she have? None. And she hates that, too.

Kiana pulls off Beachfront, into a paved lot near the pier. A pair of wooden posts remain stranded on this side of the concrete barricade. She pulls into a space where, decades ago, surfers would park for a day at the beach. It's hard to imagine now: suntanned boys and girls in bright swimwear, hoisting surfboards from convertibles and tramping across the sand. No wall between them, the welcoming waves. Now, there are maybe half a dozen other cars in the lot. In the post-seawall era, the pier has become a popular spot for drug parties and backseat teenage sex.

Kiana steps out of the car, and the cold wet air slaps her face. She activates the door lock on her watch and waits to hear the mechanism click into place. As she walks through the parking lot, she refrains from peering into windows. Her focus is on the lone figure standing in the shadows of the pier's decaying stairwell. Salt stings her tongue, and a shiver rattles her stride. She can now make out the red hoodie that the seller mentioned in her email. Kiana's own hoodie is canary yellow, a beacon in the night—the seller must see her. Kiana raises her hand in silent greeting. The red hoodie acknowledges her with a nod.

"Nadine?"

"Mm-hm." The seller's expression is implacable. "And you are?"

When emailing, Kiana never offered her name. "The buyer."

Nadine smiles, just barely. Her face is more attractive than Kiana expected—her brown skin smoother than the pock-faced weasel who sold her the busted ventilator, her teeth straighter than the dealer who sells morphine to Kiana from the back of a van.

Nadine opens a messenger bag and pulls out a sleek black rectangle, its surface shiny in the pale light. The unit looks sturdier—brawnier—than her terminal at home.

"It's unregulated?" Though the vendor has already emailed Kiana a brief clip of the impressive results of a speed test run on what would appear to be that very same terminal, she feels the need to be reassured. Once she makes the buy, she'll be stuck with what she gets.

"Sure is." Nadine sounds bored, which somehow reassures Kiana. Eager salespeople always strike her as liars.

Kiana tugs a folded-up envelope from the pocket of her jeans. Inside the envelope is two thousand dollars in cash. That's most of their savings—or what's left of it. Her heart feels sick as she hands the money to Nadine. The heft of the terminal, now in her hands, could drag her out to sea.

"Police! Don't move!"

The shout hits Kiana from behind like an electric jolt, a deep freeze—both at once, in an instant.

"Set the device on the ground." A man's gruff voice, closer now.

Kiana hesitates. She looks to Nadine, as if the black-market seller might offer a solution. No. Instead, she's waving shining objects at Kiana. A gold police badge, a black gun. Nadine is a fucking undercover cop.

Kiana complies.

"You're under arrest," says Nadine—or whoever she really is.

The male cop wrenches one arm behind Kiana's back, then the other. Cold metal smacks her wrists.

Now she's being led across the parking lot, as the words of the Miranda Warning evaporate into the wet salt air. They're heading for a big brown sedan, with a steel grate that divides the front seat from the back. This can't be happening.

As the male cop opens the door, Kiana gets her first look at him. Older, fat, and balding—a lumpy man in a shit-brown suit. "Watch your head," he growls, then folds her into the back of the sedan.

They have her now. They'll lock her away for who knows how long. And what will happen to Javi? The state will take him away. They'll leave him to rot in some frightening hospice ward.

Anguish bunches in Kiana's throat, burns the back of her eyes.

No, she can't let her husband die that way. She has to get out of this.

As the sedan lurches onto Beachfront Drive, lightning sparks across the sky. A second later, thunder booms and rain pours down.

Kiana lowers her face and quietly sobs. She hasn't felt so helpless in years. She wants her mother, right now, alive and at her side.

CHAPTER FOUR

OCTOBER, 2040

E llen fell back from her daughter's side, slowing her pace while she peeled off her orange hoodie. A faint breeze carried the zest of salt water up from the bay, to the footpath that wound along the cliff. The Santa Cruz afternoon was cloudy and cool, but the mile-long walk from Pacific Garden Mall had warmed her up. Just the other day, Ellen read that the average global surface temperature had risen one-point-two degrees Fahrenheit over the past twenty years—the same amount of time that elapsed since she gave birth to Kiana. A nearly catastrophic surge of heat.

By the time Ellen had tied the hoodie around her waist, Kiana's golden brown ponytail was bouncing just ahead on the path. Ellen hurried her stride, to catch up. She resumed her spot alongside Kiana, walking to her daughter's left so that Ellen could listen with her good right ear. This adaptation went back to childhood, a bout of meningitis.

Ellen had met Kiana in town a couple of hours before after riding the city bus down from her mountain home. Kiana had bussed over the hill from San Jose. They'd had lunch at a food cart, then browsed for a while at Bookshop Santa Cruz, where neither woman had committed to a purchase. Ellen got all her reading material from the library. Kiana was a scholarship student at San Jose State and worked part-time at Best Buy, which didn't leave her much disposable income. Whose income was disposable nowadays? Not Ellen's. She worked part-time doing accounting for the Bear Claw Café, the coffee shop down the road from her house. The Korean barbecue tofu wrap she'd bought for lunch was a luxury. And spending the afternoon in town constituted a major outing for Ellen. She didn't like to stray from her comfort zone. She'd spent the last twenty years avoiding being seen.

But she relished the opportunity to have her daughter all to herself. Mostly, Kiana came to the Small House for visits. And, inevitably, Alex would emerge from the Big House and insert herself into their company. It was only natural that she would do so. "Aunt" Alex had been a constant presence in Kiana's life since day one. Ellen hated feeling resentful toward Alex, who really was like a sister to her. Even if—maybe, probably—Alex had always hoped for a different kind of bond between them.

"So, after next quarter," Kiana was saying, "I should have enough credits to complete my History minor."

"Oh?" Ellen thought Kiana had stopped taking history classes, after changing majors sophomore year. She had lobbied hard to convince Kiana that Electronics Engineering was far more practical and would open up more career opportunities. They'd argued a lot. Thanksgiving that year had been fraught. But the world was fraught. And it wasn't getting any easier to support oneself. Ellen had once chosen a narrow path for herself, and she'd spent the last two decades living as a hermit. "That's right. I'd forgotten you'd kept that up."

Was that a sigh from Kiana? Or a normal exhale? They were walking at a good clip alongside West Cliff Drive—or what remained of it. Ellen could remember when cars still drove that scenic road. Over the last decade, the rising ocean's relentless erosion of the cliff wall had eaten away large chunks of asphalt, along with the foundations for some of the most valuable properties in Santa Cruz. Now an ugly concrete barricade interrupted views of the Pacific world below: the Boardwalk, the wharf, the surfers in their wetsuits, the murky horizon. In another decade, she supposed, the path they walked on now will have washed away, too.

"So, the history class I'm taking this term?" Kiana turned her head toward her mother.

A pointed gesture. Ellen knew that particular angling of her daughter's eyebrows. A test. Are you going to listen to me or are you going to judge me? "Yes, tell me."

"It's pretty cool. Do you know the video game Level Up?"

Just ahead, a cop strode quickly around the corner. A husky guy, stuffed into a dark blue uniform. He came toward them on the path, head lowered to read whatever message was being transmitted to his watch. A staticky voice leaked from his earbud, the transmission tinny and indistinct from that distance.

Ellen's nerves pulsed, a million tiny alarms. She pushed her sunglasses up her nose. She reached for the brim of a cap she wasn't wearing. Damnit. She'd left herself exposed, too easily recognizable. She'd gotten lax. Her hair had grown back out— the hair she'd once hastily chopped off in Alex's guest bathroom, her first night on the lam. And she had long ago stopped dying it the cranberry red that had once marked her transformation, from wanted criminal Taylor Ellen Olsen to a new woman without a past: Ellen Taylor.

As the cop drew nearer, blood revved through her body.

She dropped behind Kiana, single file—even though the path was plenty wide enough for the cop to pass.

"Copy that. On my way." The cop clicked his watch and broke into a shuffling jog. As he passed Ellen, his gaze remained on the path ahead.

Ellen returned to her daughter's side. For several seconds, neither spoke.

"Mom."

"Level Up. I heard you."

"No. Okay, yeah. But what was *that* just now?" Kiana smirked. "You don't honestly think, after all these years, that some beat cop is going to recognize you and—?"

"Force of habit, all right?" Ellen sighed. For the last several years now, she'd been asking herself the same question: was she being paranoid or appropriately cautious? Was her image among those whom the FBI or the NSA automatically checked against video footage collated from CCTV cameras, police body cams, and surveillance footage of protest gatherings? Or had the authorities abandoned her case years ago?

"I mean, the gray alone," Kiana said. With a wry smile, she swept her fingertips through Ellen's hair.

"Yeah, yeah." She batted away Kiana's hand. "Stop being mean to your elderly mother."

"Elderly?" Kiana snorted a laugh. "Sure thing, Mom. You're like, what? Forty-five?"

"Yep." Ellen was forty-six, but why quibble? She was glad to know her daughter didn't think of her as old yet. But fifty was approaching rapidly. A blip later, she'd be sixty. And another blip: a senile and shriveled thing, stashed away in a nursing home, some poor stranger mopping up her drool. She couldn't imagine a more horrifying end.

"So, anyway," Kiana said. "Level Up is virtual reality, world-building software. The basic idea is, you create an avatar of yourself and a cool place to live, awesome job, hot lover, whatever. The world is your oyster. And the world of Level Up is way better than this one, right? Climate's great, everyone's employed, et cetera."

"Makes sense." A virtual world would have to offer an improvement, to appeal to anyone with common sense. Although, back in her youth, plenty of boys Ellen knew had played those first-person shooter games that took place in seedy underworlds and wartime hellscapes. Some people just seemed to enjoy wallowing in shit. "But what does this video game have to do with history?"

"Okay, good question. The software for Level Up is so good at recreating houses, neighborhoods, entire cities ... it's so realistic that historians have started using it to recreate places from the past. For example, the Battle of Gettysburg or daily life in Colonial Rio de Janeiro. Those examples being two of my classmates' projects."

Ellen nodded. "And what's your project?"

"Right. So. Yeah." Kiana's voice turned circumspect. She stared down at her sneakers while she walked. "My project is the Beacon Hill neighborhood of Seattle in the 1970s."

"I see." That's when and where Ellen's mother grew up. Lindsay Zelenko, daughter of habitually unemployed airline mechanic and chronic gambler Harry and emotionally absent Patty. It wasn't just history Kiana was investigating, but *family* history. Ellen's least favorite history. She hadn't spoken to any of her relatives since before Kiana was born. Occasionally, she searched for news online. That's how she'd discovered that her mom had died, three years ago now. Her father, Greg Olsen, appeared to remain among the living. The year Kiana turned sixteen, Ellen had finally relented to her daughter's incessant pleas and presented her with a list of names. Along with the identities of Kiana's grandparents, those of her great-grandparents: Frank Olsen and Ilse Schmidt, Harry Zelenko and Beverly Wallace. Also, the name of Kiana's father: Sam Mahi'ai. Ellen had stipulated that, should Kiana reach out to any of these people, she wasn't permitted to reveal the current whereabouts of Taylor Ellen Olsen. She'd also made clear that she didn't want to know whatever news Kiana might discover. Ellen didn't exactly hate her father, or anyone from her family of origin. But she had cut herself off from her former life completely. And she didn't believe in looking back. The past and the present became volatile when mixed. All that mattered was here and now. As for history? Ellen didn't see any value in it.

"Just a small section of Seattle," Kiana was saying. "Between Beacon Avenue and the interstate. The tough part is the names of businesses, what certain buildings looked like prior to remodeling or demolition. But Level Up is amazing at synthesizing various sources of information—scans of old photos, digitized video footage, text from newspaper articles—and converting that data into city blocks and landscapes. And my project is part of a global, collaborative effort. Open source, shared knowledge. To get credit in the class, I just have to add a few new, well-researched elements, myself. Which is fair. But tricky, of course."

Kiana was babbling, a nervous habit Ellen had witnessed time and again. Her chest cramped with guilt. She'd been dismissive of her daughter's passion project. "Well, that all sounds really cool, honey."

"It *is* pretty incredible." The path angled toward the west. As Kiana turned her head to speak, the hazy sun caused her to squint. "I can put on a pair of VR glasses and, like, *walk around* Cold War Berlin. Only, without the foul smells and dank air."

"Well," Ellen said, "maybe they'll add that later. Like with the feelies, in *Brave New World*."

"Oh, right. I remember that seemed kind of creepy in the novel." Kiana shrugged her typical change-of-subject shrug, and Ellen heard the words—*so, anyway*—a moment before her daughter spoke them: "So, anyway. This project got me thinking about my last name. How Taylor is only *my* last name because you changed *your* last name. But Taylor doesn't say anything about where I come from, you know?"

"This is true." And just as well, it seemed to Ellen.

"So, I was thinking of changing my last name to Olsen. Maybe after I graduate? To honor my heritage. I mean, if that feels okay to you, Mom?"

Possible replies in the form of questions piled up on Ellen's tongue. Why Olsen and not Mahi'ai? Why not Zelenko, Schmidt, or Wallace? Had Kiana spoken to Ellen's father, met him in person? If so, had Kiana's conversation with Greg Olsen somehow inspired her choice of surnames? And did that mean the man had changed? Or had tales of some elder Olsen led to Kiana's decision? Ellen herself had always admired her grandfather Frank and his father, Einar.

Ellen swallowed all the questions down. It didn't matter. And, she reminded herself, she didn't want to know. "Sure, honey. Of course." She forced a smile. "It sounds important to you. So that's what you should do."

"Thanks, Mom." Kiana wrapped her fingers around Ellen's forearm, gave a squeeze.

They walked in silence for a while. A comfortable quietude. Though Ellen didn't really believe in New Age stuff like auras or energy fields, some detectable atmospheric shift had occurred just now between her and Kiana. An ease that only sometimes manifested itself between their bodies—two bodies that had once felt to her like a single body. Not so long ago. Only twenty years. Two decades in which everything had deteriorated: Ellen's knees, the plumbing at the Bear Claw, the cliff on which she walked, civility in America, the value of the dollar, species diversity across the planet. Shit. Did anything change for the better? Okay, yes, one thing did: her daughter. Kiana had grown into a healthy and intelligent woman. Her young mind continued to expand, to welcome new philosophies. If one of those philosophies included her family of origin, then maybe—

The ground shook, violent and sudden. An explosion?

"Earthquake!" Kiana grabbed Ellen's wrist and pulled her off the path.

They stumbled into a vacant lot, overgrown with grass. Ellen's every other footstep seemed to miss the earth, then her next landed with a jarring stamp. Before them stood the crumbled remains of a bulldozed house. Why were they running toward that house? Nothing made sense. One thudding step later, Ellen understood: Kiana was leading her away from danger. Away from the eroding cliff. Away from the overhead power lines that draped among the dying palm trees. Into an open space. After a lifetime in California, Ellen should have known what to do. But the rumbling earth, it blanked her mind completely, every goddamn time.

They stopped before the ruins of the house and wrapped their arms around one another.

A terrible sound—sharp yet deep, a sundering sound—made Ellen jump. Her heartbeat flew, her breath cinched tight. The earth was splitting. The end had come.

"Wow, look," Kiana said. She lifted an arm from their embrace and pointed at a place where a section of the concrete barrier had cracked in two.

"Oh," Ellen said. Then she realized the trembling had ceased. Another ordinary California quake. Sudden tumult, some damage here and there, then it's over. And yet, when caught in the middle of it, the primal fear struck her every time:

this was the end. The final cleaving of the San Andreas. And that singular fear conjured others. Some great annihilating event always loomed just over the horizon. The flood that breaches the sea walls. Nationwide total blackout. Another global pandemic. Nuclear catastrophe. The world engulfed in flames.

These terrible endings formed a knot in Ellen's chest. She held tightly to Kiana, to the life she had created. From the day her daughter was born, Ellen never should have let her go. She desperately wanted never to let her go again.

A moment later, Kiana peeled away—as easily as shedding an unneeded hoodie. She turned to Ellen, mouth slack and hazel eyes wide. "Well, that was scary."

Ellen stood there, staring mutely at her daughter. "Mm-hm," she finally managed.

Just by muttering those syllables, she began to relax. The surrounding world opened back up to her. She heard the sound of crashing waves, felt the warmth of the sun. Only now did she realize that a scattering of tents lay pitched across the vacant lot. People had emerged from the soiled nylon flaps. Scruffy beards, brittle hair, frayed clothes, faces smudged with grime. More and more people went homeless every year.

And here she and Kiana stood, in a place these people had staked for themselves. Ellen felt like a spectacle. She needed to get out that not-so-vacant lot, to escape hectic Santa Cruz, to slink back up to her little house in the woods. She tugged at Kiana's sleeve, then started walking back toward the path, toward the bus that would ferry her back up the mountain.

Kiana fell in step alongside her. "Hey, Mom. Would it be okay if I maybe spent the night at home tonight?"

"Of course, honey. You're always welcome." Ellen's eyes dampened. Was she feeling sentimental? Or was the shock from the quake wearing off? Maybe both. At that moment, nothing sounded better to Ellen than a simple meal at home with her daughter. And Alex, too.

"Always?" A sly grin squeezed into the corners of Kiana's lips. "Even after I change my last name to Olsen?"

Ellen felt her lips stretch into a smile. The cinched-up knot in her chest loosened, just a touch more. "Yeah, even then."

CHAPTER FIVE

FEBRUARY, 2057

A wet chill seeps through the gray concrete walls of the holding cell, where Kiana sits alone on a steel bench. She rubs her hands up and down her arms, trying to warm her blood. The air smells of piss and toxic sweat. After getting fingerprinted and strip-searched, after forfeiting her wallet and watch and wedding ring, after getting her mug shots taken, she's spent the last twenty minutes staring through steel bars at the clock in the hallway. 9:03. Two hours since she drove away from home. Every slap of the second hand wears away at hope. She's never felt so far from Javier. How stupid of her, to have left his side.

A uniformed cop—Eckhart, his name tag says—opens the jail cell door. "The detectives are ready for you now."

When she stands, her entire body aches. From digging, from sleeping like shit, from the weight of worry. That weight wants to drag her down to the floor. It compels her to let go, to cry, to release. But she can't start grieving yet.

Eckhart holds out a pair of handcuffs. "Turn around for me, please. Hands behind your back."

Kiana follows his orders. Any notion of choice—of free will—has deserted her.

"This way." Eckhart grips her elbow, guides her out into the hallway. He pushes her along, like she's a child lost at the shopping mall, or a lamb destined for slaughter. It's a short walk down the nondescript hall. Kiana had expected more from the police station's interior, given its pompous façade of Roman arch and Ionic columns. But it's all just California stucco. Same as the courthouse, right next door. All the times Kiana drove past this building, she never imagined that she'd one day be locked up inside.

Eckhart unlocks the door to Interrogation Room 2 and leads her inside the dim, windowless space. A jagged crack runs along one of the pale green walls. The moldy acoustic ceiling tiles are like the surface of the moon gone rotten. Even still, the room is an improvement over the holding cell.

Kiana is marched around a gray metal desk. Its surface is tarnished, the embedded glass control panels scratched. Eckhart uncuffs her, points to an ugly chair. Aluminum legs and a molded plastic seat in navy blue. Or maybe that color started life as a royal blue, before the grime of so many criminal asses dulled its sheen.

Kiana sits. Is she now a criminal, too? Just for buying a damn terminal?

In walk the two plainclothes cops who arrested her: Detectives Nick Turley and Olivia Bell, as they identified themselves on the drive to the station. Officer Eckhart slips out of the room behind them, and the door clicks shut. Turley peers into a retinal scanner mounted to the wall. Outmoded security, but secure enough to trap Kiana inside. A deadbolt locks with a jarring thud.

Detective Bell has changed out of the frumpy hoodie and into a mustard yellow blouse, black slacks, and fitted blazer.

With her shallow crow's feet and that smidgeon of gray in her afro, she can't be too far north of forty years old. Turley suffers by comparison. His doughy physique is bundled in a lumpy beige suit. He looks to be in his mid-sixties, maybe older. No one can afford to retire anymore.

The detectives sit across from Kiana. Neither says a word. Is their silence is meant to claw away at her already tattered nerves? Well, the strategy is working. They each tap their panels, log into their systems. Holographic screens light up before them. But all Kiana sees are the encrypted backs of their screens, a pair of image-scrambled blurs.

Right away, Turley's screen flickers off. Then on again, then off. On, off. On, off. He grumbles and mutters, jabs his thick finger at the controls.

When a technical problem presents itself, Kiana's brain switches into work mode. At the moment, she welcomes the distraction. She suspects a haptic calibration issue with the hologram. Or maybe frayed wiring to the projector. Or the Western Interconnection's withering power grid. Maybe all of the above. At the desal plant, she would have the proper tools to diagnose the issue. She'd dispatch a repair droid or order a new part. But, clearly, the Costa Perdida Police Department doesn't get the caliber of municipal funding that the desal plant enjoys.

Detective Bell raises a skeptical eyebrow at her partner's senseless pawing. Kiana notices the look, but Turley doesn't seem to. Or maybe he's immune to criticism from his younger, darker-skinned, female colleague. Old white guys, they never change.

At last, his screen pulses back to life. He smiles, far too satisfied with his role in the cycle of happenstance. "Okay, initiating interview." He squints his baggy eyes, clears his throat. "It's now 9:07 p.m., Friday, February 9, 2057. Present are

Detectives Nick Turley and Olivia Bell. Our suspect is Kiana Alexandra Olsen."

The surname she plucked from her family tree. An homage to her great-grandfather, Frank Olsen, and his father, Einar. In his later years, Frank Olsen devoted his life to gay rights for military personnel. And Einar Olsen, after commanding one of the first racially integrated squadrons during World War 2, became a civil rights ally. In 1963, he drove from his Minnesota home to Alabama, where he was arrested during a demonstration. After a few hours in jail, his case was dismissed. Kiana doubts she'll be so lucky.

"Date of birth," Turley continues, "Is November 8, 2020. The suspect's address is ... nothing but a PO Box?" He looks at Kiana and his face sags. "We'll need a street address for our records."

There is no mailbox at the end of their driveway, no number affixed to their house, no street address listed on any document. Not even their employers have this information in their files. Kiana and Javier don't want the government watching over them.

"That PO Box, it's my official address."

"We'll circle back around to that," Turley grumbles. "Our suspect is being questioned in regards to the attempted purchase of this unregulated, uh, portal at Pier—"

"Terminal," Bell murmurs.

Kiana catches Turley's sidelong look at his partner, his flare of irritation. "Unregulated *terminal*." His rheumy eyes turn back to Kiana. "Anyhow. Occupation?"

She studies the two detectives. This info must be on their screens. They probably want to get her talking, in the hopes she'll divulge some crucial piece of information. She's too tired to talk. "I work at the desal plant. Process Control Specialist."

Olivia Bell leans back in her chair. "You got your BA in Engineering at San Jose State, isn't that right?"

Kiana nods. Her head feels like an anvil, weighting down her neck and shoulders, compressing her spine into the hard plastic chair.

"Hey," Bell says. "That's my alma mater, too." A warm smile creeps across her lips. "What year did you graduate?"

What's with the casual we're-just-chatting-here approach? Kiana isn't buying it. "2041. I'm surprised that date is missing from your records."

"Oh, here it is." Bell's smile flattens. "And is that where you met your husband, Javier Gallegos?"

Kiana's gut corkscrews. She doesn't like his name hovering in the stale air of the interrogation room. She breathes into the fear, plunges it down. "No. We met after I moved down here."

"Married in Mexico. June 16, 2046."

"That's right." A small ceremony on a beach in Baja. Just family and a few close friends. A warm, wet wind skimmed of the surf, slapping Kiana's hair across her face while she earnestly recited her vows. She could tell by the strain of Javi's lips that he was trying hard not to laugh—mostly for his parents' sake. The newlyweds cracked up about it later that night, on their honeymoon, in a roadside motel. Anza was conceived somewhere on that languid drive back up the Pacific coastline. In a campground, maybe, or—

"And where is your husband right now?" Bell aims her finger at Kiana.

But staring down the barrel of her chipped fuchsia nail polish isn't going to fluster Kiana. Not like back at the pier, when an actual steel revolver was aimed at her chest. "My husband's at home right now, waiting for me to call back, to let him know much bail's going to cost."

Bell's finger drifts off-target, inscribing a loose spiral in the air. "The amount of bail depends on what we charge you with."

Turley leans forward, resting his hands on the desk. "And how is Javier? In good health? Happy with his job?"

Kiana tries hard not to react, to keep herself from flinching. "I don't know what this has to do with ... Javier's fine. His job is fine."

"Interesting." Turley smirks. "Because, when I called his place of work just now, the guy who answered said Javier hadn't been there in a long time. So I asked if this prolonged absence was due to illness. The guy got skittish and hung up."

Should she refute Turley's interpretation of the phone call? No, better to keep her mouth shut. Kiana shrugs.

"You know what's a funny coincidence?" Bell says. "A month or so back, we busted a black market vendor for selling unregistered medical supplies, including refurbished ventilators. We were able to track down a couple of his buyers, but not all of them. We did get descriptions, though. Here's one of them: *female, mid-to late-thirties, medium height, slender build, chin-length light brown hair streaked with purple, green eyes.* And, get this, *maybe kinda Asian or something.* A perfect match for you, Kiana. Wouldn't you say?"

Heat rises in her chest. That weasley little prick betrayed her. It's a good thing he didn't see Kiana's distinctive tattoo. Like tonight, the sleeve of her hoodie was covering the cursive *Anza* inked into her forearm. She didn't want her daughter's name mixed in with this shit.

Kiana shakes her head at Detective Bell, as if she were babbling in Vietnamese or Bengali—one of those endangered languages from before the Great Submersion. "I don't know. Most people say my eyes are hazel."

"Okay, then." Bell snorts. "So, your husband isn't deathly

ill? Because that's where the evidence is pointing here. And, if he is, why hide it?"

"What this sounds like to me?" Turley tugs at his saggy chin. "Sounds like the behavior of someone who's uploading their mind—"

"Or the mind of someone in their care," Bell adds.

Turley acknowledges his partner with a begrudging tip of his head. "Who's uploading their—or someone else's mind. Maybe to a Level Up profile."

"Come on, Nick," Bell says with mock incredulity. "Isn't it illegal for anyone other than a nationally licensed neurosurgeon to encode and upload a person's cognitive processes?"

"Why, yes, Olivia. A felony crime, in fact. Punishable by up to ten years in prison." Turley smiles coldly at Kiana.

She's nodding along, or believes she is. The detectives' words and gestures are barely registering, barely perceptible through the haze of fear. They know—or at least suspect—far more than Kiana thought they did. Javier's illness, Level Up. She has to get out of this interrogation room, out of this police station. Find another unregulated terminal, somehow. She's so close to preserving Javi's mind. And so fucking tired.

"Hey, Kiana?" Detective Turley waves his big clumsy hand in her face.

"Sorry, what?"

"Is that your plan?" He snuffles, wipes his knuckle under his nose. "To upload Javier?"

"No," she manages. The word sounds puny to her, a worthless protest. The detectives are grinding down her will. She's letting them win.

"No, huh?" Detective Bell's gaze bores deep into Kiana's eyes. Right pupil, left pupil, right again. Those tiny black portals, they can reveal so much. Too much. "Then why don't you just give us your home address? We'll check on your husband. If he's as peachy as you claim, we'll slap you with a light fine and cut you loose. What do you say?"

Kiana stares back. She's not uttering a single word this time.

Turley sighs. "We'll figure it out ourselves. Sometime in the next forty-eight hours."

Worry skitters across Kiana's chest, frantic as a swarm of beetles exposed to danger. "What do you mean?"

"You heard right." A smirk dances across Turley's lips. "We can hold you up to forty-eight hours before charging you with a crime."

Time, time, time. She has so little time left with Javi. Every minute since the detectives arrested her is an erosion of that time. And more time will be eroded still. Kiana understands now: the police aren't going to charge her until they've run down every lead. And, until they do charge her, bail can't be set. And, until she pays bail, she can't get out of there. And, even then, she still won't have the piece of hardware she so desperately needs.

Misery churns like a sickness in her gut. She should have stolen the terminal from the server room at work. But, just a couple of hours ago, Kiana thought she would be able to get away with everything. How fucking naive.

"You know what would really help your case?" Bell nods at Kiana encouragingly. "Giving us your home address right now. We tend to look favorably on suspects who volunteer information. Judges feel the same way. Lighter sentencing, reduced fines. That kind of thing."

First a threat, and now cajoling. But Kiana can't give in. Not when she pictures the detectives driving out to her house and finding Javi hooked up to that black market ventilator. Which she only bought because their worthless health insurance wouldn't provide for his care beyond the first round of chemo. Limited coverage for Foreseeable Natural Consequences—of breathing the air, they mean. So now the police would charge Kiana with yet another illegal purchase, and she'd go to jail for even longer. She'd never see Javi again.

That thought makes a fist around her heart. Then the fist grabs her by the throat. She can't get out of this situation on her own. "I want a lawyer."

"A lawyer?" Turley tilts her head and smiles at Kiana as if she were a child who's asked for something fantastical and absurd. *May I please have a unicorn on a tricycle?* "We're just talking here, Kiana."

"Yeah," Bell adds. "A friendly conversation, is all." She opens her hands, palms raised, an atlas of lifelines and lovelines exposed.

But Kiana's no palm reader. Maybe Olivia Bell will live to a hundred, or she might die alone tomorrow. She doesn't wear a wedding ring, anyway. Neither does Nick Turley—though his left ring finger retains a pale crease from an old wedding band. Divorced? No, Kiana guesses he's a widower.

She'll be joining that club soon. Way too soon. Under the table, she twists her slim gold band around her finger. How long will she wait before removing that ring? Days, months, years? No, it can't happen. Why would it? Kiana will never be a widow, she tells herself, because Javier will never die.

Except he will die. His lungs have failed. And the machine that keeps him alive could also fail.

"I mean it," Kiana tells them. "I'm not saying another word until I consult with an attorney."

Turley rears back. For a second, his sagging face shores up, gathers a hostile edge. She thinks he might slap her. Then he deflates with a sigh. "Fine." He starts typing on his touch panel. "I'll put in the request."

"Gonna be a while, though," Bell says. "Jane Hamamura, she's the only public defender in Costa Perdida working at this hour. And she's with a triple homicide suspect right now."

"Walter Brogan," Kiana mumbles.

Detective Bell grimaces. "Anyway." With a sigh, she gets up, unlocks the door to the interrogation room, and summons Officer Eckhart back in.

"We'll fetch you when your lawyer's available," Turley says.

Kiana is cuffed and trundled out of the room, led back down the hall. The same set of metal bars await her. Eckhart opens the door to the holding cell, removes her handcuffs, and sends her off with a light shove, like he's pushing a rowboat out to sea. The door clanks shut behind her. Its echo makes Kiana shiver. Her heart stammers. She'll never get out of there. She'll never see Javier again. Tears rise to her eyes.

Then she notices she's not alone. Tucked into the far corner of the dusky cell, a woman sits on the metal bench attached to the concrete wall. Adrenaline zips through Kiana. Who is this stranger she's confined with? A step closer, and she sees her very pregnant belly—a perfect hemisphere beneath an old denim shirt. Large brown eyes watch Kiana, black brows pinched with worry. But her youthful skin—a warm shade of brown—doesn't wrinkle. Kiana thinks she might even a teenager still. The young woman wraps her arms over her belly, as if guarding her unborn child.

Her presence stifles Kiana's sadness. She sits, slowly, at the far end of the bench. She tries to smile reassuringly at her cell-mate, but the tightness in her face tells her she's failed. She's in no position to reassure anyone. "Hey."

The young woman eyes Kiana warily, as if her introduction might be some form of trap. "Hey."

"I'm Kiana."

"Suheera."

"Pretty name."

A smile pulses to her lips. "Yours, too."

How did this girl land in that cell, in their mutual purgatory? Is it okay to ask? Kiana doesn't know the etiquette.

Her lips part, but Suheera is quicker. "So, what did they arrest you for?"

Reflexively, Kiana says, "It's a long story." Then she shakes her head—the detectives have provided her with a neatly abridged version. "The purchase of regulated goods."

"Oh, uh-huh." Suheera nods, but the bend in her eyebrows is uncertain.

Kiana can't blame her. Her crime sounds innocuous, trivial. Maybe Turley and Bell will come to the same conclusion and let her walk free? What a fantasy.

"How about you?" she asks Sueheera.

"Aiding and abetting an armed robbery. Pharmaceuticals. But I didn't ...." Water blinks from her eyes. "I didn't know that's what he was doing."

"Who?"

"My boyfriend, Tommy." Suheera shakes her head. "He's an assistant manager at Walgreen's. He told me there was something he forgot to do at work, that he'd get fired if he didn't fix it before tomorrow morning. With the baby coming, we can't afford him losing his job, right?"

Kiana nods. When Anza was born, she and Javi were struggling to make ends meet. They both had low-level positions back then. Javier worked nights, tending to the algae tanks. Kiana worked days, replacing fuses and fixing gauges—maintenance tasks she now supervises.

"So, I drive Tommy back to work. The place is closed. He tells me to wait outside, that he'll just be a minute."

"Mm-hm." Kiana tries not to wince. She sees what's coming. What a terrible plan. The only Walgreen's in town is just three blocks from where they sit right now—on the same street as the police station.

"Tommy's only been gone for, like, a minute when I hear sirens. I look in the rearview mirror, and cop cars are racing down the street. Some bad shit's happening somewhere, but what else is new? A second later, Tommy runs out carrying a bag full of stuff. That's when I know: the bad shit's happening to *us*. So, I to start the car, and guess what? Piece of shit stalls. Meanwhile, the cops are almost there. So I yell out the window for Tommy to run. And that's what he does." She snorts a bitter laugh. "Not even a second's hesitation. Can you believe it? Fucking coward, just turns and runs away. Abandons me and his unborn child." Suheera shakes her head. "By the time I managed to haul myself out from behind the steering wheel, the cops had me surrounded." She chokes back a sob. "Sorry."

"It's okay." A sigh shakes out of Kiana. "I'm scared shitless, too."

"What am I gonna do?" Suheera stares down at her stomach. "I can't have a baby in jail. Oh, fuck." She covers her face with her hands.

Kiana's known guys like this Tommy. Stupid boys, overgrown children. What Suheera needs is an adult. Someone who'll tell her to make a deal with the cops: a reduced charge in exchange for telling them where her idiot boyfriend is hiding out. But Kiana's in no position to offer legal advice. That's what lawyers are for. Once they show up.

Looking at Suheera, Kiana can't help but think of her own mother, when she was pregnant with her. The choices she made. The lives that changed.

CHAPTER SIX

MARCH, 2020

Taylor drove the surface streets of Santa Cruz, avoiding Highway 1. Since fleeing Modesto that morning, she'd taken as many back roads as possible, stretching a two-hour drive into four. Her hands hadn't stopped shaking.

A concrete bridge carried her over a wide green gully—the San Lorenzo River, according to a road sign, but only a stream trickled below. From the crew's trip here last fall, she remembered that so-called river emptying into the bay, near the Beach Boardwalk, where she'd stood around eating an ice cream cone while Sam and Becca rode the rollercoaster. The thrill-seekers paired off together, Taylor cast aside.

Turning from Water Street onto River, Taylor heard the word "Modesto" on the radio. She punched up the volume.

"—where three suspects have been arrested following a shootout early this morning. The incident occurred at a chicken processing plant. Preliminary reports indicate that the suspects belong to an ecoterrorist organization called the Wildlife Liberation Front. Both a police officer at the scene and one of the *suspects have been rushed to Memorial Medical Center and are listed in critical condition at this time. We have word that a fourth suspect remains at large. We'll have more on this story as it develops. Now for the latest on COVID-19. Today, the World Health Organization declared that the rapidly spreading coronavirus is now a global pandemic. It's estimated that more than four thou—"*

Taylor smacked the car stereo's power button, as if it were a mosquito, a tiny buzzing threat. *Critical condition.* Fuck. Reckless Becca. The moment she showed them the gun, they should have called off the action.

The crew's newest member—big, bald, bulky Leon—had already gotten them into the processing plant: the bolt on the side gate cut, alarms disabled. They'd gathered in a hallway outside the first room in the slaughtering process—a room unironically named Reception.

Taylor's nerves were already frayed. She'd been sleeping poorly, and last night had been particularly rough. Another run-down motel room, her turn to crash on the floor. And the deep-fried zucchini sticks she'd eaten for dinner had left her queasy. She'd woken up in the middle of the night, stumbled into the bathroom, and puked into the same acrid toilet bowl that everyone else in the crew had pissed in the night before. *If it's yellow, let it mellow.* Fucking hippies. At some point Taylor, herself, had become one.

With his hand on the door latch to Reception, Sam had reminded everyone of their brief window of time before the plant's lone security guard returned from his coffee break. That's when Becca hitched up her maroon hoodie, revealing the handgun wedged into the waistband of her jeans. "He won't be a problem," she'd said.

"Are you fucking crazy?" Taylor had hissed the words, and

the tiniest fleck of saliva had landed on Becca's face. A face that, six months ago, Taylor had thought beautiful, irresistible, kissable.

Sam had wedged himself between them, as he so often did. "Hey!" he whispered. Then he unleashed that calming smile of his on Taylor. That look in his hazel eyes that still warmed her blood. That golden brown skin, that dark mess of hair streaked copper by surf and sun. He was twenty-six—the same age as Taylor—but his body remained boyish and lean. Every time she stood near him, she could still taste the dewy salt-sweat on his skin. With a one-second look, Sam had neutralized Taylor. Then he'd turned his smile on Becca. With a wink he told her, "Just keep it in your pants, all right?"

Somehow, that had settled the matter, and they entered Reception.

Immediately, the room's nasty, fetid smell had flooded into Taylor, rushing from nostrils to gut. The stench of fear and death. Chicken shit, blood and decay. Patches of white-brown slurry pock-marked the concrete floor, below the assembly line of metal slots used to hang the chickens upside down for elec-tro-hydraulic immobilization and live slaughter. The Wildlife Liberation Front had targeted this particular facility due to its citations for substandard conditions and charges of animal cruelty. Now those conditions were assaulting Taylor like a physical force. Her stomach shuddered. She clamped her hand across her mouth, turned, and bolted. Sam's hushed shouts died as the door shut behind her.

She stood on the concrete walkway that ran between the building and the gate they'd broken into. Most of the property was covered in gravel. Her gut roiled once more, and the taste of sick burbled up her throat. But she held it in. Too vulnerable there in the cool pre-dawn air. Exposed. She didn't want to leave any forensic trace of herself behind.

Beyond the fence stood a grove of oak trees that bordered the Tuolumne River. Taylor dashed out the gate, across a cracked-asphalt road, and into the sheltering oaks. She braced her hand against the rough bark of a sturdy trunk. Her torso buckled, and vomit streamed from her mouth to the bed of dried leaves below. Once the upheaval ended, she wiped her mouth with the back of her hand, straightened slowly, and pressed her back to the tree.

As Taylor stood there catching her breath, the truth smacked her, hard. She counted backward, just to be sure. Five weeks since her last period. Four weeks since the night in Bakersfield with Sam, after they'd raided an animal testing facility in East LA. The one and only time they'd fucked since Sam and Becca cast her aside.

A baby. Motherhood. Taylor had never truly contemplated this for herself. The idea had always hovered in the fantastical distance, like an alien spacecraft. And yet. In that moment in the woods, the wanting overwhelmed her. A button in her brain had been tapped. Yes, she would bring a child into the world. Nothing else mattered.

Taylor had driven to the crew to the plant that morning. She'd parked her silver Honda Accord on a dirt service road within the patch of trees. She now found herself walking toward the car. What had she been doing in that awful place? Why had she allowed a crazy person into her heart? As her thoughts spiraled free, a strange calm settled like a coolness on her cheeks. The enclosed quietude of the woods felt like a balm. She ducked under low branches, and fallen leaves crackled beneath the treads of her sneakers. Through gaps in the overstory, dawn's pinking light bled through.

Maybe, Taylor thought, she could rejoin normal society. Get her master's degree, take a real stab at a career in architecture. That had been her major in college. Before meeting Sam and becoming an activist, she'd worked a couple of soulless assistant jobs at architectural firms—early attempts at playing yuppie. She wouldn't even have to sell out her ideals. She could remain involved with the WLF: volunteer to run a safe house, become one of the anonymous donors who kept the collective afloat. A perfect dream. All she had to do was get in the car and drive away.

A siren screamed into the air. No, two sirens. Police, fire, ambulance? The howling, already loud, grew louder. Taylor saw a flash of movement through the trees. Between the branches and leaves, she caught sight of a pair of SUVs. In the dim light, she could just make out the gold stars on white doors. Highway Patrol. She raced back to the others.

By the time Taylor reached the edge of the grove, the SUVs were skidding to a halt before the chain link fence. Cops emerged, guns raised, and charged the door of the chicken processing plant.

Taylor had stood completely still beneath the umbrella of a mighty oak. Her heartbeat throbbed in her head. A single thought had whirled through her brain: *I should do something.* But the thought gained no momentum. *I should do something.* It accumulated no weight. *I should do something.* No purpose.

From inside the building, a gunshot echoed out into the air.

Taylor turned and ran.

Now she drove narrow Highway 9 into the Santa Cruz Mountains, winding her way up through ancient redwoods. Time and again, her eyes darted up to the rearview mirror. Only one car trailed behind her: a harmless orange Volkswagen Beetle. The landscape—evergreen boughs and long-fronded ferns—looked familiar, from the crew's journey up this same road back in October. Taylor, Sam, and Becca had come to Santa Cruz to participate in a climate protest and had stayed one night with a WLF donor named Alex Hemley.

Alex lived by herself in a house in the hills. Around thirty years old, she worked remotely, something to do with computers. Taylor and Alex had stayed up late, talking by themselves. Alex's calm exterior and quiet convictions had grounded Taylor during a time when she'd felt especially alienated from Becca and Sam. And she'd gotten the sense that Alex enjoyed her company, too.

Based on that lone encounter, Taylor chose Alex's place as her potential refuge. A crazy impulse, she knew. She was a veritable stranger. But Taylor had few good options. Assuming the police knew her identity, family members could be monitored. Not that she was close to any of her relatives, anyway. Mom had shacked up with a new boyfriend, a creepy dietician in Santa Barbara. It drove Taylor crazy, the way Lindsay kept bouncing from one identity to the next: EMT, web designer, organic farmer, and now publicist for a health guru. And forget about Dad. He had his new family, a bunch of clean-living Christian guilt-trippers. Taylor's one aunt, Shelley, was an uptight investment broker on the verge of divorce, according to Taylor's cousin, Opal. And Taylor's grandparents were either dead or stashed away in retirement communities.

Desperate, Taylor drove on. In addition to the very real possibility that Alex would simply turn her away, Taylor faced another complication: she was navigating entirely from memory. Her phone sat inert on the passenger seat, a useless chunk of plastic. After speeding away from the processing plant, she'd pulled off to the side of a rural highway, yanked out her phone's SIM card, and snapped it in two. Then she'd popped open the back of the phone and disconnected the battery. In the process of rendering herself untraceable, she'd also forfeited her address book, her GPS, her lifeline to the modern world.

Since leaving Modesto, Taylor had relied on an old California state map—creased, faded, and coffee-stained—that the car's previous owner must have left in the glove compartment.

At a small town along the way, she'd stopped at a convenience store. She'd worn her sunglasses inside, her cap pulled down low. The girl working the front counter kept checking her phone, then glancing up. Taylor's hands shook as she grabbed items from the shelves—water, chips, pregnancy test. She was sure the cops would surround the store at any moment. When she took her items up to the front, Taylor glimpsed the checkout girl's phone: horse photos. The girl, after glumly ringing up the items, had pointed to a key that hung from a hook. "Restroom's around back, if you want." Between gray aluminum walls, Taylor had peed on a stick, watched as two bright pink lines had materialized in the little oval window. *Pregnant.* It was the verdict she'd both hoped for and dreaded. The gray walls had tightened around her chest. She'd dropped the peed-on plastic stick into the paper bag, pushed her way out of that restroom, and staggered out into the immense California sunshine.

Taylor gripped the steering wheel tight, tighter. Her knuckles blanched white. The words *critical condition* kept circling her brain. She hated herself for hoping it was Becca or Leon. Just, please, not Sam. Not the father of her child.

The other phrase that ran through her head: *suspect at large.* Did the authorities have her name, her photo, the make and model of her car? Fuck. Just yesterday, Taylor would have sworn that she was prepared to be imprisoned for following her beliefs, for placing the lives of animals before those of the humans who'd fucked the planet. Not anymore.

She took a deep breath and flexed her stiff neck, once to the right and once to the left. She finished off the bottle of water she'd bought at the convenience store.

The dim woodlands gave way to a sunny clearing. Fenced yards and houses appeared. Soon after, a town. Bank, gas station, realtor's office, organic grocery. Taylor followed jots of memories through the tiny town. There, that Mexican restaurant. The crew had eaten lunch on the outdoor patio.

She came to the town's lone stoplight, a line of traffic accumulating behind her. She checked the rearview. An old muscle car, a pickup. The third car back had some metal apparatus mounted to its roof: emergency lights or a ski rack? Taylor swallowed, and saliva stuck in her throat. The light turned green. She stamped the gas, and the Honda jolted forward. She passed a fire station, a school. The two-lane highway carved deeper into the hills, and the town thinned out. Redwood trees towered high again, allowing scant sunlight through. On a wide curve, Taylor glimpsed the flank of the third car: a police cruiser. Her breaths quickened—shallow breaths that seemed to overlap, to cancel each other out. Her pulse hammered.

Where was that turnoff to Alex's? Across the street from a coffee shop, if she remembered right. For all she knew, she'd already passed it. Or she still had miles to go.

The cruiser maintained its distance behind her. She had no idea whether the local police might already be on the lookout for her silver Honda. Did they have her plate number? Taylor's fingers drummed a rapid beat on the steering wheel.

As she rounded the next curve, the Bear Claw Café appeared. And there, across the road, stood the sign for Alex's street: Ridge Way. She almost flicked on her left turn signal. Instead, she pulled off to the right, into the coffee shop's parking lot. She held her breath, waiting for the cop to swing in behind her, to arrest her. She watched the muscle car pass, then the pickup. Next, the police cruiser. It flashed right past the coffee shop, rounded a bend, and disappeared.

When Taylor exhaled, the air shook from her chest. No other cars were parked in the Bear Claw's lot. A closed sign hung from the front door. She sat and stared ahead at the wrap-around porch, waiting for her pulse to slow its pounding in her head. But she felt conspicuous in that empty space. She turned the Honda around and crossed the highway.

Ridge Way climbed steeply, a straight shot uphill, golden light glancing through the redwoods. Taylor edged down the window, and the sweetly spiced air brought an inkling of respite to her whirring mind. That smell, those trees, the quietude that enveloped her: this was the kind of environment where she could envision raising a child. Maybe she could find a place to rent in the area. A landlord who valued discretion. She could pay in cash. Find a job washing dishes, or landscaping, or cleaning houses. For the rest of her life? No, she couldn't think that far ahead. First things first. Beg Alex to stay at her place, just for a night or two.

Wild bushes, grasses, and patches of ivy lined the roadside embankments. At occasional breaks in the undergrowth, drive-ways appeared. Mailboxes on tilting posts, gravel lanes that plunged further into the woods, houses secluded from the watching world.

She spotted the name, HEMLEY, painted in black on a small wooden sign next to a dirt driveway. As Taylor guided her car down the rutted lane, her nerves lit up with worry. If Alex turned her away, she couldn't cope with finding another place to hide.

The ranch style house was just as Taylor remembered it. A front door painted chocolate brown, two picture windows with cream curtains drawn shut. The property had no lawn, no arti-ficial landscaping. With its natural wood stains, Alex's house blended into the surrounding forest.

Just as she came to a stop in the driveway, the garage door

groaned and rolled slowly upward. In the dim space beyond, a pair of sneakers materialized, followed by Alex's lean legs, loose-fitting shorts, a plain yellow tee, lanky arms. She had pale skin and a sheet of strawberry blonde hair that rested on her shoulders.

Taylor tentatively raised a hand in greeting, and Alex waved her ahead.

Anxious to get the car out of sight, Taylor pulled into the garage. As she emerged from the car, words babbled from her mouth: "Alex, hi. Thanks. So, I don't know if you remember me? I'm—"

"Hi, Taylor. Of course I remember you." On Alex's thin pink lips, the hint of a smile. "And, as of five minutes ago, I'm afraid everyone knows who you are." She held up her phone.

On the glass screen, Taylor's own face stared back at her. The photo came from the personnel file of her last official job, at an architecture firm in San Francisco, three years earlier. Back then, Taylor had still followed society's rules for how a woman should present herself in the workplace. Those neat waves in her hair, the mascara and lip gloss, the silver hoop earrings. Below that baffling image: *Taylor Ellen Olsen*. It jolted her, seeing her full name like that. As if she were someone infamous, like an assassin. The others had also been identified: *Rebecca Marie Smith, Samuel Thomas Mahi'ai, Leonard Benjamin Vitola*. They seemed like the names of total strangers.

"Fuck," Taylor said.

Alex nodded. "Yep."

"I'm sorry. I didn't know where else to go. I made sure no one followed me. At least, I'm pretty sure."

"You're good," Alex said. "I've got a security camera at the end of the drive. I saw you coming in. There's no one else around."

A knot of worry unraveled in Taylor's chest.

Alex pushed a button, and the garage door began its moaning descent. She opened the door behind her. "Come on in."

Taylor grabbed her backpack from the trunk and followed Alex into a small foyer that opened into the living room. Though she was only five or so years older than Taylor, Alex lived in an utterly grownup house. White walls, hardwood floors, a matching taupe sofa set that looked to have come from a Pottery Barn catalog. Taylor had slept on that couch last fall. The familiar setting eased the bunched-up muscles in Taylor's neck and shoulders.

Alex sat in a chair, and Taylor sank into the couch, opposite her. Taylor automatically angled herself in her seat, her good right ear aimed at her interlocutor.

"So," Alex said. "I read the news, but I want to hear it from you. What really happened?"

"It was crazy," Taylor said. "We'd just broken into the plant. The smell was just ... I ran outside, into the woods to ... well, to throw up." Heat rushed to her face. She didn't want to come across as frail, but she wasn't ready yet to divulge her pregnancy to someone she barely knew. "Then I heard sirens. The highway patrol rushed in. A gun went off. I got the hell out of there."

"Fucking cops." Alex shook her head, an angry rattle. "They just opened fire?"

"Oh." Taylor looked down. She felt ashamed, the decisions of one crew member speaking for them all. "Becca. She got hold of a gun somehow. Brought it with her. Maybe she .... or, who knows, maybe the police shot first. I guess it doesn't matter now." Taylor shrugged. Fatigue fell over her, like a collapsing ceiling.

Alex's face settled into a frown. "Okay, so. But wait." Her

eyes narrowed. "You said you'd just broken in. How long did it take for the cops to show up?"

"Hm, I don't know." Taylor tried to reconstruct the passage of time that morning. They'd had the entire action planned to the second. But those plans didn't account for one of them abandoning the action. "Three minutes, maybe four."

"Seems awfully fast," Alex said. "Especially for state police to get there."

Taylor nodded. She tried to speak, but everything bunched up in her throat: words, fear, exhaustion. Betrayal. Now that Alex had pointed it out, the truth seemed obvious. Tears stung her eyes. She swallowed hard. "Someone in the organization ... maybe even someone in my crew must have ...."

"Exactly." Alex's face hardened. "One of the people who stayed here in my house last fall might be working undercover, or as an informer."

Taylor's chest tightened. "I don't know. Look, I'm sorry. Maybe I shouldn't have come here." She planted her palms on the couch cushion, started to push her body upright.

"No, hey." Alex held up both her hands: stop and stop.

Taylor froze, stuck between the worlds of staying and leaving. The story of her life. But she was tired of her life story. Her muscles went slack, and she fell back onto the couch.

"Let's work through this." Alex leaned forward. "So, there was the couple that you were here with in the fall. Sam and Becca. Could either of them have alerted the cops?"

An image of Sam sparked in Taylor's mind, from when they first met, fresh out of college, working low-level jobs. His hair was even shaggier then, his face even more boyish. They'd both signed up for weekend volunteer shifts to gather signatures for Prop 67, a ban on plastic single-use carryout bags. They joined Greenpeace together, participated in sit-ins and protests together. Then they heard about an underground organization with a more radical agenda. "Not Sam," Taylor said. "I've known him way too long."

"And Becca?"

Taylor had a hard time trusting the person who'd maneuvered Sam away from her. That aside, the intensity of Becca's dedication to the WLF would have been hard to fake. And now Becca's extreme devotion had brought about terrible consequences. "Not her, either," Taylor said.

"I agree." Alex made a sour face. "If she was with the cops, she wouldn't have gotten involved in a shootout."

"It could be Leon," Taylor said. "He's the newest member of the crew. Strong and quiet type. But, I don't know. He has an arrest record. I verified it online."

"The record could've been faked." Alex nodded slowly. "Or ...."

In that pause, Taylor's stomach turned acidic—sharper than morning sickness. "Or what?"

"Or, it could've been you."

Taylor felt herself go slack, as if she'd fallen out of her own body. "What?"

"It's just that, you know, everyone but you got arrested."

"But—"

"Look." Alex frowned. "I'm just not used to ...." She stood, and her long legs carried her in quick strides over to the fireplace along the far wall. Somewhere, the second hand of a clock ticked loudly. Alex heaved a sigh and turned. "I don't let very many people into my life. That time I hosted you guys, that was the one and only time I volunteered for that. Now, months later, those same faces that were here in my house? They're on the news, and people have been shot. It makes me nervous." She shook her head, and a laugh tumbled loose. "But the really stupid thing is, I'm actually glad to see you."

"Yeah?" Taylor plunged back into her skin. Heat prickled

her chest and tears threatened to well up in her eyes. "I promise you, it wasn't me."

Alex continued her pacing, back and forth before the fireplace. "You know what? I believe you."

"You do?"

"I've read about this before," Alex said. "When agents are working deep cover, they let themselves get arrested. Pretend to be interrogated along with everybody else. Helps with the confessions, I guess."

"Right," Taylor murmured. She pictured Sam sitting in a windowless interview room, men in suits looming over him. She pictured Becca in a hospital bed, her body connected to the machines keeping her alive. And she pictured Leon, ditching his dusty Carhartts for a crisp suit—the same suit worn by the agents interrogating Sam.

Then the images of her crew members parted like clouds, and Taylor realized she'd been gazing into the painting that hung across from where she sat. The canvas was thick with oils. Abstract shapes, but not too busy. Strangely calming, in fact. The painting's bold colors contrasted perfectly with the taupe chair.

"I like it," Taylor said, turning to Alex, who was smiling at her. Taylor got the feeling Alex had been watching her for a while now.

"A local artist, Nathaniel Birch," Alex said. "His wife, Gloria, is a midwife. They're regulars at the coffee shop down the road."

"The Bear Claw," Taylor said.

"Right. Sometimes I get stir crazy and work from there on my laptop. Otherwise, here I am."

Taylor was relieved to talk about something else, anything else. "Here is good." She smiled. "I like it here, hidden away in the woods."

"Hidden away." Alex grinned. "Is that why you came here?" In an instant, her smile turned uncertain, vulnerable.

"I don't know." Taylor shook her head. "It just felt right. Like I could trust you."

"Oh, hey. Thanks." Alex's cheeks pinked. She looked down at the floor. "Well, hey, you must be tired." Her long legs sprang back into motion. "I'll show you to the guest room. I think Sam and Becca stayed there last time?"

"Yeah," Taylor said. "I think you're right."

She hefted up her backpack and followed Alex down a long hallway. They passed an office, a bathroom, and what Taylor guessed must be a linen closet. Alex entered the next room down the hall.

Taylor found herself lingering outside. At the very end of the hallway: a door with a sturdy steel latch, a keypad built in. She tried to imagine the blueprint of the house and where that door might lead. A basement, she decided.

"Here we are."

Alex's voice drew Taylor inside the guest room. Double bed, pine dresser, bookshelf stuffed with paperbacks, a smallish TV. On the twin bed, a lightweight floral blanket. Its cheery tropical pattern reminded Taylor of visiting Sam's mom, near Honolulu. Kiana Mahi'ai had converted her son's former bedroom into an office with a guest bed. Sam had complained about the "girly" overhaul of his former dude lair, but Taylor had loved it.

She sat on the edge of Alex's guest bed, tested its bounce. With gentle strokes, she smoothed the blanket.

"This is where Mom stays when she visits."

Taylor blinked herself out of her daydream. "Where does she live?"

"Boise. That's where I grew up."

"What about your dad?"

"My parents are divorced," Alex said. "And Dad hates to travel. Which, hey, I can relate. Ha, ha. Like I said, I barely leave the house."

Taylor liked knowing that Alex's mother enjoyed floral prints. The sense of coziness. A homey quality that was otherwise somewhat lacking in Alex's realm. A floral blanket to balance out the steel door. "Can I ask a nosy question?"

Alex smirked, a playful twist of lips that dimpled her cheeks. "Wondering where that door leads?"

"You read my mind," Taylor said.

Alex turned, waving Taylor back into the hall. At the mysterious door, she punched numbers into the keypad, and the door swung the door open. "I should warn you. Certain family members refer to me as paranoid." She flicked on a light and started down the stairwell. "Personally, I like to think of myself as prepared."

Taylor paused, watching the other woman's descent. In a horror film, this would be the part where the heroine gets locked up in a dungeon.

At the bottom of the stairs, Alex flipped another switch. Fluorescent lights stuttered awake, lighting the realm below.

As if plunging into unknown waters, Taylor all but threw herself down the steps.

"Welcome to the bunker," Alex said.

Taylor found herself in a concrete basement, bare walls lined with shelving units. She wandered the space, glancing at canned goods, boxes and bags of dry goods, rolls and packets of paper goods, all the imaginable goods. Bottles of water. Lumber and power tools. Gardening supplies. Bunk beds in the corner.

"Remember the swine flu, about ten years ago?" Alex said.

"Mm-hm." Taylor had been a teenager then, sharing a yurt with her mom at Seabreeze Organic Farm. Her best friend,

Brendan Wardell, had lived in the main house. He'd contracted swine flu and had battled fevers for weeks.

"That was the last official pandemic," Alex said. "While everyone else went about their lives like nothing was happening, I pretty much stayed inside for two months straight. I was living alone in an apartment in San Jose, coding for work from my bedroom. That's when this little obsession started."

Taylor peeked inside a freezer chest packed with boxed dinners and vegetables. An incredible array. How long could a person survive down here? Or two people, or three. "Man, you are definitely prepared." She laughed, surprising herself. When had she last laughed?

Behind Taylor, no response. Total silence. All her fears boomeranged back. She was instantly certain that Alex had snuck back upstairs and locked her in the bunker. That she would call the cops. That Alex was the one who had infiltrated the WLF. Taylor's heart thudded. She spun around, ready to charge up the stairs.

But Alex hadn't moved. She stood, head bent over her phone, forehead wrinkled in concern.

Bad news.

Taylor clasped her hands together, gripping tight. "Is everything okay?"

"No, actually. Everything is pretty much fucked. Three TSA workers at the airport in San Jose have been diagnosed with COVID. It's our backyard now." Alex looked up, mouth slack. "This virus is going to get really bad, really fast." Her green eyes glistened. "Lots of people are going to die."

Taylor searched those eyes, saw only caring. Why had she mistrusted Alex just a moment earlier? The answer, she realized, had nothing to do with Alex. It was everyone else. From her feckless parents to whomever informed the police that very day, so few people had proven themselves trustworthy. And yet,

Taylor had no choice. In order to create a new life, she would have to place her trust in others.

"Shit, that's terrible," she said. Taylor felt relieved that the news wasn't about Becca or the cop, then guilty about finding relief in such awful news. She'd experienced too many emotions that day, a drunken swirl of feelings. "It's a good time to be a prepper, though, right?" With a clumsy wave, she gestured at the plentiful shelves. "Meanwhile, I am totally unprepared." Why hadn't she planned ahead, thought of the future? "I don't know what I ..." Her head was too light, her stomach queasy. This time, the pregnancy wasn't to blame. She was just exhausted. Scraped fucking raw, that's how she felt. "I mean, I really don't know." She tried to laugh it off—a sharp and jangling sound, totally false, that echoed off the concrete walls. She swallowed the laugh, and a sob caught in her throat, ugly and wet. She turned away. "I'm sorry."

"It's all right." Alex lay her hand on Taylor's shoulder. "You're welcome to stay here. I mean, until we figure out what's going on. What your next move should be."

That's exactly what Taylor was hoping to hear. Now she felt guilty for wrangling the invitation. She faced Alex squarely. "You shouldn't feel obligated."

"Hey, it's not like I'm going anywhere." That playful smirk surfaced again on Alex's face. Those dimples, so earnest. "And, with the virus spreading like it is, I'm not letting my mom leave her house, much less come down here to visit. So the guest room is all yours."

Taylor smiled. A house in the woods. A floral blanket. A bunker crammed with food. She couldn't ask for more. But she also couldn't accept the offer. Not yet.

"Okay, before I say yes?" Taylor's hand went to her belly. The contour hadn't changed in the last five weeks. No outward signs of life. But she felt a connection there beneath her palm, a continuous circuit of flesh and blood and some deeper energy. The connection grounded her, settling her stomach and calming her nerves. The connection spoke to her. That tadpole in her womb, it liked this house. It liked Alex, too. "There's something else I need to tell you."

CHAPTER SEVEN

FEBRUARY, 2057

Clack-clack-clack-clack! The sound jolts down Kiana's spine. Gunfire in the police station?

Suheera points up to the plaster ceiling of the jail cell. "I think it's just a hailstorm," she says.

Kiana nods quickly. Now she recognizes the sound.

Seconds later, the ruckus dies, and the holding cell goes quiet.

Suheera's gaze returns to the concrete wall opposite where they sit, lost in a daydreamy stare.

Kiana also feels lost, somewhere between past and present. She longs for the comfort of Alex's land—the sanctuary of her childhood. Kiana's mother gave birth to her in that house. The midwife was Alex's friend, Gloria Birch. She and Nathaniel were among the very few visitors to the house during Kiana's childhood. Early on, she didn't mind the lack of company. Alex and her mom met her every need. That house—and the three acres of surrounding woodlands—was Kiana's entire world. Her mom made her first contribution to the property while still pregnant. In a sunny patch behind the house, she dug a vegetable garden, supplying the family with dirt-fresh carrots, lettuce, tomatoes, artichoke, and berries for many years. Kiana grew up on that land. But not always in Alex's house. Eventually, she and her mother outgrew the guest room. When Kiana was five or six years old, her mom designed a separate space for the two of them. Based on her blueprints, she, Alex, Nathaniel, and Gloria erected the Small House. Their home.

Alex still lives in the main house—the safe house, the house on the ridge. Even before Kiana's mom tumbled into Alex's life, she kept her address unlisted, had all her mail delivered to a post office box. Kiana learned that particular trick from Alex. That, and many others: coding, some basic electronics. But Kiana never learned how Alex managed to make Ellen Taylor appear from out of nowhere, the creation of a new identity. Did Alex bribe a courthouse official? Hack into the county's computer network? Pay off an expert forger? *It's best you don't know*, they always told Kiana.

Alex is nearly seventy now. The average life expectancy in America drops with each passing year. Another reason for Kiana to get herself free.

When she looks to Suheera again, the softness in her eyes has turned brittle. Maybe her nostalgia for the past has turned to despair for the future. Or maybe Kiana's projecting.

"Where did you grow up?" she asks Suheera.

"Houston," the girl says, her voice smeared with disdain. "Both sets of my grandparents fled Syria, and that's where the government resettled them. There's a small Syrian community there, but plenty more racist white people." Suheera studies Kiana's face for a moment. "No offense?"

She smiles, shakes her head.

"Anyway. My parents were kids at the time. They grew up together, attended the same mosque. They swore they'd leave Houston someday. But, with the Submersion, so many of us lost our homes. Everyone was sick all the time and too poor to move anywhere else. I'm the only one I know who got out of there. My friends and family thought I was crazy for moving to California." Suheera glances around the cell, before her focus settles on her belly. "Maybe they were right."

Kiana is lost for words. What could she say? Suheera has made some questionable choices. But so has she.

Footsteps echo in the hall. Officer Eckhart emerges, his profile flickering between the metal bars of the holding cell. Beside him walks a man in handcuffs. He's tall and broad-shouldered with buzzed-short brown hair and a mustache. Chinos and a button-down shirt. The prisoner turns to look at the women. In his eyes: nothing. Beyond nothing. A frightening vacancy. For that single second that she's immersed in his stare, Kiana fails to breathe. It's not until after he's removed from her sight and she hears the door clank shut on the holding cell next door that she exhales again.

"That's him," Suheera whispers in her ear. "The killer on the news."

Kiana nods and whispers back, "Walter Brogan." Already, his name seems foreboding, like he's the bogeyman.

Eckhart returns and stops at the cell door. "All right, Ms. Olsen. Your attorney'll see you now. You know the drill, right?"

Kiana does: stand, turn, hands behind her back. Before rising, she gives Suheera's shoulder a squeeze. "Be brave."

She smiles sadly at Kiana. "You, too."

As Eckhart slaps the handcuffs around Kiana's wrists, Suheera grimaces. That empathy will make her a good mother. Outside of prison, Kiana hopes.

Eckhart marches her back to the same interrogation room, as if she's trapped in a loop. Has she already been found guilty, and this grinding repetition is her sentence? Except, the variables change each time Kiana reenters a space. Now, in place of

Detectives Turley and Bell, a woman in a peach pantsuit sits at the gray metal desk.

And the terminal is gone.

Locked away in an evidence room, she assumes. Kiana knew she'd never walk out of here with that precious object in her hands, but its absence is crushing. Another acre of hope, turned to dust.

Eckhart unshackles Kiana, then positions himself near the door. A houseplant with a gun.

The woman stands. She's petite, like Kiana. She wears a charcoal-gray pant suit and a saffron-colored blouse. Her neat brunette bob forms parentheses around her slender face. "Kiana Olsen?" She smiles tightly, briefly. "Hi, I'm Jane Hamamura, the public defender assigned to your case."

They shake hands. Such a banal formality, and yet Kiana's emotionally moved by the gesture. To be treated like a human being! Then it hits her: the lawyer probably shook Walter Brogan's hand, too. That's her job. Each person is just a cog in that particular machinery, grinding through their roles: lawyer, suspect, detective, guard. Only, Kiana never intended to play her role.

She takes the same seat as before. Another purgatorial recurrence.

Hamamura pulls her chair up alongside Kiana's. From an attaché, the lawyer pulls out her phone and sets it on the desk between them. A holo-screen pops up. "Let's go over your case file," she says. The lawyer begins her recitation, but the words skim right past Kiana. She knows she should be attending to each and every sentence—not *as if* her future depended on doing so, but *because* it does.

And yet. All she can focus on is a sound from the corner of the room: the metronomic splatting of water on water. It's seeping through the moldy ceiling tiles and dripping into a strategically placed bucket. The ice from the hailstorm must be melting on the flat roof of the police station, slipping through the cracks and seams. *Splat, splat, splat.*

"Is this making sense, Kiana?"

Jane Hamamura's teak-colored eyes are scanning her own.

"Sorry," Kiana says. She can feel her face crumpling—all those tiny muscles bunching in ugly ways—but she can't control it. She looks away. "I'm really tired."

"Of course you are." Hamamura pats her shoulder, like Kiana's a kid who fell off a bike.

But she doesn't need this woman's pity. With a deep inhale, Kiana straightens her spine. "Okay. Explain to me what my options are."

This apparent change of attitude earns her a crisp nod of approval from Hamamura. "Option number one: you supply the detectives with your street address. Apparently, this is a real sticking point. I've been assured that doing so will get the charges against you reduced from a Misdemeanor B to a C, with a recommendation for community service instead of thirty days prison time. There's also a minimum fine of ten thousand dollars."

Kiana gasps. That's more than she and Javier have in savings. "And what happens with option two, the Misdemeanor B?"

"Thirty days to six months in prison and a fine of twenty thousand. That's *if* you plead guilty before the judge at an arraignment hearing, which would likely occur tomorrow morning. Keep in mind that Governor Jenkins is really adamant that this particular offense be prosecuted. It's part of her whole One Life Is All You Need campaign. So, if you don't cut a deal with the police right now, you'll probably get the maximum sentence. And a steep bail fee."

"Shit. Okay." Kiana's head is swimming. "And what is the third—"

The interrogation room goes dim. Kiana wonders if she's passing out. No, it's the overhead lights, pulsing at half power. A moment later, they jolt back to life. Then they semi-falter again.

Officer Eckhart takes one step away from his spot against the wall, his hand on his holstered gun. His eyes lock on Kiana's, a silent warning to stay put.

For a few seconds, everyone remains frozen in place. The interrogation room is bathed in a soft ambience, as if candlelit. Then, total darkness.

What happens to the locks when the power is out? Kiana could take a chance: vault over the desk, bust out of the room, charge down the hall. There's another door at the end, tended by a security droid. She tries to remember the layout of the police station. Which way did she turn, after Bell and Turley had her booked? She remembers a desk sergeant and a wall of bulletproof glass. Beyond that, a sprint across the lobby and—

The lights clack back on: full-force, blindingly bright.

Eckhart is blocking the door, gun drawn, barrel pointed at the ground. Even still, seeing that little death machine out in the open scares the hell out of Kiana. She was smart to have stayed put. And also cowardly. She needs to be braver.

Eckhart mutters something like, "That ain't supposed to happen." Then he holsters his gun and resumes his post.

At the desalination plant, the backup generators would have kicked in immediately. Of course, unlike the police, the desal plant doesn't have to rely on scant municipal funding. They have droids who fix things like leaking roofs, long before the electrical wiring is compromised.

Jane Hamamura laughs with forced levity, then clears her throat. "Now, where were we?"

Kiana shakes her head, the trail lost.

"Right," Hamamura says. "The third option. Plead not guilty at the arraignment, and we go to trial." She stares Kiana down. "I do not recommend this option."

To Kiana, this sounds like her last chance to win over a sympathetic jury, to beat the odds. "Why not?"

The lawyer sighs. "First, if you're unable to afford bail, you'll be remanded into custody until the trial starts. Given the current backlog, that could take months. The prosecution would then have plenty of time to build their case against you. And it's my understanding that the police have additional leads they might choose to pursue. If more evidence is acquired, prosecution could add charges to your case. You might be looking at a Misdemeanor A, which is a minimum of one year in prison and two-hundred thousand in fines."

Kiana's lungs tighten, her throat clamps. "Mm-hm," is all she manages to reply. If that black market weasel were to identify her, then Turley and Bell could nail Kiana for the ventilator. One more dire factor to weigh. It's all too much. Isn't it enough that her child is dead? That her husband is dying?

"What about medical records? Can the police look into those?"

Hamamura frowns. "I'm afraid so. HIPPA doesn't protect against subpoenas."

More potential evidence, more potential jail time. One month, six months, a year: it makes no difference. Kiana can't afford to lose a single day. Already, too many days have slipped away. She should have attended to every moment with Javier, nurtured every memory. She wants transcripts of every conversation, audio samples of every idiotic burst of laughter, video clips of every time she walked into a room and Javi's mouth lifted into a smile. A dozen years, spilled into a mental blotch.

A dozen years since the day they met. That morning, Kiana remembers.

She'd been working full time at the desal plant for four years then. On nights and weekends, she studied for the national licensing exam to become an electrical engineer, which would allow her to qualify for a promotion. She'd lived in a yurt behind the yellow house that she and Javi now call home. Even with paying only minimal rent to the Wardells, Kiana could barely afford food, fuel cells, and her share of the internet bill. She also didn't maintain the old Honda as well back then. On a drizzly January morning in 2045, while she drove through the valley outside Costa Perdida, the car lost power. Kiana was stooped beneath the propped-open hood when a motorcycle growled past. The rider pulled a U-turn and circled back. A sage green bike. A man in faded denim, brown leather boots, and scuffed black helmet. His goatee shined darkly in the mist. His hair, which was longer back then, draped below his helmet, clinging to the collar of his jacket. When he flipped up his visor, Kiana was immediately lost in the kindness of his eyes, in the genuine concern that his thick black eyebrows inscribed onto his broad forehead. The first words Javi spoke to her: "Is it the engine?" Kiana loved the assumption he'd made—that she'd already diagnosed the problem. She smiled. "The alternator, I think." An educated guess, which would later prove correct. "Shit, that sucks," he said. Then the corner of his mouth puckered in concentration—the left corner, always the left, as Kiana would come to learn. "I know a guy up in Point Nada, works at the auto yard. If he has the part, I could help you replace it." A laugh bubbled out of her. Who was this guy? Javi half-smiled—momentarily uncertain, he would later admit, whether she was making fun of him—and then his mouth widened into his glorious smile. "Wow, are you sure?" she asked. "I'm heading that way anyway," he said. They exchanged numbers, shook hands. As Kiana watched Javi stomp his bike into a roar, the future shuddered brightly in her mind: the rides they would take along the Pacific Coast, her arms wrapped around his thick torso, the thrill of hard turns and bracing cold. All the adventures that life would bring them.

"Kiana."

Jane Hamamura's sharp tone pulls her back into the interrogation room. The air is damp and cold, just like on that ride to Point Nada. And yet the air is completely different. Twelve years ago, the air smelled of freedom.

Wrapping her arms around herself, Kiana looks to her lawyer. "What were you saying?"

"That I highly recommend you cooperate with the police. Give them the information they want now, before they investigate further. It's my understanding that the offer of Misdemeanor C has a short lifespan."

Kiana stares down at the literal table before her. The ugly gray metal slab where her hands are resting. No, not resting. Shaking. Her mind has gone numb, but her hands are shaking. From digging into the unforgiving earth. The one hole down to the junction vault. And the other. The grave.

Javier asked to be buried alongside their home. Returned to the soil, so his decaying flesh can feed the starving planet. And Kiana will do anything to fulfill Javi's dying wish.

Except there's nothing she can do now. The system has her. They'll keep moving her from place to place—from holding cell to interrogation room, from courthouse to jail. She can't escape the loop.

If there is a way out, it must be through her mind. Somewhere amid the galaxy of neurons inside her head, a wormhole must exist. Some sort of calculation, or astral projection. An escape route to the other side.

"Kiana? I can give you a minute to think this over. But the detectives are waiting. And between you and me? You don't want to make Nick Turley any grouchier than he already is."

Kiana can't understand why Jane Hamamura is wasting her time like this. She should be talking to Suheera, who still has a chance to help herself and her unborn child.

"Look," Hamamura says. "There's only one way you're walking out the front door of this police station tonight." She points to the corner of the interrogation room where the water continues to drip, drip, drip. "And time is running out on that option."

That front door. The detectives led Kiana through there, earlier tonight. A slab of grimy glass beneath the faux-Roman arch. The earthquake of 2040 left a prominent lightning-bolt crack in the off-white stucco. If only she could squeeze through that jagged crack.

Her lawyer clears her throat. "Do you understand what I'm saying?"

"Yeah." Kiana blinks hard. She understands that she can choose from options one, two, or three. But there is no good choice. She's trapped in a labyrinth without an exit. "But I can't decide."

Jane Hamamura inhales sharply through her nostrils. The breath deflates slowly through pursed lips. "All right," she says. "I'll let the detectives know. I'm sure they'll want to speak with you again."

Seconds later, Kiana's lawyer has evaporated from the room, as if she never existed in the first place. Now it's just Eckhart standing by the door. The armed houseplant. Kiana stares past him, and he past her, their thoughts wandering separate galaxies. Where is the wormhole in hers?

CHAPTER EIGHT

MARCH, 1964

Ilse Schmidt took a deep breath and slipped beneath the surface of the cold bath water. The shock turned her body electric. To prepare for her swim, she was trying to simulate the winter temperatures of the River Spree. The one time she'd added ice cubes to the bath, her mother had commented on their absence from the freezer compartment. Such were the hazards of continuing to live with her parents. In a police state, even the prying eyes of one's own family could prove fatal.

Tonight, Ilse would escape those prying eyes.

She stared up at the bathroom ceiling. White, like the East Berlin sky that day, suffocated by fog. The kind of sky a person could dissolve into. Ilse imagined that a gentler sky hung over the Western half of the city. That the air itself would taste sweet.

Sweeter than the stale stench of her father's cigarettes, the motor oil from the garage where he worked, the vodka he sweated from his pores, the acrid gunpowder from his hunting rifle, the bitter frustration that clung to his breath, the cruel scent of his leather belt. Horst Schmidt, formerly a corporal in the German Wehrmacht, some two decades past. Ilse was only three years old at the time the war ended. Her first memory is of her father's return from the front. A veritable stranger. She still thought of him that way.

Soon, Ilse would put her father in the past, where he belonged. Same with her nervous mother, Gerda. She worked the ticket window at a U-Bahn station. She was cold to passengers and cold to Ilse. All of East Germany was cold, indifferent. Soon, Ilse would put the whole frozen-hearted country in her past.

She had planned her escape carefully. First, she'd chosen her method. By water, of course. She'd spent most of her young life in the pool, training to win Olympic gold. At the age of eight, her swimming skills earned her placement at a sports boarding school. There, she received paltry academic instruction, while her strokes were honed for hours each day. And what good had all that training done her? In 1960, at the age of seventeen, Ilse swam one-point-three seconds too slow to qualify for the East German Olympic team. In the trials for the 1962 European Aquatics Championships, she had fared worse. Every year, a new crop of teenage girls emerged who swam faster and faster. She knew she had no hope of making the Olympic team this summer.

At twenty-one years old, Ilse Schmidt was a failure. A secretary at a textile plant, the Democratic Republic had doubled her work hours, from part-time to full-time. Her swim coach had been reassigned. Ilse had become just another worker cog. Swimming for her country no longer mattered.

Tonight, she would swim for herself: for a chance at a new life in a free land.

Prior to the summer of 1961, the citizens of East Berlin had enjoyed more liberties. They could pass with relative ease from their Soviet-controlled half of the city to the Western sectors nominally controlled by Allied forces: American, British, French. Then, on the night of August 13, 1961, the German Democratic Republic stretched a barbed-wire fence along the political border, dividing the city in two. Within two weeks, they erected a crude concrete edifice in its place: the first incarnation of the Wall. Now that terrifying monstrosity separated Cold War enemies, as well as friends, colleagues, family members, lovers. And, as if the Wall weren't formidable enough on its own, watchtowers had also been erected at various intervals. From these watchtowers, Volkspolizei used searchlights and rifles to protect the border, by any means necessary.

A few East Berliners had attempted to escape by swimming across the Spree. The meandering river divided Berlin between north and south, more or less. Along certain stretches, it also coincided with the political border between East and West. In these places, the grotesque Wall menaced the riverbanks, making it nearly impossible to even approach the water, much less swim its breadth. Those who'd tried, the VoPo had shot dead.

Ilse could imagine only one way to escape. She would swim under the Wall.

As she lay submerged in the bathtub, she envisioned the spot for her start dive. Near Friedrichstrasse Station, along the Reichstagufer promenade, only a simple metal handrail stood between everyday pedestrians and the polluted river water below. Presumably, the East Germans deemed the promenade a safe distance from the Western shore. Ilse would enter there, about 100 meters from where the Wall crossed the river, along Marschall Bridge.

But, even after swimming under the Wall, her journey would be far from over. Beyond the bridge, the border cruelly stretched one extra city block further along the southern bank of the Spree. Her exit point would be the first stretch of

Western land beyond the Wall: the shoreline before the Reichstag building. Ilse had estimated the entire distance from dive to safety at 250 meters. A difficult swim for most people, even under normal conditions. And Ilse's conditions would be far from normal. For instance, she would have to swim without being seen, which meant swimming underwater. And who could swim that far underwater?

Ilse could.

Every evening after work, in the public pool at Stadtbad Mitte, she swam and swam. Her head submerged, she'd steadily built up the capacity of her lungs, one Olympic lap at a time. Frog kick, breaststroke, glide. One lap per minute. The rhythm suited Ilse. Her body worked more efficiently, in harmony with the water instead of fighting against it. Until her lungs ran out of air, that is. Then her body wrestled against her mind until she was forced to breech the surface. But the work had paid off. In two long breaths, she could swim to West Berlin.

Just five laps to freedom.

Ilse lifted her head from the bath water and took in deep breaths of air. She wouldn't push herself any further—not right before her swim. She pulled the stopper from the drain, stepped out of the tub, and slid into her threadbare cotton robe. She stood before the bathroom mirror and towel-dried her lemon-blonde hair, which she kept "short as a boy's," as her mother often complained. But then, her mother complained about everything. Ilse wouldn't miss her sour rants.

In the living room, her father sat in his wingback chair, the evening paper stretched before him. How many column inches of propaganda did he absorb every day? Unfathomable. Her mother sat on the ugly old couch, flipping through the latest issue of *Sibylle*, a magazine of fashions neither she nor Ilse could afford.

Her father lowered the paper with a snap. "There you are!"

He always barked his words, as if commanding an Allied soldier to halt. "In the water all the time. The swimming pool after work, the bathtub after dinner. Are you hoping to grow fins and gills? You think this will make you swim faster? Ha!"

Her mother looked up at Ilse from a stylish photo spread. She had a way of frowning and smiling at once, each expression faltering and straining against the other. "It's Sunday night. Shouldn't you be getting ready to visit Helga?"

"Yes, I'm leaving soon." Inside, Ilse beamed. She had trained her mother well to notice this new routine. Helga was her paternal great aunt. A recent widow, her eyesight had begun to fail her. Once a week, Ilse road the tram out north to Prenzlauer Berg to keep the old woman company. But not tonight.

In her bedroom, Ilse slipped her hand under the mattress and withdrew an envelope. It contained a single photograph, an address jotted on a scrap of paper, and the paltry funds she'd managed to set aside: two hundred Marks der Deutschen Notenbank, as the money in the East was now called. She'd heard that banks in the West might not even recognize her Marks as legal tender. But she had nothing else to build her future on.

The address—on Prinzenstraße, in the Kreuzberg district—belonged to Renate Maier, her only friend in West Berlin. Ilse had known Renate since childhood, when they swam together at sports camp. Her family had defected to West Berlin before the Wall. Though the girls hadn't seen one another in nearly three years, they had maintained a correspondence through the mail. Of course, the Stasi almost certainly read these letters. Ilse had therefore never revealed to Renate— or to anyone—her intention to escape.

Just thinking of the Ministry for State Security made Ilse's stomach jitter. She concentrated on the photo.

In the black-and-white image, she and her older brother, Arnold, stood between their parents on the shore of Wannsee Lake. On the far side of the glittering waters, a dark smudge of trees, against which Ilse's hair appeared ghostly white. She was eight years old that summer and already tall and lean. Ilse got her long bones and broad shoulders from her father, her blonde hair and wide mouth from her mother. Arnold and her father had darker hair, shadowed eyes. Scarce smiles. The photo was the lone image of the Schmidt family where everyone looked happy. There would never be another. Arnold had defected five years ago and now lived in Duisburg, in the West. With luck, Ilse would see her brother again soon.

She sealed the envelope and wrapped it in cellophane. She would take nothing else to the other side. Ilse peeled off her bathrobe and, with long strips of Sellotape, bound the envelope to her abdomen. Then she tugged on her one-piece black swimsuit, put on a gray overcoat, and slipped into a pair of flats. Unnoticeable clothing, disposable. Like the rest of her life in East Berlin.

That included her parents, who, when Ilse entered the living room again, remained fixed in their usual spots. She could swim around the globe, and they wouldn't have budged a millimeter. Ilse grabbed her handbag from where it hung by the front door. Would this be the last time she saw her parents? Or this apartment? Her family had lived between these thin walls for the past nineteen years, since the bombing of their Charlottenburg house during the war. Leaving seemed impossible. Her head felt light, her legs weighted down. She clung tight to the doorknob. After a deep breath, the dizziness passed. She forced a smile, made her voice light against the sudden heaviness in her limbs. "Auf weidersein!"

Neither of her parents bothered lifting their eyes. "Auf

weidersein," her mother sighed. Her father merely cleared his throat.

Good. Indifference was good. Ilse shut the door behind her, and the weight dispersed, like the bursting of a dam. Right before the fastest swims of her life, this same surge of energy had propelled her through the water. Ilse breezed down the stairwell to the ground floor, out the door, and into the bitter winter night.

The narrow street was quiet and dim. The sky remained enshrouded in fog.

She turned onto Friedrichstrasse, toward the train station. Through the haze, her neighborhood appeared unfamiliar, sinister. The true East Berlin. When fully visible, the streets were often too familiar. They tricked her mind into forgetting about the institutionalized crushing of free will.

From out of the fog, Friedrichstrasse Station appeared. The windowed walls glowed eerily in the wet, white air. Ilse paused on the sidewalk, as an S-Bahn train roared over the bridge and slowed for its approach. If she were truly going to visit Great Aunt Helga, she would catch the yellow tram just outside the station.

It would be so simple to board that tram. So simple to sit in Helga's ugly tenement flat making idle chatter. So simple to return to her mindless job on Monday morning and suffer the petty insults of her smug boss, Frau Kessler. So simple to endure her parents. So maddeningly simple to swim lap after lap for a country that had never believed in her. To give up, simplest of all.

Ilse drew nervous breaths through pursed lips, as if poised at the edge of the swimming pool, waiting for the starting whistle. But no coach or referee would compel her next move. And so her legs decided for her. They propelled Ilse toward the river. Like a fish, she slipped through the wave of people disembarking the station. Tired faces, eyes gone flat with resignation. Everyone headed the opposite direction, to the cramped apartments that awaited them—apartments like the one Ilse had just left behind.

A fetid smell rose from the river just ahead. A strange beckoning. Through the fog, the yellow glow cast by lampposts caught the black metal handrail that ran along the Reichstagufer. Ilse couldn't see the far riverbank—just a smear of marquee lights from the theater on Schiffbauerdamm. She turned west. The cobblestone roadway was deserted. The sidewalk, too. Good. She didn't want to be noticed.

But, walking alone, would she stand out to the watchful Vopos? The nearer she drew to the Wall, the more attention she would call to herself. She had to appear as if she belonged on that esplanade. But Ilse didn't belong on land. Certainly not on East German land. She only felt a sense of belonging while in the water.

With her mental stopwatch, Ilse timed the sweep of the searchlight from the watchtower that stood at the edge of the death strip. She counted the seconds: *Eins, zwei, drei, vier, fünf.* When the beam of light turned its back on her, she began to shed the layers that bound her to the terrestrial plane. First, her handbag. The purse was empty, worn just for show. Its strap slid down her arm and the bag landed with a muffled thud.

Upriver, the dark outline of Marschall Bridge emerged from the fog. A trio of graceful arches, topped by the graceless Wall. Beyond, she could just make out the tall, clean lines of the Reichstag building. Her beacon in the West. Just five minutes away, beneath the icy waters of the Spree. When she emerged, she would take deep breaths of sweet Western air.

Unless, of course, her lungs emptied, forcing her to breech the surface. Then she would get a bullet in the back of her skull. Through that imagined hole, fear crept in. Fear wanted

Ilse to stop in her tracks. Fear wanted her to stare nervously up at the watchtower, to search the shadows of nearby doorways for informers, to turn back. But Ilse's legs kept her moving.

She was nearing her dive spot, where Bunsenstraße met the Reichstagufer. Any further, and she risked detection from the watchtower. With each new step, Ilse freed one of the buttons on her overcoat. She charted the arc of the searchlight. The yellow beam passed closer now, then struck out across the water. Ilse shrugged off her coat: the rolling of shoulders, the sweeping of hands. The heavy fabric sloughed cleanly down her back. She was certain a fellow pedestrian would call out to her: *Fraulein, your coat!* Or a Vopo would leap in front of her, rifle drawn, shouting: *Halt!* But the only noise was the clatter of a train across the river.

Ilse kicked off her flats. Now she wore only her swimsuit, with the envelope Sellotaped to her stomach beneath. The damp, freezing air gripped her bare limbs. She shivered once, then pushed the cold from her mind. Quickly, she climbed over the handrail and stood at the precipice of the retaining wall. Below, a sheer drop of several meters into the blue-black Spree. She was accustomed to meditating at the lip of the pool, her toes neatly aligned, her thoughts organized, her breath steady. She hadn't thrown herself headlong into a body of water since she was a child, since the summertime outings to Wannsee, where she and Arnold would take turns climbing onto their father's broad shoulders and leaping into the lake. Now, as the searchlight prowled back across the Spree, she had no time to linger. She aimed herself toward the Reichstag and dove.

Ilse concentrated on the alignment of her limbs, on straightening her jackknifed torso. It was only halfway through her brief descent that she remembered: air! With a deep gulp, she filled her lungs. Her fingertips sliced into the water and, in the instant before her head submerged, she clamped her mouth shut.

A clean entry, which meant a quiet splash. Ilse herself couldn't hear a thing. In the dense underwater silence, her mind calmed immediately and her body took control, steering her upriver. The current was slow, posing only slight opposition to her progress. No current could compare to barbed wire and bullets, or to the machinations of an entire regime. Also, she knew that the current was weakest along the river's edge. With each stroke of her arms, the fingertips of her left hand grazed the stone retaining wall, its surface worn smooth. That tactile check kept her on course. Otherwise, she swam nearly blind through the contaminated water—a miasma of gasoline and sewage that occluded what little light penetrated the surface.

Ilse shut her stinging eyes and counted her strokes: *Eins, zwei, drei, vier, fünf.* She would try to maintain her ideal rate of ten strokes and kicks per fifty meters. After twenty strokes, she would reach her temporary haven beneath Marschall Bridge.

Ilse's legs shot back and flared out, kicking like a frog. From the years of repetition, her limbs moved in perfect unity, fluid as the water itself. Kick, stroke, glide. Kick, stroke, glide. She focused on tabulating her progress: *acht, neun, zehn.* With that tenth stroke, Ilse had swum her first fifty meters. One minute gone. Her lungs still felt full of air. And, thanks to her cold-water baths, the frigid waters of the Spree hardly bothered her. In fact, she felt invigorated, alive for the first time in months. She could remain submerged for days, could swim forever.

Ten strokes to go. Then she could surface. She restarted her count: *Eins, zwei, drei.*

Yellow light. Even through closed eyelids, she sensed the beam of the searchlight passing nearby. Ilse opened her eyes, suffering the water's sting. A jaundiced glow lit the surface of the Spree. Uncertain how far down the light could penetrate, Ilse glided lower, into the darkness.

Sechs.

Her chest tightened, but Ilse reminded herself not to panic. A mere itching for air, that was all.

Sieben, acht.

With each pass, the searchlight grew brighter, stronger. The Wall was exerting its will against her. She could feel the Vopos itching for action, the selfish blood-tug of her parents, the stricture beneath her sternum. All of these forces, telling Ilse to retreat.

Her limbs kept churning.

Neun, fünf.

A moment later, the bright light disappeared. Marschall Bridge. She must be directly underneath. Now was Ilse's chance to breathe.

As she began to rise, a second light skimmed the water, just beyond the shadow of the bridge. Ilse had known all along that another watchtower stood on the opposite bank, further upriver, but she had misjudged the scope of its vision. Her arms flung out, breaking her upward momentum. Her lips parted in surprise, and precious air billowed from her lungs.

She hovered there underwater, watching and waiting for the arc of the searchlight to pass—seconds that felt like hours. When darkness returned, Ilse pushed against the water and shot up. The moment she broke the surface, her mouth opened wide, like the beak of a hungry baby bird. For the first time in two minutes, she swallowed deep breaths of air.

At that same moment, an engine rumbled over Marschall Bridge. As she bobbed there in the water, Ilse traced the vehicle's path overhead, to the far side of the Spree. Her gaze landed on a small boat. It floated near the opposite bank, at the base of the bridge, maybe fifty meters away. She could just make out the dark shape of a hunched body: the back of an overcoat, the slant of a cap. The figure was facing East—the way she'd just come. A Vopo, guarding the borderland.

Ilse clung as best she could to the damp stone abutment, staring at that shadowy shape. Now that the noisy engine had passed, even the lightest lapping of water echoed off the underside of the bridge. She breathed as quietly as possible, waiting to recover, to refill her lungs. But the longer she remained still, the deeper the cold seeped inside her. Ilse had to move. After one last gulp of air, she slipped her head beneath the water, planted her feet against the abutment, and thrust herself upriver.

She counted her strokes: *Eins, zwei, drei.*

Ilse's muscles began to strain. But she was no stranger to the burn, to the aching of shoulders and hips. She could endure the pain. If her lungs held out, then her body would carry her to the end.

She focused on an image of herself, standing tall before the Reichstag building. That vision, she clutched to her mind.

Now where was she? Oh, yes. *Acht, neun, zehn.*

Just one hundred meters to go. The cycle began again. *Eins, zwei, drei.*

Everything hurt now. The cold bit into Ilse's bones. Her chest grew tighter and tighter. And her limbs struggled through every stroke. She hadn't rested long enough under Marschall Bridge. Her lungs yearned for the oxygenated realm that stretched above her, tantalizingly close. No, she wouldn't succumb to that traitorous urge.

Pressure mounted in her bladder, as always happened at this late stage of her underwater swims. A petty bodily demand, not worth fighting against. She relinquished control, and, for a moment, relished the warmth that clouded around her shivering thighs...

What was her stroke count? *Secht? Acht?* Oh, god. Fear rushed through her. She'd lost herself in time. Now she wouldn't know when she could safely swim ashore. But had she ever? The distance from her dive spot to the Reichstag was only an estimate. And what was an estimate but a calculated guess? Ilse had guessed with her life.

Her entire body trembled, as if the weight of the Wall lay upon her back. The Soviet will, it turned the river to concrete. Her country willed her to fail now. Was failure Ilse's destiny? When she tried out for the 1960 Olympic team, her muscles had knotted. She had struggled to the lip of the pool, humiliated, and dragged herself out of the water. Now she had failed to properly execute her escape plan. Her exhausted arms and legs pushed hopelessly against the concrete water.

Then, a flutter in her chest. Was she having a heart attack? Ilse swam another stroke, and the seizure struck again—below her heart, below her lungs. A spasm in her diaphragm. Her limbs froze and her throat clamped shut. The spasm buckled Ilse's torso, folding her like a pocketknife. All the air, gone from her lungs.

Up. She had to go up. Her hands and feet shoved against the concrete water, launching her toward the golden light that danced on the wavering surface above. She was nearly there, nearly there.

Her head burst free of the water, and she gasped for air. She felt dizzy, disoriented. Her surroundings made no sense. Why darkness? Why fog? Where was she? Then she snapped into focus. Ilse looked up, and there stood the mighty tower of the Reichstag.

A shout cracked the air: "Halt!"

Ilse captured a quick breath, tucked her chin, and dove. How far to safety? Fifty meters? Just one more Olympic lap. Ten kicks, ten strokes. *Eins, zwei, drei.*

The cold had numbed Ilse clean through. Her limbs felt foreign—like crude wooden levers screwed into her torso. Her anatomy—that strange machine—transported her to another world.

A sharp sound, like a cough in her ear. A trail of bubbles streaked before her eyes. A bullet. She pushed through its trail, through her terror.

Another cough, this one quiet and polite. A dash of bubbles in her periphery.

On her eighth stroke, just as her legs frogged back together, something struck her right calf. The force of the blow rippled through her, shaking her muscles into chaos, obliterating form. Now the streaks of bubbles came from Ilse, spurting from her shock-parted lips. Her mind knew only one thought: *I'm going to bleed out and die.* But her body wouldn't listen. From its state of chaos, it realigned itself. Her arms fanned out and back. Her left leg flexed out and kicked, and her wounded right did its best to follow.

Arms raking through the water, her fingers reached and reached. Nothing. When she reached again, she touched the stone retaining wall. Stretching higher, her palm landed flat on the shore. The concrete path before the Reichstag.

The West. She'd made it. Though too numb to feel its textures, her hand now resided in West Berlin.

But her submerged body remained in hostile territory. East Germany controlled the full breadth of the Spree.

Ilse raised her head out of the river. She couldn't believe that all of it lay before her: the curving pathway, the sloping grass embankment, and the Reichstag building itself, looming majestically above it all. She pressed her other palm to the concrete and, with a final dolphin kick, flung her chest onto the walkway.

A man came running toward her through the dark and fog,

the tails of his coat lifting like sails, like wings. As he skidded down the slick lawn, his face emerged from the shadows: square jaw clamped tight, brown eyes, dark blue cap on his head, a matching dark blue coat. The man kept repeating the same two words. English words. *My god, my god.*

Ilse tried to pull herself from the river, but she had no strength left.

The man crouched low and hooked his hands under her arms. He lifted her from the water.

Ilse wanted to thank the man, but her teeth were chattering too hard.

He laid her on the grass, on Western soil. He yanked off his dark blue coat and draped it over Ilse, like a woolen blanket. The man wore a light blue military jersey. Stitched across one breast pocket were the words US AIR FORCE. Across the other, OLSEN.

His eyes darted—from Ilse's face to her bleeding leg and back again. "I go. Telephone. Hospital," Olsen said, his German barely comprehensible.

She knew a little English. How to communicate that all she really wanted was assistance in getting to the address of her dear old friend Renate? She opened her mouth to speak, but Olsen had already dashed away, toward the Reichstag.

Ilse pulled his coat tight around her shoulders. Despite the cold and damp of the grass beneath her, she felt warmer already. Sleepy and warm. Cradled by the welcoming soil of West Berlin. Her trembling lips lifted into a smile.

CHAPTER NINE

FEBRUARY, 2057

O nce again, the two detectives sit across from Kiana.
Nick Turley brought the remains of his dinner back into the interrogation room: half a Sub Atomic sandwich in his hand. A greasy smell makes its way across the table, invading Kiana's sinuses. How can Turley stomach those things? The flatbread comes from the usual mass-production sources: a mixture of chemically enhanced wheat flour and processed filler. And that protein patty? Atrocious. One of Javi's coworkers—a former Sub Atomic employee—claimed to have obtained inside information on exactly which animals they mash, press, and fry to produce them. Javi and Kiana were sitting on the couch when he told her. Then he slipped into his boyish grin and did a really bad hillbilly impersonation: "Mmm, I sure do like me some of them critter patties." They laughed so hard that César started barking at them.

"So...." Bell gives Kiana a funny look.

Was she laughing out loud? And her cheeks are wet. Now Kiana feels the heat of shame there, too. She swipes away the tears, tries to compose her errant face. "Yeah?"

"We talked with Jane Hamamura outside," Bell says. "No deal on the street address? Is that where we're at?"

Kiana reconsiders her options. If she withholds the information, she's making a huge mistake. If she relents and leads them to Javier, she's making a different huge mistake.

"I don't know," Kiana replies. All of this mental processing—laws, decisions, consequences—has become impossible. Despite the nauseating odor of Turley's critter patty, her empty stomach is distracting her. She feels lightheaded. When was the last time she had a meal? Food has so little appeal for Kiana anymore. She forgets to eat. To think, she used to complain about always having the same thing for dinner: sautéed veggies and the free noodles that Javi brought home from Pastalgae. She got really good at inventing new sauces to cover the same boring entree. Red sauce, garlic sauce, cream sauces, curries. Anza would always ask for cheese sauce. Children and their love of bland foods. In every other way, she was vivid, electric, always playing. Javier and Kiana would stand in the kitchen, chopping and stirring up dinner, while they watched Anza in the yard. Swinging from a tire tied to the oak tree, or jumping rope with friends, or throwing a tennis ball for César, who was just a floppy-eared puppy then.

Then, then, then. Six years ago, now. In 2051, Anza was a happy and healthy child. The world was overflowing with happy and healthy children. Or, at least, living children. Then came spectral fever. Scalding the blood of Kiana's baby girl, passing its gray shroud beneath the surface of her skin. In just sixteen awful days, she was dead. Reduced to a digital avatar. She deserved so much more.

Detective Bell snaps her fingers at Kiana. "Hey, are you with me?"

"Hm?" She's starting to wobble again. Bell just asked her

something. To commit to a choice, of course. Yes or no, night or day, prison or the illusion of freedom.

Meanwhile, that constant drip in the corner is driving Kiana insane. How can the detectives just sit there placidly? Have they become inured to that maddening sound? To the depressing ambience of the police station? To the dysfunction of society?

Everyone is working too hard for too little in return. Especially now that androids occupy so much of the labor force, companies can get away with underpaying their human employees. Like Javier and Kiana. They both have managerial jobs, they grow their own veggies and raise their own chickens, rarely go out, avoid extravagances. And yet, they can't afford to buy a house. But they did manage to scrape together enough cash for an old Airstream trailer. And Javi's Subaru has a trailer hitch. That is the entirety of their retirement plan. Drive to Alex's land, park the Airstream, and live out the rest of their days in the Santa Cruz Mountains.

That *was* their plan, their days. Now hers alone.

Kiana turns to check the clock. 10:02. The secondhand jolts, and it feels like a slap. With every tick, she tries not to think about her husband—his sunken cheeks, his pale skin, his cracked lips, his body lying so still. Every other second, she fails. Every other breath, she falters. Kiana's every other thought runs back to Javier.

Detective Turley's mouth smacks wetly open. "Come on, Kiana. You don't want to end up like your old man, do you?" He consults his screen. "A laundry list of convictions. Involuntary manslaughter, three counts of vandalism, multiple B and Es. A grand total of twenty-five years in Victorville Federal Penitentiary. Ouch."

Kiana first wrote to her father, Sam Mahi'ai, the year she turned eighteen. The letter began: *You don't know me, but I'm your daughter.* How embarrassing. She spent hours laboring over that terrible opening line. What a mindfuck that must have been for him. And Kiana couldn't offer much proof of her claim, since she assumed the mail was inspected. If she'd mentioned the name Taylor Ellen Olsen, the FBI would have hounded Kiana for ages. Instead, she relied on the power of her name: Kiana was also his mother's name. In his reply, Sam wrote: *A daughter? That the best news I've heard in a very long time.* After a few letters back and forth, he asked Kiana to visit him in prison. Spring break, freshman year at San Jose State, she drove down I-5 to Bakersfield—where, her mother once told her, she was conceived at a Motel 6—and cut east across the Mojave Desert. She remembers only a panorama of beige. When she arrived at the prison, Kiana was patted down and bodily scanned, escorted through locked passageways, and deposited into the visitation room, where plastic tables and stools were bolted to the concrete floor. When the guards brought her father in, she recognized him instantly, despite the awful orange outfit and the gray at his temples. Kiana had imprinted the images of his younger self into her mind. Yearbook portraits, group photos from protest rallies. Even the courtroom sketches from the trial of *People v. Samuel Mahi'ai.* Even the sketch that showed only the back of her father's head—a minor detail in the artist's rendering of the testimony given by Federal Agent Edgar Ozola, the prosecution's star witness, a bald and burly man whom her parents had known as Leon Vitola. But, on that first meeting, Kiana and her father didn't talk about the Wildlife Liberation Front, the arrest at the San Joaquin Valley Pipeline valve station, Becca Smith's death following the explosion, the ensuing trial. He only wanted to hear about his newfound daughter, how she spent her days in college, what she hoped for her future. The girl who sat in that visitation room feels remote to Kiana now. She wanted to become a history professor, didn't care if she ever married or had children, and envisioned herself living in a more progressive country, like Denmark or New Zealand. She couldn't have imagined that she'd remain stuck in California, mother to a dead child, wife of a dying husband. Or that the man she sat across from that day in the visitation room would be killed in a prison riot three years later, robbed of the opportunity to redeem the failures of his youth.

Does Kiana want to die in prison? Of course not. But she won't give Nick Turley the satisfaction of a reply. His eyes on her are almost as revolting as the smell of the critter patty. She looks away, watches a drop of water plummet into the bucket.

The splashing water shifts Kiana's focus to the pressing demand of her full bladder. She leans toward Detective Bell. "May I use the restroom?"

"Sure thing. We could all probably use a little break, hm?" When Turley replies with a noncommittal nod, Bell pushes her chair back from the desk. "Come on," she says. "I'll escort you."

Kiana was expecting Eckhart to be summoned. That's how the loop operates: he places her in handcuffs and walks her down the hall, back and forth, back and forth, until the end of time. Kiana stands. She takes tentative steps toward the door, which Detective Bell has unlocked and holds open for her. It's like in those old movies, where uniformed employees of nice hotels were paid to facilitate the easy commuting of guests. The only good thing about being stuck in a loop is knowing what to expect. Kiana holds her arms out, wrists exposed.

Bell gives her a weary look, then nods toward the hallway, indicating a right turn instead of the left Kiana has grown accustomed to. "Just stay one pace ahead of me. And don't try anything stupid, all right?"

"Yeah, no, okay," Kiana mutters. As soon as she steps out of the interrogation room, she realizes the folly of her earlier escape fantasy. At the end of the hallway, guarding the door, is an armored security droid. Burly metal body painted police blue, big simian arms, small brainless head, eyes glowing yellow. And, because droids are battery-powered, they remain active during power outages. Also, that particular model might have night vision. Kiana isn't sure. The security droids at the desal plant are far less imposing.

"Hold up," Bell says. "Back to the wall, please." She steps around Kiana, opens the door for the women's restroom, and glances inside. "All right, we're clear. Let's go."

It's an ordinary restroom. Linoleum floors the color of a smoggy sky, a row of sinks, three gray metal stalls. Kiana drifts toward the first one, pauses, raises her eyebrows at Detective Bell. The unordinary conditions of the ordinary restroom visit have rendered her infantile and mute.

"Take your pick," Bell says.

Kiana chides herself for her timidity. She needs to be stronger, more decisive. She chooses the middle stall, because choosing the first would be too easy. When she slides the flimsy latch on the stall door, she realizes this might be her last chance for a long time to close herself into a space that she's chosen.

Kiana unbuttons her jeans, sits, and pees. The relief is immediate, a loosening of every muscle in her body. Slumped forward, elbows on knees, she peers under the stall door. The heels of Bell's black sneakers stand by the row of sinks.

A fat drop of water splats against the top of Kiana's head. Her entire body tenses again. She cranes her neck back. The restroom ceiling is made of the same mildewed acoustic tiles as in the interrogation room. She pictures the space between roof and drop ceiling, the water pooling there, like in a damp coastal cave.

"Damn humidity," Bell says. "Fucking with my hairdo."

Kiana tears off two squares of toilet paper. It's become

subconscious, the imperative to conserve precious resources. Even this cheap, flimsy, abrasive toilet paper must be conserved.

"Oops!"

An object—red, plastic—hits the floor near the detective's feet. Kiana watches it skitter across the linoleum. A hair pick. It clack-clack-clacks as it dances away from the shuffling pursuit of black sneakers. "Shit," Bell mutters.

Kiana stands, pulls up her jeans.

The lights shudder. A moment later, the restroom goes dark.

In that interstitial moment—less than a second—Kiana decided. Now, without another thought, she acts. Her own sneakers find their way onto the toilet seat, then the lid of the tank.

"Stay where you are, Kiana." Bell's voice echoes off the walls. "Do not fucking move."

In the hallway, someone shouts.

Kiana pops the acoustic tile loose, pushes it aside. She reaches into the unknown space above, searching for a sturdy handhold. She's worked in spaces like these. The aluminum grid that holds the ceiling tiles and fluorescent light fixtures is typically suspended from the rafters by slender guide wires. The apparatus isn't designed to support a person's weight.

The air cracks, then cracks again. Gunfire.

Kiana flinches, freezes. Blood pounds through her body, beating against her skin. Is Olivia Bell trying to kill her? Then she realizes the shots came from somewhere else in the police station. More shouts break out: warnings, calls for backup. Someone yells the name Brogan. A woman screams.

"Kiana!" Bell's voice is near. Is the detective right beside her, there in the stall?

A wooden beam. Kiana's fingers wrap around the two-by-four. With a jump and a tug, she pulls herself slowly upward. A virtual memory flashes to her mind: Ilse Schmidt, swimming toward the Western shore. In the ultra-highspeed era, Kiana had inhabited her great-grandmother's avatar, had felt the frigid density of the river against her muscles. She'd understood intellectually what Ilse had known bone-deep in her every stroke: to fail is to perish. Kiana clenches her jaw. Her triceps pulse with the strain. She pretends she's climbing in the arroyo, inching her way skyward, toward the next rock ledge. She flings one arm over the beam, then the other. With a final push, she hoists herself up into the crawl space.

When she rises to a squat, the crown of her head bangs against a beam. Kiana muffles a grunt, winces against the ringing pain. She tries to gauge her surroundings, but there in the rafters, the blackout is even blacker. Instinctively, she reaches for her watch. She could use its flashlight app. But, of course, the cops took her watch when they booked her. Her other senses will need to compensate. Through the thrumming in her head, she listens for signs of Detective Bell.

A second later, three more gunshots erupt in the police station. Outside, a siren screeches. Kiana hears thuds and cracks, from who knows what. Chaos rules the world below. She takes advantage of the noise to set the acoustic tile back in place.

"Kiana!" Bell calls out. "Wherever you are, get down on the ground and stay down. You hear me?"

She hears but won't obey. She has to move. Now. Before the power returns and the chaos subsides. But which direction? Her hands grope the space around her, tracing the pattern formed by the network of beams. The verticals run in rows of tight angles, a crosshatching that would be tricky to navigate even under ideal circumstances. She pivots, reaches out. Another horizontal beam, parallel to the one supporting her now, lies two feet away. Okay, good. She can crawl from one beam to the next.

Now she notices an interruption in the darkness. The glow of a rectangular light. A window, maybe? Kiana maps the building in her mind: hallways, doors, rooms. The courthouse sits on one side of the police station, a vacant property on the other. If she's right, the glow will lead her away from the courthouse. She crawls toward the glow.

Progress is infuriatingly slow. Kiana feels like an infant. Each movement is frighteningly new. Was that how Anza felt when she first made her way across the living room rug? No, she had smiled and laughed, encouraged by her mama's happy face. But no one is cheering on Kiana. Only the thought of returning to Javier keeps her fumbling onward.

She reaches out for the next beam, and a chasm opens before her—an opportunity to fail. On the sixth beam, her palm slides on damp wood. Hand slips free. Wrist smacks. The whoosh in her gut informs her of a certain plummet through open space. In a flash of fear, Kiana sees everything that will happen: She'll crash through the flimsy ceiling tiles and land at the feet of the detectives. Years will be added to her jail term. She'll be completely fucked. But Kiana's limbs act independently from her scared-stupid mind. They know to grab, to brace against, to wrap around, to hold on tight. Somehow, she's managed to right herself. After three deep breaths, she crawls on.

The shouting below has stopped. But the sirens wail on, near and far, as if the police cars were crying out to one another across downtown Costa Perdida. Their urgent, whining dialogue rings in Kiana's ears: *Have you found Walter Brogan yet? No, not yet. What about Kiana Olsen? You mean that idiot lady who tried to buy a black market terminal? Yeah, that's the one. No, not her either.*

A spider web smears itself onto Kiana's face. Black widow? Brown recluse? Is it on her? Shit, shit. Kiana shakes her head, swipes at her face, wobbles on the beams. But she doesn't feel anything creepy-crawly. Fucking arachnids. What kind of a world does she live in where dolphins and cheetahs have gone extinct, but venomous bugs live on?

As Kiana crawls ahead, the rectangular glow takes on distinct properties. It's not a solid shape after all, but a series of luminous yellow slits. A vent in the wall?

At least the light is strong enough now that she can discern the outlines of the beams. Her infantile trek gets easier, her movements quicker. She thought she'd never reach the wall, and now she's there.

Sure enough, the source of the glow is an aluminum gable vent, mounted to the wooden frame of the police station's exterior wall. A corner of the vent hangs loose, a screw gone missing. Two of the louvers are bent, and rust is setting in. Kiana estimates the dimensions of the crappy old vent. If she can pry it loose, the hole that's left should be just the right size for her to squeeze through. If only she had her utility knife, she could make quick work of those screws. But the cops took that from her, too.

Kiana peers between the louvers to see what awaits her on the other side. A cold slap of damp air. The blue-black night. A rain so light, it makes no sound as it falls on the roof of the vacant building that abuts the police station. The drop down looks short, maybe four or five feet. On the next block over is a functioning streetlamp—the light source that drew Kiana, moth-like, to this spot. But from what she can tell, the blackout in the police station extends to the entire block, maybe further. Good. In the darkness, those whining police cars will be less likely to spot her.

With one hand gripping a vertical beam for support, Kiana

slips her fingers around the limp edge of the vent and pulls. The thin metal starts to bend back from the wooden frame, just a bit. She leans back, tugs harder. The blood-rush to her brain makes her woozy. Her arms are shaking, always shaking. But the effort isn't good enough. She needs more torque. Kiana scoots across to the other side of the vent. Turning sideways, she sits on a horizontal beam and plants the soles of her sneakers against two nearby verticals. She feels unsteady in this pose, but, this way, she can use her entire body. The moment she grabs hold of the vent again, a flash of memory hits her. She's on a rowing machine in the gym at San Jose State. One of the few pieces of aging equipment that still functioned, Kiana used that machine a lot. Her kinesthetic self remembers the motion: pushing with her legs and glutes, pulling with her arms and back. *Row*, she thinks, *row*. As her legs thrust out, her upper body pivots back, like the reclining of an easy chair. The vent begins to peel away. The metal edge digs into Kiana's fingers—it hurts like hell. Teeth clamped tight, she focuses on the screw at the bottom corner of the vent. She watches it struggle to maintain its hold, its threads worming through the mealy old wood. When the screw finally gives, it caroms off Kiana's shin and disappears below. With one border free, the vent peels back more readily. The aluminum creases, like folding construction paper. As a child, Kiana did that, folded construction paper. But for what purpose? The flicker of memory disappears. Her hands fall away. She's exhausted, but she did it. She's created a small window to freedom.

Her breaths are rapid, her brow covered in sweat. She should rest. There's no time to rest.

Through the opening, Kiana climbs out backward: feet, legs, hips, and belly slide over the ledge. Her chest scrapes against the wood. She hangs there, scared to relinquish her grip. She's used to climbing in bright daylight, used to seeing where she'll land. Javi would tell her to have faith. Not in any super-natural power, but in herself. Kiana lets go.

The soles of her sneakers land firmly on the rainy roof. Already, her face is wet, sweat washing away, skin cooling in the night. It feels wonderful. In air like this, Kiana could run all the way home. Yes, and she'll call up Javi on the way. He'll make hot cocoa—three steaming mugs. And the family will huddle together on the couch. And—

The loud, fast beating of her blood tramples Kiana's thoughts. Her throat is closing up. Nerve ends gone frantic. She's standing on a rooftop, in the middle of a blackout, and she can't breathe. The rain is soaking through her clothes, there's a murderer on the loose, sirens are screeching across the town, and her chest is convulsing. As if a creature inside Kiana is trying to rip itself from her gut, to clamber up her throat, to fly screaming into the night. But she can't let it out. And she can't run home yet. And Javier isn't going to be making any hot cocoa. Not tonight, not ever again. Not in this reality. But maybe in Level Up? Sure, yes, good. Maybe her husband's avatar is performing that lovely domestic task right now. And he wouldn't be using the powdered shit that's mixed with microwaved desal water, but real melted chocolate and pan-heated milk. And maybe, when Anza drinks that hot cocoa, the taste and feel will be perfect on her tongue, and she'll be glad she's stranded in her phony digital world and not the one in which her parents live.

Is it the distance between those two worlds that Kiana is unable to reconcile? Unlike Javi, who *is* prepared to bridge that distance, to move from this world to the next. But only if Kiana finds another unregulated terminal.

She knows where she has to go. Her normal life is over, anyway. She may as well forfeit her career.

Kiana's breaths are steady now. The creature, satisfied with having rattled its host, has slithered back into its miserable home. Kiana sighs. Why does she always fight to repress the painful truth, when she knows the pain will escape to the surface?

Her own escape isn't yet complete. She still has to get off this roof.

A rumble in the air, from the back of the building. A car engine turning over. In a low crouch, Kiana makes her way along the wall, to the edge of the roof. Below is a small parking lot for whatever business once operated in the building below her feet. She's used that lot several times over the years, when doing business in town. The space is separated from the police station's parking lot by a knee-high chainlink fence, its outline barely visible in the blackout night. Kiana cranes her head around the wall. She can just make out the dark shapes of cruisers and sedans. A pair of headlights pierces the darkness, and Kiana ducks back into the shadows. The car pulls out of the lot, glides past on the street below, and disappears into the night.

With every cop in Costa Perdida scouring the town, she can't imagine how she'll ever make it home. But, first things first. Kiana surveys her rooftop realm. On the far side is a boxy protrusion. An access hatch to a ladder maybe? Or just an HVAC unit? She stays low as she makes her way toward it. Squinting into the dimness, she blinks rain from her eyes.

That whoosh hits her gut again. The plunge. It happens so fast that, by the time Kiana registers the fact that she's falling, her body is already thudding to the ground.

CHAPTER TEN

JANUARY, 1991

G reg parked his 1982 Mazda hatchback halfway up the block. His buddy Yosef had scribbled out the address, a mile or south of UCLA—Greg's alma mater, as of last June. In the yellow glow of streetlights, ragged palm trees drooped before apartment complexes painted every shade of beige. But the address for the party belonged to a shambling old house. What kind of party? Greg didn't know. He only knew that Yosef would be there, likely in pursuit of some girl. And Greg welcomed the diversion: people, drinks, music. Maybe he could make some extra cash while he was there.

He patted the inside pocket of his linen blazer, checking on the baggie plump with Ritalin. He had been legitimately prescribed the drug to combat the effects of ADHD. Was it his fault that his doctor had accidentally scripted ten times the number of pills Greg required? And that his dad's insurance provider kept paying for the surplus of drugs? Greg had more or less felt obliged to become a dealer.

From his crappy speakers came the moody throb of Depeche Mode. Greg didn't think much of Jesus, personal or otherwise. He'd been raised agnostic, at most. His gay dad and the Christian church certainly didn't see eye to eye. And his German mother had grown up in the godless Soviet empire.

Earlier that night, Greg had met his maternal grandfather, Horst Schmidt, for the first time. After the Berlin Wall fell last year, the old widower had decided to track down his family in America. Apparently, he'd found Greg's mother through an archived newspaper article that had profiled the wedding of Ilse Schmidt and Frank Olsen, the woman who escaped from East Berlin and the Air Force pilot who'd found her washed ashore. A different article had mentioned their relocation two years later to Denver, Colorado. Greg's mom had refused to see her estranged father. She'd also warned her children to stay away. Greg's younger sister, Shelley, had sided with their mom, as she typically did these days. Shelley had stayed close to home for college. She'd gotten her BA at CU Boulder and was now working toward an MBA there, too. Though his sister had always been more ambitious than Greg, he lauded himself for being the adventurous sibling. When the call came from Horst, he'd been unable to resist.

* * *

They'd met at a dive bar in El Segundo, down the street from the motel where his grandfather was staying, near LAX. Having arrived early, Greg chose a table near the door and ordered a rum and coke. Exactly at eight o'clock, Horst Schmidt entered the smoky room. Greg recognized him immediately from the one family photo his mother had brought with her from East Berlin. The old man still cut an imposing figure: broad-shouldered, brown hair gone silver, a burning light in his blue eyes. With a crisp formality, Horst shook Greg's hand across the formica table, then signaled the waitress before sitting. "Stolichnaya," he ordered. When the waitress asked "Rocks?", his grandfather narrowed his eyes and sneered, as if the poor woman had offered to hock a loogie into his glass. "Ice," Greg said, his laugh lacking the levity he'd intended. "Rocks means with ice," he explained. "Ja," Horst said to Greg. "I know this." Then he'd turned back to the waitress and his hand cut through the air. "No rocks."

Horst's hard stare pivoted back on Greg. With a terrifying intensity, his grandfather interrogated him about his life. None of Greg's responses seemed to please the old German. With each revelation—about Greg's participation in sports (minimal), about his scholastic prowess (moderate), about the reasons why his parents' marriage had "failed" (a complicated subject)—Horst had commanded still more information. "Ja, and what else." Greg had found himself shrugging a lot.

Eventually, he'd attempted to deflect the inquisition with questions about his grandfather's life.

"What's it like in East Berlin since the Wall came down?"

"Fewer people live there now."

Greg tried a more personal tack: "What about my grandmother? What was she like?"

"Gerda worked for the Ministry of Transport. In 1982, she died of pneumonia."

"Oh." Follow-up questions about his grandmother withered on Greg's tongue. "So, what's your plan now? Stay where you are? Relocate somewhere in West Germany? Move to America?"

Horst frowned. "Undecided."

His grandfather had then nodded to the TV above the bar, where flashes of explosions lit up the sky behind a newscaster's head.

"This war in Arabia," Horst said. "You will join army, ja? You will fight."

Since the start of the Gulf War in August, Greg had watched hours of CNN every night. Now that US troops were involved, he lived in a state of perpetual anxiety that the war would drag on for years, that he would be drafted and shipped off to some foreign desert, where he would be shot between the eyes. These daily imaginings had invaded his dreams. He woke up gasping, his tongue dry as sand.

Greg had just sucked down his third rum and Coke. "I'm registered for the draft," was all he'd replied.

A smile crept into the corners of Horst's mouth. "I was a corporal in the Fürher's Wehrmacht, you know." His grandfather explained that, during the first few years of World War II, he worked as a mechanic in a factory, building trucks and tanks. Then, in 1944, he was called into battle. "At this time, your mother was perhaps two years old and your uncle, four." Horst's chest seemed to inflate as he launched into a speech about troop camaraderie and defending the fatherland against foreign invaders.

His eyes had then lit up. "Ah, I have a good war story to tell."

A revelation from his grandfather, at last. Greg had leaned his forearms on the barroom table.

Horst explained that his regiment had been fighting for months in a German forest near the Belgian border. Countless casualties on both sides. Horst described the dark of the pines, November's bitter cold rising off the nearby stream, the mist that hung in the valley, the smoke from artillery fire that blighted the air. He had lost track of his squadron. As he broke through a thatch of trees, he found himself face to face with a US infantryman. "I had my rifle at the ready, as did the American. There was little space between us, and so we wrestled. Soon enough, I had him pinned to the ground. I thrust my combat knife into his abdomen." Horst lunged across the

table and jabbed his finger at Greg's diaphragm. "Right here."
His grandfather was smiling as he did this—a strange and
frozen smile that caused Greg to shiver. Then, as Horst
remained poised over the Formica table, his expression soured,
his eyelids emptied. At last, he collapsed back in his seat. His
eyes trembled as he gulped down his third glass of Stoli. A
moment later, Horst complained of jet lag, and the evening
ended.

* * *

Headlights flooded the rear-view mirror as another car pulled
up behind Greg's. He blew out a puff of bad grandpa vibes and
shook his head like a dog. That left his brain nice and blurry.
He killed the ignition and Depeche Mode cut out. Greg
checked the firmness of his well-moussed hair in the mirror,
creaked upon his car door, and stepped out into the mild Los
Angeles night. Still buzzed on rum and Cokes, he swayed like a
California palm.

As he neared the old house, the knucklehead drums and
farting guitars of some hair rock band pounded into the air. He
didn't spot any Greek letters on the off-white stucco façade. So,
not an official frat party. All the same, Greg had his doubts. But
he needed to keep his buzz going. And he'd promised Yosef he
would be there.

The front door was propped open, as if to suggest that even
the uninvited were welcome. Greg walked into a living room
straight out of his 1970s childhood: brown faux-wood paneling
on the walls, shag carpet the color of overripe avocados, and a
soft buttery light cast by yellow lampshades. College kids
mingled in clusters on tatty couches or wedged into corners of
the room. Greg recognized a short guy in an orange rayon shirt.
Henderson? Hendrickson? They'd taken Spanish 201 together.

Greg had been a junior, Rayon Shirt a sophomore. He stood by himself, nodding his head to the unmissable beat.

Greg smiled wide and made his approach. "Hey-ey, man!"

Rayon Shirt lifted his chin in greeting. "What up, Olsen." He shifted a blue plastic tumbler from right hand to left, sloshing beer foam, which the furry carpet instantly absorbed. "Long time, no see."

They fist bumped—Greg's preferred level of physical intimacy with other guys. And emotional intimacy, for that matter.

Rayon Shirt had gained weight over the last couple of years. He'd frosted his hair, likely an attempt to compensate. The attempt had failed.

"Looking good," Greg shouted over the music. "Senior year, right? How's school going?"

Rayon Shirt shook his head, slugged back some beer. "Biochem is a bitch, bro."

"Yeah, I bet."

Greg had majored in geology. He'd amazed himself when he'd parlayed his BA into a salaried job, back in July. An environmental research assistant, he now spent his days driving around a hydrologist and helping her collect water samples. She was analyzing the effect of California's current four-year drought on salinity and algal bloom in rivers and streams. She probably understood biochemistry. Meanwhile, Greg was the one squatting on muddy banks, capturing un-fresh water in sterile bottles. Despite his meager salary, the job itself was all right. He liked getting out into nature. But his boss would only listen to classical music in the car, which made the long rural drives feel that much longer.

At the moment, Greg would gladly take Beethoven over Bon Jovi, or whoever the fuck was wailing away on the stereo upstairs.

"Say, bro." Rayon Shirt leaned in close. "I've got this killer exam coming up on Monday, and I'm going to have to cram my ass off tomorrow. You got any of those magic pills handy?"

Exactly the words Greg was hoping to hear. He pulled the baggie from his blazer pocket, but kept it close to his chest. "I got you covered, man. Five bucks a pop." He lay his hand on Rayon Shirt's shoulder—a gesture of professional reassurance he'd copied from his own doctor. "How many do you need?"

Seconds later, Greg was folding a twenty into his wallet and heading for the bright, white kitchen.

He walked in on a scrum of Neanderthals in sports jerseys and Polo shirts. They were whooping it up and downing shots from a bottle of Jägermeister. Greg recognized a couple of the guys from classes. They all played for the Bruins football team.

As did Brody Claypool. In his fifth year at UCLA, Brody was an all-conference left tackle and king of the campus Neanderthals. Greg was hoping to avoid his massive presence. Brody's girlfriend, Tracy Battaglia, was among Greg's regular buyers. And, sometimes, more than a buyer. Last fall, during midterms, he'd paid a few professional visits to her dorm room. Both times, they wound up drunk and mostly naked in Tracy's bed. According to her, she and Brody were "pretty much broken up" at the time. Based on recent rumors, Greg had gotten the impression that Brody had a different perspective on their relationship status. Now Greg wasn't sure where he stood with either of them.

Before he could duck out of the kitchen, one of the Neanderthals handed Greg a glass. He dreaded the taste yet craved the buzz. Also, due to the sheer mass of steroidal humanity that now surrounded him, he felt obliged to imbibe. He downed the liquor in one speedy gulp. That awful taste—licorice and cough syrup—stuck like varnish to his tongue.

Several pairs of bleary eyes were staring down at him, as if awaiting his verdict.

"Ah!" he said, and the Neanderthals laughed.

So, they were all good drinking buddies now? Greg considered breaking out the Ritalin, but he doubted these guys were the type.

A blockhead with curly red hair loomed over Greg. "I know you, right?" His breath smelled of corn chips and Jägermeister. "What's your name again?"

He could give a false name, but what if they caught him lying? "Greg."

"Right," said Blockhead. "We had a class together, I think. What's your last name again?"

The warm breath of another oaf steamed the back of Greg's neck. Did all of these guys smell like corn chips? "Olsen."

"Right, right. Greg Olsen." Blockhead nodded, and Greg pictured an anvil balanced precariously over his skull. "So, you must be a friend of Brody's, since you're here at his house."

Greg felt the kitchen tip off axis. Brody fucking Claypool's kitchen. "Yeah, well." He took a half-step back and thumped into a chunky wall of humanity. "Me and Brody, we know each other from around campus."

"Sure, sure." Blockhead's eyes narrowed. For several seconds, he said nothing. A guitar solo screeched through the kitchen. Then he broke into a wide smile. "All right, Greg Olsen. Enjoy the party."

With a stinging clap on the shoulder, Greg was dismissed. The wall of Neanderthals parted, and he escaped, back into the living room that time forgot. There was the front door. He could just leave. Hadn't the day gone on long enough? He'd already driven his boss all over San Bernardino, collecting bottles of murky water and listening to Bach. Then that fucked-up encounter with his German grandfather.

Even as Greg tallied his waking hours, he found himself climbing the stairs to the second floor. He'd promised Yosef.

And he still had that bulging baggie and plenty more potential buyers to find.

When he reached the landing, Greg started down a long hallway, then wandered through the first open door. The only source of light in the room was a large screen TV. Three guys sat on a couch, aiming black plastic pistols at the digital creatures who blinked to life on the screen. The enemies looked humanoid and cast an eerie glow. Were they the inhabitants of some alien world or a catastrophic future Earth? The game pinged, bleeped, and chimed, clashing with the power chords and thundering drums that blasted down the hall.

If Greg were going to waste his time on a video game, it would have to be more like real life. Only way better. He would live in a much nicer house than this. He would have a cool job, maybe designing solar-powered cars. And, of course, he would have a smart and sexy wife—a beautiful keyboardist who was also a mountain climber. And they would live in a world without drought. A world without war. Now that would be a game worth playing.

Along the far wall, a trio of girls huddled by an old stereo console, its dull brown wood surface littered with empty beer bottles. The girls' faces were slack with boredom. They'd all put so much effort into looking cute—short-skirted floral dresses, faces painted on, hair primped and sprayed into place—just to hang out in some noisy cave and shout gossip in each other's ears, while their boyfriends blew up aliens.

Greg drifted over. He recognized a blonde girl with a tight perm. She had perpetually mournful brown eyes, like a Cocker Spaniel condemned to wait at the window for humans who would never come home. A fellow geology major a year behind Greg, their schedules had occasionally overlapped. He was pretty sure she knew Yosef, too. And her name was?

He placed himself in the girls' close orbit. His eyes linked with Tight Perm's. "Hey," he said. "Have you seen—?"

"Greg, hi. Omigod, I was just saying." Tight Perm turned to her friends. "Wasn't I just saying? This is the guy!" Her eyes landed on Greg's again. In the dim light, they seemed less mournful, more lonesome and buzzed. "All last year, whenever I needed to pull an all-nighter, I was telling them, Greg Olsen totally hooked me up." She wrapped a curl of golden hair around her finger and smiled.

"Yeah?" Greg said. "That's cool."

She always flirted with him, and he sometimes flirted back, but mostly because she was buying drugs off him. The exchanges always left a bad taste in his mouth—almost Jäger-meister bad.

He looked to the guys on the couch. Which one of those doofuses was ignoring this lonesome girl? Playing with their toy guns. Blasting away at fake enemies. Meanwhile, actual US soldiers fought in a real war. What if the Persian Gulf turned into the next Vietnam? Or World War III? In last night's dream, Greg had found himself in full combat gear. He needed to scale a high dune, but his boots kept filling with sand, and the weight of his guns and ammo were pulling him under.

He could almost admire Horst Schmidt for having survived the war. If only his grandfather had fought for the right side.

Greg's other grandfather, Einar Olsen, had been a sergeant in the US Army. He'd emigrated from Sweden in 1936, married an American gal named Betty the following year, and had a son named Frank the year after that. Einar, too, had fought on the Western Front, where he was shot in the leg. Beyond that fact, Greg didn't know a single detail. Maybe he'd killed dozens of enemy soldiers. Now he was just Grandpa Einar, a stolid old man whom Greg had visited every summer of his childhood. As for Greg's dad, Frank Olsen had never harmed anyone, in combat or otherwise. Frank was an Air Force pilot during the Cold War. He was stationed in Berlin when he met Greg's mom. His service obligation ended right before America's involvement in Vietnam escalated. Thankfully, neither Frank nor Einar had ever voiced any expectations that Greg might follow in their bootsteps.

"So, do you, like, have any on you tonight?"

He squinted at Tight Perm, hoping either to make her image clearer in his mind or to make her disappear. He wasn't sure what he wanted. Another drink, maybe.

She leaned in closer, smiled slyly. "You know, Ritalin?"

"Right, yeah." He whipped out the baggie. "How many?"

"Oh, just a couple. No, make it four." Tight Perm gave an embarrassed smile. She wrinkled her nose like a little bunny rabbit.

As Greg shook the round white pills into her open palm, one of the doofuses on the couch cried out in mock anguish.

I thrust my combat knife into his abdomen. Greg could still feel Horst Schmidt's finger pressed to his diaphragm.

"Hey," he said to Tight Perm. "Did your grandfather kill anybody in World War II?"

"What?" She laughed and playfully pawed his arm. "Greg, you are so random."

"Yeah." He shrugged. "Never mind." A wave of tiredness crashed over his brain. He would find Yosef, then go home and get some sleep. "Well, see you around."

"Oh?" Tight Perm's smile faltered. "Okay. Bye, I guess."

Greg wandered out into the hall. A pair of Neanderthals stood at the far end, mean looks on their faces. Or maybe they always appeared dyspeptic.

He opened the nearest door and ducked into an empty bedroom. A king-sized bed. Posters of girls and cars. Crown molding gone to hell. A glass door that opened onto a balcony.

Long ago, the house might have been grand—before succumbing to the habits of college kids.

Greg stepped outside. The Los Angeles sky was choked by an orange haze. A chorus of backyard voices smeared the nighttime air.

"Hey." Tracy Battaglia stood at the far end of the balcony, forearms braced against a wrought iron railing, a plastic tumbler in one hand and a cigarette in the other. In the gauzy light and swirls of smoke, she looked like an interstellar being from that video game. Or a newscaster reporting from a nighttime desert war. A cautious smile played on her lips. "So, are we no longer on speaking terms, or what?"

"Sorry," Greg said, and walked over to stand beside her. He imitated her lean, sharing her view of the patchy lawn, the concrete patio, the empty pool, the beautiful young people who laughed and drank, pranced and posed. He looked for Yosef's bushy hair, his stick-figure limbs. No, just a bunch of anonymous college kids. When gathered among them, Greg could convince himself that he still belonged in their world. But not from the height of that balcony. He'd become someone else, hadn't he? An interloper. A small-time dealer, crashing a party. A regular grownup from the workaday world. None of those kids down there had tasted real life. And maybe Greg hadn't either. But he kept getting whiffs of it, and the stench grew deeper with each passing day. The bitter murk of still water, the stale sweat of war-terror, the astringency of vodka and hatred on an old man's breath.

I had him pinned to the ground. Thanks to his grandfather, Greg could now add to his combat fears that he might be forced to kill someone at close range. A complete fucking stranger. Some Iraqi dude who likely shared Greg's same goal of not dying in a war.

He spoke softly, out into the night. "Were either of your grandfathers in World War II?"

"Hmm." Tracy swirled her glass. An eddy of melting ice in an amber sea. She sipped her drink. "One of them was in the Navy, and I think he fought in that war. Or maybe it was Korea? I don't remember. Why?"

Greg studied her eyes, the pinch of frown between them. He tried to read a message in the curious poise of her lips. Maybe he should be kissing Tracy Battaglia, instead of talking about some evil shit from fifty years ago. "Oh. No reason." He shrugged, light and easy. In a moment, the distance between them would collapse. Maybe, with her body against his own, his mind would take a rest.

"So, Greg. You got any pills on you?"

He flinched. Tracy's lips now seemed light years away. "Yeah. Why else would I be here, right?" Reflexively, his hand withdrew the baggie from the pocket of his blazer. "How many?"

From the doorway, a voice barked at his back: "Olsen? What the fuck!"

Hands raised, Greg turned to face Brody Claypool. He felt himself smile. Where others fought or fled, Greg's instinct was to charm the beast that threatened him. "Oh, hey, man. I just happened to run into—"

"Get the hell out of my house." Two hands, like metal claws, grabbed at Greg's chest. Brody was a machine designed solely to uproot objects—a truth Greg understood in the moment his feet lifted from the patio.

"Brody, no!"

Tracy's command rang loudly in Greg's ear, but seemed to have no effect on the physics at play. Greg's spine smacked against the railing. Then the roof went whirling past his upended shoes. A millisecond later came the blurring of lawn, of concrete, of human shapes.

Greg must have landed, but he had no awareness of that fact. All sensory information seemed to arrive across a chasm of yawning time. Even when sights and sounds and pressures finally reached him, they made so little sense. Voices? Sirens? Was he lifting from the ground? A pair of doors slammed shut, or they had slammed shut some time ago. What was she asking, the woman who hovered over him?

Greg heard himself say, "The year."

"Yeah." As she spoke, the woman's face came into focus. She had reddish brown hair pulled back in a ponytail and eyes the silvery green of eucalyptus leaves. She looked young, maybe around his same age. "Can you tell me what year it is?"

He watched her voice leave her mouth. An instant later, it reached his ears. His brain was clearing, as if emerging from underwater. Like when he swam at the public pool at Celebrity Sports Center in Denver, in the 1970s and '80s. But now he lived in Los Angeles, didn't he? "Um, 1990. No, January of '91."

"Good." She said this flatly, without the praise that Greg felt he needed in that moment. After all, he was riding in an ambulance, strapped down to a gurney, a throbbing in his skull. An ambulance?

"And what's the name of our current president?" She pumped a blood pressure cuff while she asked, her eyes trained on the task. Her blue shirt made her look like a cop. Or an airline pilot, like Greg's dad. Such a serious face she had. She, too, belonged to the regular grownups of the workaday world. Her name was stitched above her left breast: Lindsay Zelenko. On her arm: Emergency Medical Technician, AmbuRide. Even in the bright artificial light, the planes of her face shone beautifully. If she wore any makeup, she kept it simple. Greg couldn't imagine her dolled up, like the girlfriends of the video gamers back at the party. They already seemed so distant in his mind. Wait, what had Lindsay the EMT just asked?

"The president," Greg mumbled. "George Bush." The Commander in Chief, declarer of war. The stench of the world flooded back, its ugly faces. He felt queasy. The squeezing at his bicep didn't help. Neither did the swerving of the ambulance, the little bumps in the road. His low back seized in pain. He'd liked the world better a few minutes ago, when he hadn't felt anything.

"Indeed he is," Lindsey sighed. "Now wiggle your toes for me? Good."

She shined a penlight in his left eye, then his right. "Dilation is normal," she said, scribbling notes on a clipboard. "Blood pressure is slightly elevated, but that's typical with a concussion. They'll examine you further at the hospital."

"UCLA Medical Center?"

"Yeah. We're almost there." Lindsay's posture eased. She sat back on her bench.

Greg nearly laughed. What a strange return to his alma mater. Not as a student or a petty Ritalin dealer, but as a patient. Somehow, it seemed an appropriate ending to a night that began in the presence of Horst Schmidt.

Greg turned his head to look at Lindsay, and blood pulsed in his ears. His vision blurred, then stilled. Was he still drunk or still concussed? Maybe a little of both. "Can I ask you a weird question?"

Her eucalyptus-green eyes focused on his. It was the first time, Greg realized, that she'd looked at him as a person instead of a patient. She seemed to be examining him in a new way, her head tilted and plain lips pursed, as if judging an amateur painting. Good? Terrible? A certain odd appeal? "Fire away," she said.

"Were either of your grandfathers in World War II?"

"That *is* a weird question." Her smile bloomed at an uneven angle. "Yeah, one of them."

Greg nodded once, slowly, and his brain felt like slush. "Do you know, did he kill anyone during the war?"

Lindsay leaned forward, elbows on navy blue thighs. "So, my dad's dad, he was born in the Ukraine. Danylo Zelenko." She pointed to the last name on her chest. Greg made a point of keeping his attention on her face. "The Soviet Army conscripted him when he only sixteen or seventeen. He spent the next two years in combat duty. He never talked about what happened—not to me, anyway. But I got the impression some pretty fucked-up shit went down." That slanted smile again, the angle of irony not quite masking a distant sadness in her eyes.

Then she pivoted on her seat and called out to the front of the ambulance, "What about you, Corey? Your grandpas kill anybody in World War II?"

"Nope," a voice replied. "Too old, the both of them."

"Dude, *you're* too old!" Lindsey leaned back over Greg. "He's, like, thirty-two."

"Ancient." Greg smiled his most charming smile. In his position, what effect could it have? Anyway, maybe he'd lost his charm—exchanged it for a diploma and a paycheck. Outside of college, was he just another asshole? Because, who else gets tossed off balconies?

"And you?" Lindsay said. "Did your grandfather kill anybody in the war?"

Greg tried to picture Horst Schmidt back in 1944. A young man in uniform. Greg's mother had only one photograph of her father. Black and white, snapped in the Fifties, the Schmidt family in their swimsuits, posed on the shore of a lake. Whenever Greg returned home to Denver, he would dig up that photo. In the face of the younger Horst, Greg had come to recognize his own features: the boxy jaw, the protruding brow. The same as his Uncle Arnold's. Meanwhile, the women—his grandmother, Gerda, and his mother, Ilse—were blessed with blonde hair, slender faces, long limbs. Some genetic traits, one could never escape. But cruelty? How much further would an asshole have to fall before turning cruel?

"Yeah," Greg said. "I just found out tonight. He was in the German Army. He killed an American soldier. In cold blood." The phrase, a cliché from courtroom dramas, had leapt off his tongue. But it sounded right. The cold November air, the knife-drawn blood.

"Well, shit." Lindsay's features scrunched with distaste. There was something about her face in that moment—her lack of makeup, the realness of her expression, her evident sympathy—that caused Greg's heart to rush.

"It's weird," he said. "Finding out my grandfather was a fucking Nazi."

"Maybe," Lindsay said. "Not everyone in the Wehrmacht was a Nazi. Lots of the officers, yeah. But the enlisted? Not necessarily." She shrugged. "I have an associate's degree in history. I'm actually hoping to transfer to UCLA one of these days. After I do this for a while, save up the tuition."

"Cool," Greg said. "You totally should." He knew he'd been fortunate. His father had a good job and lived in San Francisco now, so Greg had gotten in-state tuition. Not that he'd paid the bills himself. Now he wanted to know Lindsay Zelenko's story. What had occurred between her Ukrainian grandfather fighting for the Russians and her enrollment at community college? Why hadn't her parents been able to start a college fund for their daughter? And where did she get those beautiful eucalyptus eyes?

The ambulance turned, then slowed. Pain knifed his low back.

"Here we are," Lindsay said, as they rocked to a halt.

In a moment, Greg would be rolled away, and this intriguing woman would be removed from his life. On Monday, he'd go back to driving out to the boonies and standing in streams. And, come next weekend, would he find himself skulking around the dorms once more, dealing his minor stash? Or flying from another balcony?

"I wish I'd gotten the chance to hear more about your grandfather," he said. "And more about you."

"Yeah?" Lindsay smiled down at him, an even smile, absent all irony. She jotted a final note on her clipboard, tore a shred of paper, and stuffed it into the pocket of Greg's blazer, alongside his baggie of pills. "Maybe we'll trade more stories sometime soon."

Was that her phone number at his chest? Greg's lips parted. He wanted to say something clever in reply. Something a charming asshole might say. The ambulance doors swung open. He kept his grinning mouth shut.

CHAPTER ELEVEN

FEBRUARY, 2057

"Shit. You all right?" A man's voice, scratchy as steel wool. Kiana strains her eyes open. She's lying on a floor. But the floor of what? The space around her is a blur, as if painted by the motion of falling. A memory comes of a similar fall, off a balcony and down to the lawn below. Then she remembers: that had been a virtual fall, a digital reenactment of her grandfather's fateful drop. In Level Up, the landing hadn't hurt at all.

When Kiana tries to lift her head, the blur goes blood-dark. The place—room, office, storefront, wherever—is dim. The light from the streetlamp on the next block barely penetrates the smudgy plate glass windows. In that faint light, a shape coalesces: a man, standing before her.

Every part of Kiana aches. She worries some part of her is broken. Physically, incapacitatingly broken. When she raises her head this time, she's able to focus better. There are her two legs: more or less where they belong, nothing bent into hideous angles. No alarming protrusions from her stomach or chest. She lifts one hand, hesitantly probes her throbbing head. A sticky blotch of blood in her hair. Either from when she banged her skull against the rafters, or from crash landing just now. So, is she all right? Didn't someone ask her that? Right, the man by the window.

She homes in on his face. Bent nose, wrinkled and weathered skin, startled eyes. Gray beard. Lank silvery hair draping down from a tan ball cap. Words are coming from his lips: "Ma'am? You are alive, aren't you?"

"I think so." Kiana is still thinking of his first question. Had he asked another? "Alive? Yeah, I'm alive."

"Right on." The old guy smiles, a scramble of teeth and black gaps. "I never know for sure, anymore. Who's dead? Who's real? Know what I mean?"

"Sure," Kiana says. But what does he mean? Ghosts? Memories? Avatars? Droids? Voices in his head?

Slowly, Kiana props herself up onto her elbows. Beneath those sharp joints, the floor is cushioned. Kiana rubs her fingertips over wet plastic, or maybe vinyl. Beneath that, some other material yields slightly to her touch.

The man points toward her probing hand. "That's a tarp, ma'am. I duct-taped it to some poster board."

He's standing closer now. When did he move?

"It's all I could find to patch up the hole in the roof," he says. "Worked pretty good. For a while."

His words move like sludge, slow to solidify in her mind. Kiana doesn't know how to reply. And, through that hole in the roof, the rain continues to fall, soaking into her jeans. Kiana scoots back, off the tarp. She stays sitting like that, her arms wrapped around her shins.

She's trying to think clearly, to determine what to do next. But there's a buzzing in the air outside, a tiny motor growing nearer. A moment later, a harsh white light beams through the windows. Fear thumps Kiana's chest. They've found her.

The old guy drops into a crouch.

Kiana curls into herself, like the pill bugs from her mother's vegetable garden.

The light sweeps over their heads, darts along the far walls, across the room and back again. A second later, it peels away. The buzzing motor grows faint, disappears.

"Police drone," the old guy tells her. "The radio said the cops are looking for an escapee." His lips curl into a mischievous grin. "Doesn't look like your name'd be Walter Brogan, though."

"No." Her own laugh—more like a cough—surprises her. "Kiana ... my name's Kiana."

"Ma'am, my name's Jimmy Driscoll." He points to his coat, splotchy with gray and beige, where his surname is stitched in black above the words U.S. ARMY. Another detail Kiana has failed to observe.

"Jimmy." She nods. "On the radio, did they mention any other escapees?"

"Oh, I see." He cackles. "Kiana, did you just bust outta jail?"

She glances at the front door. Metal and glass. It's probably locked. Even if it weren't, she couldn't run out into the street. Not with the police station right next door.

"Aw, it's all right, ma'am." Jimmy swipes his hand at the air. "I ain't gonna turn you in."

"No?" Kiana looks to the back of the room. Either it's too dark, or her visions is too blurry. She can't see another way out. "And why's that, Jimmy?"

"Hand someone over to the cops?" A wounded expression ripples in his eyes, as if she'd slapped him. "No way. Those fuckers, they're always hassling me. Here in my own home! Can you believe that?"

His home? Kiana takes in the objects around her: a few chairs stacked in the corner, some cardboard boxes, a couple of empty wire racks, a poster that she can't make out. The place looks more like a small business than anyone's home. "Where are we?"

"The Costa Perdida Visitor Center." Jimmy grins, his bushy gray eyebrows anticipating recognition.

Kiana shakes her head.

"You never been here before?" His smile puckers into a frown. "My wife, she ran this place for years. The city closed it down in '37, not long after she died."

A dead spouse. For a brief moment, this seems like the kind of tragedy that only happens to other people. Then Kiana remembers. She clamps her jaw tight to keep from crying.

Jimmy is rummaging through one of the cardboard boxes. "A year or so later, I got evicted from our house. But I remembered that my wife held onto her key to the Visitor Center, as a memento. And the city never changed the locks, so I've been living here ever since." He extracts a wad of fabric from the box and tosses it to Kiana.

She catches it on the fly, relieved to find that her reflexes are working.

"A souvenir for ya," Jimmy says.

In her hands is a tee-shirt, ocean blue. Silkscreened to the front, a cartoonish image: a sandy beach, a row of shops in cheery pastels, green rolling hills, and a rainbow arcing across the valley beyond. Above the image, in big sun-yellow letters: *Find Yourself in Costa Perdida!* The image is baffling. Did the town ever look that sweet?

The buzzing drone returns. No, the sound is deeper this time. Louder.

"Helicopter!" Jimmy says. "Take cover!" He scrambles quickly to the front wall, ducks beneath the large window.

Kiana is crawling again. Crawling toward this stranger named Jimmy. Crazy or not, he's clearly a survivor. She tucks herself against the wall.

The beam from the helicopter's search light is orders-of-magnitude fiercer than the drone's. Brightness floods the Visitor Center, the prowling light skimming just over their heads.

Kiana looks to Jimmy for signals. His eyes stare straight ahead, at the back of the room, or someplace beyond. He's holding his hands to his chest, as if cradling some object. The pointer finger of his right-hand squeezes, again and again. An invisible trigger on an invisible gun?

At last, the searchlight sweeps away, the roar settles into a murmur.

Jimmy lifts his head, peeks out the window. "We gotta hold our position. Too many hostiles."

"Hostiles?"

He winces. "Cops, I mean. Patrol car just cruised by. And, up the block, I spotted a couple of uniforms walking this way."

"Okay," Kiana sighs. Inside, her nerves are twitching, urging her to move. She was free for, what, thirty seconds? Now she's trapped again. And so is Javi. Trapped in his bed, tethered by a narrow plastic tube to the oxygen keeping him alive. No, she can't think of her husband like that right now. She can't afford to spiral down. If only she possessed Javi's optimism. Despite all evidence to the contrary, he always sees the potential for improvement in the world. For eleven years, Kiana has inhabited the aura of his positivity. But that aura has never penetrated her own anxious hide. The next form of ruin is always on the wing, soon to strike.

Jimmy checks the street again. "Okay. All clear, for the moment. Now, let's get ourselves someplace less exposed."

With a grunt, he rises into a crouch and waves toward the back of the Visitor Center.

Once more, Kiana finds herself following Jimmy. Because he walks in a hunch, so does she. In the last few minutes, she's acquired a fear of searchlights, of standing fully erect. She trails Jimmy around an empty display case, its glass front webbed with cracks. Clenched in her hand, Kiana is surprised to find the souvenir tee.

Two clanking knocks rattle the front door.

They freeze. Jimmy presses a finger to his lips. Needlessly. Kiana's too afraid to exhale, much less speak.

"This is the Costa Perdida Police Department." The voice outside is deep, measured, synthetic. An enforcement droid. Kiana pictures the hulking white metal, the glowering inhuman eyes. "Warning. An armed fugitive is currently at large. Anyone occupying these premises is required by law to come forward immediately and identify themselves."

Jimmy doesn't react, much less respond. He stares straight ahead, as if the blank back wall interests him more than a lethal robot.

Kiana supposes he's been trained to wait out circumstances such as these. Or worse. Probably worse. Then she can wait, too. Let the police droid rust away out there.

It pounds the door again. It repeats its original message verbatim.

They wait. Nothing. The next Kiana hears the droid's insistent knock, the sound is distant, echoing off some other door down the street.

Jimmy points to a door in the back corner. *Office*, a sign reads. *Employees Only*. Kiana nods, and they make a final hunched scamper into the back office. He switches on a light—an LED camping lantern—and shuts the door.

The space is small and cramped. The air is thick with a

deep human fug—the rank odors of seclusion. Kiana takes a quick inventory of her new surroundings. Industrial carpet, worn and stained. Some typical office furnishings—desk, swivel chair, ancient printer, metal filing cabinet. Also, the makings of a living quarters. A cot stretches along one wall. A battered suitcase sits propped open on the linoleum floor, clothes piled inside. A camping stove in the corner. On the desk is a can of soup, a spoon handle poking out.

Next to the can sits a small silver device: speaker on the front, dial on the side, antenna jutting from the top. Kiana remembers that Alex kept a similar device in the bunker underneath the Big House. A transistor radio, she thinks it's called. Old technology, it won't help her now. If only she had her watch, she could call Makia, ask her to watch over Javi until she gets home. If she ever gets home.

"Sorry about the mess," Jimmy says. "Ashley would've hated to see her office like this."

Kiana shakes her head, too tired to offer small words of comfort. She leans against the desk and stares at the poster on the wall. A photo of a beach at sunset. The foaming of gentle waves, the gleaming sand a mirror for the myriad hues of orange and gold bannered across the sky. Printed in looping letters at the top of the poster: *Costa Perdida!*

Life before the sea wall. The beauty hits Kiana in the gut every time: when looking at childhood photos from residents who grew up here, or scrolling through images in historical archives. What has happened to this world? If only the government had invested in the environmental war her parents fought, instead of all the bullshit wars for oil, wars against communism, wars over naming rights to god. On a dying planet, what's the point?

Now that she's standing still, the dank cold is permeating her skin, her blood.

"Jimmy?" She looks over her shoulder and holds up the blue shirt she's found herself unable to let go of. "Be a gentleman and turn around so I can change?"

His craggy face goes crimson. With a small smile, he ducks away.

Kiana unzips her damp hoodie, peels it from her arms. There's a tear in the canary yellow cotton, along one of the sleeves. As she wriggles out of her shirt—the same tee she's worn since seven in the morning, her own stench offends her. The new tee is a small, just her size. It smells a little musty, but Kiana doesn't mind: the fabric is warm and dry. Would putting the wet hoodie back on make her warmer or colder? For now, she drapes it over the back of the office chair to dry.

A scraping noise. Kiana spins around.

It's only Jimmy. He's moving aside the filling cabinet. Behind the cabinet is a door. He squints into Kiana's eyes, as if measuring what he sees inside. His smile is tentative for once. "How do you feel about tunnels?"

"Tunnels." Her weary brain puzzles over the word, expecting alternate meanings to reveal themselves.

"You never heard of the old mercantile tunnels?" Jimmy opens the door, revealing nothing but a closet. Utility shelves, mostly empty. A few cardboard boxes on the floor. He squats down, starts dragging the boxes out.

"Oh, right. I remember reading about them, years ago." In the late nineteenth century, following the gold rush, the streets of Costa Perdida had so much traffic—pedestrian, horse-drawn carriage—that merchants built a system of tunnels to transport barrels of goods from the docks to downtown shops. Years later, they became a tourist attraction. In this moment, they seem like an abstraction, a fable. "They collapsed, didn't they? In the 2040 quake?"

The epicenter was sixty miles due east, halfway between San Luis Obispo and Bakersfield. Kiana and her mom had felt the quake while on a walk in Santa Cruz, some 200 miles away. The damage in Costa Perdida was extensive. Even seventeen years later, scars from the quake remain: cracks in the façades of buildings, streets that never reopened, ruined houses left to waste away, compromised utilities networks, crumbled passageways.

"Some of the tunnels are gone, it's true." Jimmy peels back a rectangle of carpet. He pulls on a handle attached to the floor, and a trapdoor lifts open. "But not all of 'em."

From where she stands, Kiana can only see a rectangle of darkness.

"Growing up here," Jimmy says, "we went on school field trips through the tunnels every year. In the back room of the hardware store up on Fourth Street, there was a wooden stairwell. That's where the tours started." He peers into the hole and frowns. "Now I get kinda claustrophobic down there. But some folks, they sleep in the tunnels. Especially this time of year."

Strange people hiding in dark places. Kiana's stomach flutters. Is this really the only way out? The one path back to Javier? Then she'll have to go down there.

Jimmy brushes past her, starts riffling through desk drawers. "Most of 'em down there are harmless. But you oughtta take this, just in case." He places a box cutter in her palm.

The metal is cold. Kiana slides the blade out and back in again, then stuffs the box cutter into her back pocket.

Next, Jimmy hands her a white, tubular plastic object. Chapstick? *Costa Perdida*, reads a label on its side.

"A flashlight," he says. "It's souvenir crap, but better than nothing. Make sure it still works?"

Kiana twists the end, and a bulb glows weakly.

"Here, take this, too." Jimmy holds up a blue denim work shirt.

"No, I couldn't."

"We'll call it a trade." He points to her hoodie. "I know a gal that'll fit. She could really use it."

"Okay, deal." Kiana puts on the work shirt, rolls up the sleeves. When she and Javi were first dating, she would sometimes spend the night at his place in a town—a funky house teeming with roommates. Often, when dressing for work in the mornings, she would put on one of Javi's button-down shirts, which she'd wear over tights as a dress. And she'd always have to roll up the sleeves.

Now she's wearing Jimmy Driscoll's shirt. She'd expected it reek of the back office, but it actually smells like the same hand soap that Javi uses at work. As she fights off tears, it occurs to Kiana that Jimmy never questioned her sudden presence, her innocence or guilt, her motives, her morals. He simply helped her. "Thank you. For everything. I don't know what I would've done if—"

"Nah." He smiles and looks away.

For a moment, they both silently stare at the opening in the floor.

"So," Jimmy says. "Once you climb down, head left. That'll take you north, away from the police station. After maybe a hundred yards, go left at the next tunnel. Pretty soon, you'll spot an old sign for First Street hanging on the wall. There's a ladder that goes up to a metal hatch. You know that little alley off First, runs between Maple and Oak?"

Kiana nods. It's nice for an alley, or it used to be. Colorful murals painted on brick walls. An empanada cart that went out of business a while back. Once a month, for years on end, she and Javi would get takeout from there. At a nearby park, they would sit on a bench and devour the empanadas. It was always

Kiana's job to point out to Javi when the juices dribbled onto his lush, dark beard. If she halfway resented it then, she would give anything to reclaim those moments now.

"That's where you'll pop out," Jimmy says. "Well, come on now. You never know when that goddamn robot'll show up again."

Kiana squats beside the trapdoor. The thin beam from the souvenir flashlight glances off metal rungs bolted to the tunnel's red brick wall. She draws a long breath through her nose and funnels the air out through pursed lips. With the light clamped between her teeth, she begins her descent. The ground is only twelve or fifteen feet below. Compared to scaling the arroyo behind their property, the height is nothing. And the holds are child's play. Still, she grips each rung as if she might plummet to her death.

When her feet touch ground, she looks back up to the rectangle of light.

"Good luck to you," Jimmy calls out. Then the trapdoor shuts, and the darkness surrounding Kiana deepens.

The air is musty and cold, like a tomb. A chill seeps through her still-damp jeans. Breath held, she listens for voices. She hears nothing, sees little. A channel of darkness awaits her. Kiana aims the flashlight's beam on the dusty stone floor, up the old brick walls. She takes cautious steps forward, as if the ground, when troubled, might swallow her whole.

Her body starts shivering—whether from cold or from fear, Kiana doesn't know. She hurries her stride.

The roaming flashlight's beam catches a flicker of movement near her feet. She leaps back. Waves the light in frantic search. Reaches into her back pocket for the box cutter. Wrong pocket. The light lands on a small brown creature. A rat. It crouches at the base of the brick wall, red eyes looking up.

"Little fucker!" she hisses at it. "Go away."

The rat stays frozen in its place. This is its home, after all.

Kiana stalks ahead. She switches the flashlight to her left hand, readies the box cutter in her right. It's the return of adrenaline that has her limbs vibrating now. Her stupid heart is clattering away.

She's walked for another minute or so when she hears a snarl of sound, very near. She turns, aims the flashlight like a weapon. The box cutter, she clutches reflexively to her chest.

There's a niche in the wall, or a side passage that's been sealed off. A body lies curled on the floor beneath a heap of blankets. Shanks of dirty blond hair poke out from beneath a ski cap. A stubbly face, turned away. The man wheezes as he snores. His eyelids tighten against the brightness and he shrugs the blankets higher, sheltering his face.

Kiana moves on, walking deeper into the murky darkness, convinced the tunnel will never end. That she'll never get back to Javier. She wishes she could see further than a few feet in front of her. Even the flashlight app on her watch is more powerful. Are the police trying to hack into that watch right now? Well, good luck. Alex installed extra security measures on all of Kiana's and Javi's devices. The data will eat itself before the cops get their eyes on it.

She waves her sad beam of light back and forth, up and down. It lands on a pile of rubble at her feet, just as the toebox of her sneaker catches on a stray brick. Some stupid part of her mind tells Kiana to hold tight to the objects in her hands. Her right knee smacks the concrete floor, followed by her shoulder. She chokes back a cry of agony.

She tells herself that it's okay to lie there, just for a moment. To catch her breath, to hope the sharp pain dulls. Then she thinks of scurrying rats, of police droids on the hunt.

As she's readjusting her limbs, the wandering beam of her flashlight lands on another figure, just a few feet ahead. A woman's figure, turned away. No blankets or sleeping bag. She must be freezing. Her shining black hair fanned across the gritty stone. She wears a dark gray pant suit. A terrible understanding clamps round Kiana's lungs: that's her lawyer lying there.

"No, no, no, no." Kiana crawls over. "Jane!" She grabs the other woman's shoulder, rolls her flat onto her back. Open eyes gaze straight up at the brick ceiling. Kiana doesn't see any obvious wounds. She lifts Jane's limp arm, feels for a pulse at her wrist.

"I wouldn't bother."

His voice, low and flat, empties Kiana out. Walter Brogan is right behind her. As she pivots slowly on her knees, the sharp pain returns, awakening her mind. Terror swarms her synapses.

Brogan stands in a gaping void in the wall. In the shadows behind him, a rockslide. In his beige chinos and muted dress shirt, he looks innocuous, like a salesperson. Aside from the gun in his hand.

Very calmly, he states: "Put down the box cutter."

Kiana looks at the thing in her hand. She'd forgotten it was even there. Her grip falls open, and the box cutter clanks sharply against the concrete floor.

As Brogan lowers his gun, Kiana keep the flashlight's beam on his face, searching for signs of what might happen next.

"Get that fucking light out of my eyes," he says.

Kiana gasps, a tiny sucking sound through her teeth. She lowers the beam. His left hand is clamped across the edge of his stomach, where a small black-red lake of blood stains his checkered button-up shirt. In his right hand, the pistol drapes wearily at his side.

How did Brogan even get a gun?

Then, in a flash, she sees it: He must have taken it from whichever cop was nearest when the power went out. And he used Jane Hamamura as a human shield to get out of the police station. Then he dragged her down here. *In the back room of the hardware store up on Fourth Street, there was a wooden stairwell.* The hardware store is less than a block from the police station. *We went on school field trips.*

"You grew up here," she says.

Brogan nods, his eyes on Kiana's, yet also not. "My entire life, I lived here." He shrugs. "Guess I'll die here, too." His brown mustache disguises any emotion that his lips might otherwise reveal.

Death. Doesn't it mean anything to him? He killed his wife and child. He killed Jane Hamamura.

Or, maybe death means everything to him. Does Walter Brogan see himself as some sort of Chiron, ferrying souls to the other side? And here's Kiana, kneeling before him. But she can't die yet.

The first thought that comes to her, Kiana blurts: "You helped your wife and child."

Brogan's eyebrows raise, just barely. His breaths come out in shallow pants. The bloodstain on his shirt is slowly spreading.

"Really, I understand," she says. "My own husband, he's dying. Right now. He's dying at home." When Kiana tries to swallow, the dust of the underworld catches in her throat. "And I have to help him, Walter." Vials of morphine, locked in a metal box, stashed high in the bedroom closet. A needle in Javi's vein. Then it will be over. She's imagined the procedure so many times, on so many sleepless nights, in so many livid dreams, that she often wakes up in the morning convinced that she's already killed him. "It ... it doesn't matter what the law says. Walter, they arrested me, too. And I was only trying to help my husband. Just like you, with your family. Just like you helped them to escape this shitty world. Right?"

"Escape this shitty world," Brogan echoes. "Yes, that's exactly right. Isn't that what all of us want anymore?"

He raises his gun.

A sensation like vertigo rushes through Kiana: the collision of what cannot happen and what almost certainly will. Future collapsing into past. She's inhabited this conflictive space before, has seen it through the eyes of—

CHAPTER TWELVE

JANUARY, 1945

From his spot in the trench, Sergeant Einar Olsen watched the morning sky turn from black to gray. The snow-laden boughs of the German woodlands looked the same as yesterday, and all the previous days he could remember. Moments from his life before the war became less and less tangible. His past felt more remote than memories, as if gleaned from a storybook or motion picture. Even when he looked at the most recent photo of his family back in St. Cloud, his wife and children grew fainter in his mind. Betty Olsen, with her dark curls and wide-set eyes: was she really Einar's wife? And the two children, Frank and Adelaide, he truly no longer knew them. Frank was six years old and Addy four. Betty's letters from home chronicled their children's changes, but Einar struggled to reimagine Frank and Addy. They changed so much with each passing month. And so many months had passed.

Each day, the cold ate deeper into his bones. Einar had grown up in Sweden, on a dairy farm outside Örebro. For the last eight years, since emigrating to America, he'd lived in rural

Minnesota. Before this winter, Einar had believed himself invulnerable to cold.

He had also believed himself invulnerable to constipation. No, that's not quite right. Prior to his deployment on the Western Front, Einar had never much considered the workings of his bowels. The movements occurred with simple regularity, like the rising of that pale German sun. But, over the last two weeks, he'd become horribly preoccupied with his inability to take a measly crap. He thought of this more than he thought of death.

Two of Einar's men, Gianetti and Clarke, appeared from the gray-lit woods. Patrol completed, they walked heavily toward the trench. Their gloved hands clung to their rifles, which sat flush against the breasts of their olive drab overcoats. Their heads drooped, as if the weight of their helmets willed them down toward the snow-ridden earth. They were exhausted. All of his men were.

Eight soldiers made up his squadron, Einar included. As Gianetti and Clarke climbed down into the trench, the other men roused themselves from sleep. Or whatever passed for sleep. Drifts and snatches. Little flashes that came while slouched in the mud and ice. Dreams that felt the same as being awake: firing shots at shapes in the woods, the woods firing back. Or maybe only Einar had those dreams? No, he didn't think so. Sometimes, when dogged by wakefulness, he watched his boys sleep. That's all they were, really. As with Einar's own children, their nightmares were nearly visible through the thin flesh of twitching eyelids.

Corporal Gianetti made his way over to Einar. Through habit, they'd developed means of communication that didn't require the effort of speech. They barely had to stretch the muscles in their faces, which were frozen stiff anyway. *Spot any*

Krauts out there, Corporal? No sir, Sarge. All right, good work, get some rest. Yes sir, Sarge.

The solid mass jolted in his gut. The pressure that knew no release. He eyed the far end of the trench, which briefly cut away at a right angle. As with every trench they dug, they used that cutaway for a latrine. Last night, Einar had spent ten long minutes squatting in that cutaway, clenched and unproductive. He'd been too aware of his men nearby, his bowels alert to their movements and chatter. Ten minutes wasted on hope, just like praying to the god his parents still believed in.

What Einar needed was a moment's peace. He grabbed a shovel and, heading for the shallow end of the trench, combed his way through crouched soldiers and stacked supplies. The trench wasn't all that deep—four or five feet at most. But, unlike the other men, Einar could no longer climb over the top. During the Battle for Brest, a German paratrooper had shot him in the thigh. The medic had patched Einar up and sent him on his way, but the wound hadn't healed properly. For the last four months, he'd marched with a slight limp. And the cold only made the stiffness worse.

"Give you a hand with anything, Sarge?"

Private Jamison stood before Einar. That look on his face, it conveyed so many ideas at once: geniality, pride, eagerness, fear. Recently added to the squadron, Booker Jamison was the first colored man to serve under Einar's command. General Eisenhower had recently suspended troop segregation in the face of need. To beat the Germans, they required bodies with guns. What the hell did it matter, the color of their skin? Einar couldn't care less. And he forbade the other men from treating Jamison any differently. Only Sergeant Einar Olsen himself could address his new private as the subordinate he was.

"I don't need anyone's hand," Einar grumbled, and Jamison stepped aside. As Einar limped up the slope, he muttered: "Jag

kan torka min egen jävla röv." *I can wipe my own damn ass.*
Away from the rising sun, he walked into the forest.

✱ ✱ ✱

Corporal Horst Schmidt clomped through the snow, his rifle
nestled to his chest at patrol ready. He'd walked through the
night, afraid that if he stopped, he would freeze to death.
Hunger left him hollowed out. Isolation made his skin itch.
Every tiny sound could be the enemy. And the forest, it never
ended. Or perhaps Horst had spent the dark hours roaming in
circles. Only now, as dawn wept its first pale light, could Horst
discern east from west. The war resided in the west, his home
in the east.

He pictured the little yellow house in Charlottenburg, the
borough of Berlin where he lived with his young wife, Gerda,
and their two children, Arnold, and Ilse. With even more fondness, he pictured the neighborhood garage where he'd worked
as an auto mechanic. Repairing engines: that had also been his
duty at the start of the war. Then the Wehrmacht put a rifle in
his hand and shoved him into the back of a transport truck,
westward bound.

Now, Horst headed east through the woods. The deathly
silent woods. Perhaps the starving German troops had eaten all
the animals. Or maybe the animals had wised up and deserted
their homeland.

Would Horst's commanders deem him a deserter? He'd
heard rumors of hangings. But what should he have done,
instead? Surrendered? While the invading Americans had
rounded up the others in his squadron, he and Private Becker
had witnessed the humiliating incident from the woods, where
they'd been sent to patrol. The enemy must have attacked from
the other direction, with little apparent resistance from Horst's

compatriots. Not a single shot had cracked the air. And he hadn't spotted any casualties. Not, that is, until Becker had run out into the glade and opened fire. His one frantic gunshot had badly missed its target. A second later, the Americans had gunned Becker down. Horst had then positioned himself behind a thick pine, where he waited to be discovered, captured, and hauled away with the others. In fact, that's what he had wished for: to be locked away in a POW camp. Surely, he would be better cared for as a prisoner of the Allied than as a German soldier. So, yes, he'd nearly surrendered. But the image of Becker lying face down in the bloodied snow had kept Horst pinned to that tree.

Now, as he trudged up a slope, the woods began to thin a little. Maybe, soon, he would come to a road, a village, an abandoned shack. Any sign of civilization, to give him hope.

* * *

Einar admired the foldable shovel in his hand. This simple tool had been around for centuries, and yet the military had still thought to improve its design for use by infantry soldiers. When you hauled all of your necessities on your back, every inch mattered, every ounce. Einar folded the spade back from the handle, locked the mechanism in place, and dug away a patch of snow. He jabbed the shovel into the cleared ground— such a satisfying act.

Einar peeled off his gloves. From the inside pocket of his coat, he removed the rectangular packet of toilet paper— "tissues," as they were euphemistically labeled. Einar looked again to see that he was adequately secluded by the trees between himself and his soldiers in the trench. Then he lowered his trousers and dropped into a squat.

As if on command, the brick in his bowels shifted. Einar

thought encouraging thoughts—words of opening and welcoming into the world. He heard his father's voice in his head, speaking in the sweetly lilting Swedish tongue, coaxing a pregnant cow as she birthed her calf. How many times had Einar witnessed this event throughout his childhood? The calf's little body slicking loose, as his father tugged its ankles. What terrifying beauty. Now Einar had become the father whose children stood in awe before nature's messy unfurling. Frank had been, what, three years old when Einar helped Inga birth her calf? And Addy was just a babe, bundled in her mother's arms. The faces of his family. The Minnesota sky that morning: a boundless field of blue.

Come on, now. It's okay, little one. The world awaits you!

* * *

Horst paused mid-step, one boot lifted above the snow. Some ten meters away, a lone American soldier sat in a crouch, his back to Horst. The wooden handle of a shovel rose from the earth like a crude burial marker, and he briefly wondered if indeed the American was praying over a grave. Horst raised his rifle. His hands trembled: the cold, the fatigue, the blood. Slowly, he lowered his boot into the snow, waiting for his heel to connect with the frozen earth beneath. An eternity of millimeters. A final crunch of ice and mud.

The American's head turned, and Horst caught the corner of his eye. Then the crouching man raised his arms above his head, also with aching slowness, as if pushing against the German winter air. As the American turned to face him, the vibrations in Horst's hands carried forth into his rifle. His finger spasmed, beating like a bird's wing, on and off the trigger.

Only now, as the American faced him, did Horst realize that the enemy soldier's trousers and briefs lay bunched around his ankles, and the tip of his *schwanz* peeked out from beneath the hem of his overcoat. Horst forced his attention on the American's eyes. Those steady brown eyes, hooded by the olive-green helmet. Those unflinching eyes further unnerved Horst. Did the American believe that Horst wouldn't shoot him dead where he stood? Of course, he would!

Why, then, couldn't he control his rifle? He knew himself to be a superior marksman. His father, who had fought in the Great War, had taught young Horst to hunt deer and wild boar. By the time he was ten years old, he could shoot pheasant from the sky. So, even though Horst was late to soldiering, he could outgun most of his comrades-in-arms.

And yet, even as he wished death upon the American, his shoulder shook violently against the butt of the rifle. Horst despised his body for failing him like this.

His physique had performed so marvelously on that other day, back in November, when he'd encountered a different American soldier in a different woods. A deep fog had enshrouded Hürtgen Forest and a wet chill clung thickly to the air. Horst had lost his way. Not because he'd deserted his post—no, not exactly that. He had simply marched away from the fallen bodies. So many fallen bodies. And that made sense, didn't it? For one's own body to act in opposition to death? And so Horst had found himself lost in a thicket, drawn by the sound of running water, when he came face-to-face with an American soldier. He had tried to raise his rifle, as did the enemy—the metal barrels had banged together like ram horns. Then the American had grabbed Horst's uniform, and the two men had tumbled to the ground. Horst remembered rolling downhill, as if playing some childhood game with a school friend. Somehow, he'd wound up on top. The American went for his sidearm as Horst fumbled for his knife. Each man had grappled for the other's weapon. At one point, the pistol went off and a bullet grazed Horst's ear. In the next instant, he discovered his knife in the American's belly, his hand still wrapped around its shaft. He'd sat there for a very long time, kneeling over the American as he died. As he remained dead. Those pained blue eyes, gazing up at the pinewood overstory. For all Horst knew, he might be lying there still.

That day, his body had acted outside his will. It had saved him. Now he couldn't manage to steady his rifle long enough to aim, to draw a single breath, to fire.

The American soldier reached inside his overcoat.

* * *

Einar had lost his patience with the wide-eyed, quaking German soldier, whose rifle danced in his hands as if possessed. The barrel aimed everywhere and nowhere: at the platinum sky, down at the flat white earth, over Einar's right shoulder, then at some poor sapling to his left. Einar wanted to shout at him: *Either shoot me dead already, or lay down your arms, you idiot!* But that would only draw his men out of cover, and the German might somehow manage to kill one of them. Then Einar would have to write a condolence letter to Jamison's mother, or Gianetti's mother, or Clarke's mother. No, his best solution was to shoot the poor fool.

As Einar reached inside his overcoat, the German's head snapped back. He blinked, as if woken from a nap. Then he turned and ran.

Einar aimed his pistol at the back of the fir-colored coat that darted and wove between the trees. He had a clear shot: now, and now, and now again. But it lacked honor, shooting a man in the back. Einar thought of giving chase, but his dropped trousers bound his ankles like shackles. With a sigh, he holstered his gun and pulled up his pants.

Einar had heard that, in a life-threatening situation, a person's bowels typically loosened. His own, it seemed, had clenched tighter still. The festering bulge of K-rations had lodged itself even deeper in his gut. That goddamn idiot, he had ruined Einar's crap. If he ever saw that quivering Kraut again, he would shoot him in the face. Surely, there was honor in that.

As Einar approached the trench, weary faces looked up from cans of ham and egg, over tin mugs of instant coffee, or through the smoke of a Lucky Strike—one of the four included in their daily rations. He ordered his men to break camp in ten minutes, and the soldiers begrudgingly affirmed their sergeant's command. Soon, they would march deeper into enemy territory. Maybe that same afternoon a mortar shell or a stray German bullet would strike Einar dead. Or, more likely, his intestines would eventually rupture and he would die from his own immovable shit. In the meantime, he could only push his troops onward while pretending to himself that the snowy hills and plains would lead him away from the heart of Germany, and toward his Minnesota home. He would round a bend in the muddy road and spot his farmhouse just ahead. And there, out in the front yard, his family would be waiting for him. Betty, Frank, Addy. As Einar limped down into the trench, he promised himself for the thousandth time that he would one day see those faces again.

CHAPTER THIRTEEN

FEBRUARY, 2057

The explosion of gunfire echoes off the brick walls, the concrete floor. Kiana squeezes her eyes shut—as if, by shutting down one sense, she can free herself from all the others. Her breath is locked in her chest. Her ears are ringing. Does that mean she's alive?

Kiana opens her eyes. The souvenir flashlight remains clutched in her hand. Its beam illuminates Walter Brogan's beige slacks and brown shoes, which lie sprawled and motionless on the ground. Even as she tells herself she can't bear to witness the rest, Kiana trails the light up the seam of Brogan's checkered button-down shirt and to the mass of blood and pulp and bone where his head should be.

A strong rhythm pulses through her, a wave that ripples from her torso to the top of her skull. From a location just outside herself, she sees the problem: *My body is convulsing. I'm in shock.* A moment later, this calm astral self-plunges back into her corporeal shell. Waves of emotion—fear and sorrow and horror—crash together. She's sobbing, tears and snot. She vomits on the ground.

149

When there's nothing left inside her, Kiana turns to Jane Hamamura. She presses two shaking fingertips to the other woman's neck. No pulse. But her flesh is still warm. How long does it take for—? What should she—? Kiana opens Jane's mouth and blows hard bursts of air into her dormant lungs. Nothing happens. If only her Grandma Lindsay were here. Because Kiana has no fucking clue how to save someone's life. With the flashlight clamped between her teeth, she stacks her hands on Jane's breastplate and presses down, and again, and again, and again. The term *chest compressions* blinks hopefully to mind. But what good is knowing that? Kiana's failure is reflected in Jane's empty eyes.

She stops the compressions. It's pointless. There's no return from death. The impossibility stuns her. Just an hour ago, Jane Hamamura was very much alive.

With her husband, Kiana has had ample warning: long months of withering decline. And now Javi has so little time left. Maybe not enough time: to get the terminal, to upload his mind. To simply be with him. There's never enough time.

A light sweeps across her face, left to right across the tunnel, then back again. A crackled voice says, "What the fuck?"

Kiana aims her own light toward the voice. A woman stands before her. She's dressed in layers and layers of clothes. Her blonde hair is matted and frayed, her face a wreck of blotches, pits, and lines. She could be Kiana's age, though she looks much older.

Kiana snatches up the box cutter. She stares at the gun lying by Brogan's splayed fingers. Begins to reach for it. Stops. If the cops spot her with a gun, they'll shoot her dead.

"That's Walter Brogan," Kiana tells the woman. "From the news?"

The woman screws up her face—in distaste or incomprehension or both.

"He killed himself." Kiana points her beam at Jane. "And her, too."

"Oh, man." The woman's voice is coarse as burned wood. "I can't even ...." She shakes her head. "I mean, this is just too ...."

Kiana stands in front of her but fails to make eye contact. "Call the police, okay?"

The woman nods, vaguely.

Kiana takes this as an affirmation. She wants better for Jane, but she has to go, now.

The woman remains fixed in the middle of the passage, staring and nodding and stinking of cigarettes—another black market item, like shitty ventilators and shiny terminals used as bait.

Kiana brushes past the woman and breaks into a run. She's on her way to Javi. She can feel him, alive and beating in her chest.

What were Jimmy's instructions? Follow a different tunnel—to the left, she thinks. Kiana flicks the light from wall to wall. She runs and runs until, finally, another possible opening reveals itself. Slowing her pace, Kiana shines the light into the darkness. Not a dead-end this time.

She turns left—too abruptly. The pain in her knee reawakens with a sharp jolt. She hobbles: slowly at first, then more quickly as she adapts to a new loping stride. She fans the faint beam along the walls as she goes. In the dim underground, time and distance are incalculable. Maybe she's gone twenty feet since the turn—or twenty minutes?

The light gleams off metal. An iron rung—one of a series bolted to the wall. Just like those she descended some unknowable time ago. And there's the rusting aluminum sign that Jimmy promised her: *First Street*. Once again, Kiana holds the souvenir flashlight between her teeth. She grips the rungs and climbs.

Above her is a metal hatch. It looks solid, heavy, unmovable. Then she spots the attached metal tube. A lift assist, spring-loaded. She knows these from the desalination plant, where similar hatches are used to access the water intake tunnels. With one hand gripping the ladder, she presses the other against the metal hatch. Her arm shakes from the strain. The hatch budges, but only a millimeter.

Kiana sighs. Two hands, then. She weaves her legs through the top two metal rungs, for support. She reminds herself that she's good at climbing, that she always finds a handhold before she falls—even when staring down a scorpion. With both palms braced against the metal plate, she thrusts her torso upward. The hatch sticks, budges, sticks again. Her shoulder muscles burn. Her banged-up knee is screaming at her to stop. Her pulse drums at her temples. Just when she's sure the damn thing will never yield, the hatch jerks open, then swings smoothly upright.

Kiana clambers to the surface and shuts the hatch. City sounds rush at her: a car horn, the distant rumble of a helicopter, the thrum of urban life.

The alley is just as she remembers, but it's all wrong. The vibrant mural that spans the wall overwhelms her. Garish swirls of color, leering faces. And the savory scent of empanadas is long gone, replaced by the sickly-sweet stench of garbage rotting in Dumpsters. She's never been here at this time of night, either. Whatever time that is. The greatest wrong is Javi's absence. This was their place, together.

From the other end of the alley, someone whistles—a piercing cry. Directed at Kiana or someone else? She can only see a dark form standing there. A man's voice calls out: "Hey!"

Kiana hobbles away from the voice, to where the alley

opens onto First Street. A car glides past, and she ducks back. From a shadowy patch along the wall, she watches the far end of the alley and waits. No one appears. The whistle and shout were false signs of danger. But she can't afford to miss the true signs. And what about the signs of safety? How will she know when it's okay to venture out of the alley without getting nabbed by the police?

She peers around the corner, up and down the street. The storm has let up, but the asphalt is still wet: a slick mirror for passing headlights, break lights, street lights, and the traffic light at the nearby intersection of First and Oak. Its reflection shines green. Now yellow, now red. She watches a compact car slow to a stop. Seconds later, a brown sedan eases past. Kiana recognizes the driver by her Afro: Detective Olivia Bell. In the passenger seat, she can just make out the bulging form of Nick Turley.

Kiana's skin prickles with sudden heat. She flattens herself against the alley wall, willing herself to blend into the gaudy mural. She holds her breath until the reflection of light on the wet street cycles back to red.

The desal plant is only a mile or so away. If it weren't for the cops, she could easily walk there. She glances back at the metal hatch. How far south do the tunnels go? Probably not far enough. One-hundred-fifty years ago, the plant would have lain outside Costa Perdida, beyond the piers where cargo ships unloaded their goods. How else then? She could hail a taxi. Hope that the android driver hasn't received information about her. But she has no wallet, no watch, no way to pay the fare. Okay, but once the taxi got near the plant, she could jump out and run. No, a terrible plan. Cabbie droids are compelled to report incidents of illegal activity—it would alert the police to her location. Then she wouldn't have enough time to extract a terminal, much less get away. What about the train? The nearest stop is two blocks away. People sneak on without tickets all the time. Security droids usually snatch them up pretty quickly, but the desal plant is just two stops away. It might work.

As Kiana takes her first step out of the alley, a police cruiser turns the corner, headed her way. Once more, she jumps back, as if the sidewalk along First Street were a bed of hot coals. Fuck. She can't afford these wasted minutes away from Javi.

She watches the reflection turn once more from green to yellow to red.

Then a familiar mint-colored car passes by the mouth of the alley, slowing for the stoplight just ahead. At the wheel is Kiana's friend from work, Vanhi Briggs.

Kiana bursts from the alley and sprints to catch up to Vanhi's car. She raps her knuckles on the window, and Vanhi's wide brown eyes turn to stare at her, blankly, as if a ghost or the wind had knocked on the glass. Then she lowers the window. "Kiana?"

"I need a ride!" Without waiting for a reply, she lopes around the car's rounded hood and pulls on the passenger door's latch. Nothing.

Vanhi waves her hands frantically, as if warding off a mosquito attack. Then Kiana hears her muffled voice instructing the car: "Unlock doors." When the mechanism clicks, Kiana flings open the door and throws herself into the passenger seat.

Behind them, a horn honks.

"Oh!" Vanhi turns her attention to the road and lurches through the intersection. "Kiana, what are you doing here?" She glances over. "What's going on?"

"Nothing. My car just ... I'm not sure what's the matter ... and I need a ride to work. There's something I forgot. It's urgent."

Vanhi gives her a dubious look. Kiana knows it well: that ironic-yet-uncertain smile, the sharp angles of her eyebrows scrunched together. "What, is the plant going to explode or something?"

Kiana's excuse, she realizes, is implausible. What could she urgently need from the desal plant at this hour? She stares at the dashboard clock. 10:49. "Is that really what time it is?"

"Yeah, yeah." As they near Beachfront Drive, Vanhi flicks on her blinker. The right blinker. The desalination plant is to the left. "Listen, Kiana. The police are everywhere. There's a killer on the loose. And I'm already late for this thing I have to do," Vanhi says. "I was supposed to be there at ten."

Kiana barely recognizes the words her friend is saying. She only registers that she's going to be taken further away from where she needs to be. From Javi. She should pull the latch right now, jump out of the car. But all the energy has fled her body. "What thing?"

The light turns green. As Vanhi pulls the car to the right, Kiana feels herself slump against the door.

"It's pretty close. And it shouldn't take long." Vanhi rushes her words, a note of apology in her tone.

At uneven intervals, functional streetlights splash pools of white across their bodies. With downtown behind them, the only sound is the hum of the motor.

Pretty close. Shouldn't take long. A flint-strike of hope sparks in Kiana's brain. "Okay, sorry. But where are we going?"

"You know that neighborhood of big old empty houses down along the coast?"

"Mmh-hm."

Mansions and grand Victorians. What used to be called beachfront property. In the 2040 quake, most of the properties toppled to the ground or fell into the sea. The neighborhood is mostly condemned now. Camps of unhomed people everywhere. Squatters and meth heads. A scary scene, from what Kiana's heard.

"So, there's this guy, Neptune, that I know," Vanhi says. "He owns the old Talbot House?"

Another scrap of history flits through Kiana's head. A nineteenth century gold miner, George Talbot was Costa Perdida's first millionaire.

"The place is still pretty much standing," Vanhi says. "Neptune throws these Level Up parties there. A virtual dance club. Super glamorous. Come as your favorite avatar, right? But the hookups that happen, those are real bodies."

The whole thing sounds awful. Kiana feels her energy drain away again. A virtual sex party? Vanhi has a wife and kids. No, just one kid now: Farhan. Vanhi and Catherine also lost a daughter to shadow fever. Still, Kiana got the impression that the family pulled through the tragedy together. She can't picture Vanhi at this fake nightclub. Or how she could be late to such an event. "What happens at ten o'clock? Do they stop letting people in?"

"Well, here's the thing." Vanhi sighs. "You've heard of boost?"

"Yeah." A synthetic street drug. It's like ecstasy, from what Kiana's read. Apparently, it's particularly effective at dissolving the perceptual barriers between real life and virtual reality, making it very popular among Level Up users.

"So, Catherine's a chemistry teacher," Vanhi says. "And I get chemicals cheaply from work."

"Oh, man."

"Money's fucking tight, Kiana."

"I know."

"Cath is on dialysis. And our insurance is basically worthless. Hardly covers anything. Copays are outrageous. We're going bankrupt, Kiana." From the pocket of her door, Vanhi snatches a tissue, dabs her eyes.

"Shit. I'm sorry, Vanhi. I understand." It's the same with every procedure, every piece of equipment, and every drop of medicine required to keep Javi alive and free of suffering. "I really do."

Kiana could explain to Vanhi just why she understands, but then Vanhi would know too much. She doesn't need Kiana's crimes, in addition to her own.

They near the edge of town. A few miles ahead, the black outlines of sheer cliffs rise before them. Soon, Beachfront will merge into an intact stretch of Highway 1, which runs north through Point Nada before breaking up further along the winding coast. Instead, Vanhi steers them inland.

Still blinking away tears, Vanhi's eyes roam Kiana's face. Her expression pinches. "Okay, I hate to say it, but you look like shit." She squints. "I mean, is that actual blood on your head?"

Kiana probes her scalp. Just above her temple, her hair is a clotted tangle. At least her skull has stopped throbbing.

"Are you mixed up in some shit, Kiana?" An instant later, Vanhi shakes her head. "No, forget it. Who the hell am I to ask, right?" She snorts a sharp dry laugh and reaches into a large purse by her feet. After a moment of fumbling, she pulls out a plastic baggie and waves it between them. Dozens of pills clatter inside.

"Wow." Kiana can't think of a better reply. On a different day, she might condemn Vanhi for her choices. From what she's read, boost is highly addictive and dangerous. But, if it would save her own family, Kiana would become a drug dealer, too.

Vanhi turns them onto a pot-holed street lined with the husks of great houses. Now slumping tents and makeshift domiciles abound. People huddle around fires or walk the streets. Some of them roam solo, their bodies hunched. Others travel in packs, lean as the coyotes who died off in Kiana's youth. A gang of young men gives them menacing looks as they drive past.

Kiana looks out beyond the fallen houses and homeless camps, where the Costa Perdida elite once had beachfront decks and terraces, to where the gray seawall rises high. The formerly ritzy enclave now reminds Kiana of the post-War Berlin of her great-grandmother's childhood. The Schmidt family's little yellow cottage in Charlottenburg, bombed into oblivion. Gerda, Arnold, and Ilse had evacuated the city just two days prior. Since college, Kiana has spent countless hours poring over photo archives of that era—along with other places and times. All that tinkering away on her Level Up worlds. It seems so pointless now. So much wasted time, sitting on the couch and transferring files: images, film fragments, scans of newspaper articles and journals and blueprints and phone books. Instead, she should have been fully present in the real world around her. She should have paid attention to every tedious, exhausting, blissful minute spent in the presence of her husband and child.

The car pauses before a rolling gate in a chain link fence. Vanhi lowers the window, punches a code into a keypad, and the gate trundles open. As they pull up the drive, Kiana feels foggy, disoriented. Lost again between worlds. They park among what must be two dozen other vehicles, arrayed haphazardly in front of the Talbot House. Even in the pale cast of headlights, the mansion's decrepitude is clear: grimy clapboard facade, pitched roof covered in moss, bay windows boarded up, finials gone missing. An entire wing of the house has slid into a ravine. What a bizarre place for a party. Kiana's amazed they can even run Level Up in such a decrepit neighborhood.

An illegal fiber hookup? An unregulated terminal?

Vanhi shuts the headlights off and the house goes dark, aside from a porch light's glow.

Kiana had planned to tell her friend that she'd wait in the car. Now she has to get inside the rundown mansion. "Can I tag along, Vanhi? It's creepy around here."

Vanhi responds with a doubtful frown. Then she gets out, opens the hatchback, and rummages around. "Here, wear this."

A baseball cap is placed in Kiana's hand. People keep giving her strange articles of clothing. The logo on the cap reads: *Costa Perdida Rattlers*.

A memory comes back to Kiana: A couple of years ago, in their driveway at home, a rattlesnake was having a standoff with their César. The snake was hissing, and the dog was growling. From across the dirt yard, Kiana had watched as Javi—armed only with a patio chair—stepped between César and the snake, wrangling the rattler back into the brush. Later, while lying in bed, Kiana had asked Javi whether he'd been scared. "Nah," he'd said, but the hesitancy in his chuckle had told her otherwise.

"It's Farhan's hat, from Little League," Vanhi says. "Put it on. Let's go." The hatchback shuts with an emphatic thud.

The cap scrapes Kiana's wound as she pulls it on, but it fits her smallish head, which is apparently the size of a thirteen-year-old boy's. She throws open the passenger door and hurries to catch up with Vanhi, who locks the car by tapping a silver bracelet that winks in the porch light's glow.

For the first time since Kiana threw herself at her friend's mercy, she notices what Vanhi is wearing: dark brown trousers and a blousy orange top with a peacock feather print. A necklace and earrings to match the bracelet. Eye shadow and lipstick. A dressy outfit for dealing drugs.

As they climb the front steps, Kiana leans close to Vanhi. "How long are you planning to stay?"

"Oh, not long." Vanhi waves off her concern. "With Neptune, I always have to schmooze a little. But we'll be done in ten minutes. Fifteen, tops."

Kiana nods. That should give her just enough time. "And then you'll drop me off at work?"

"Yeah, yeah."

They step onto a sagging porch. A heavy burgundy drape hangs where the front door once stood. The entrance is guarded by a burly bouncer. Black jeans, black shirt, dark hair, dark eyes, an eerily human-like appearance. Kiana recognizes the model. A generic skindroid from the late '30s, an era before manufacturers realized that people preferred security droids who looked and talked like what they truly were: metal robots.

"The cover charge is fifty dollars," the bouncer recites in monotone. "Full VR equipment and special enhancement are included, but only if your name is on the list."

"Vanhi Briggs. And guest."

The bouncer swivels its blocky head to address Vanhi. "No cover charge for you. But you haven't been allocated a plus-one."

Kiana's debating whether to plead with Vanhi for a loan, when the drape parts, and a head pops out: a man with a thin face, neatly pointed soul patch, and platinum blond hair gathered in a high bun. "Finally!" he says to Vanhi. His smile is sickeningly false.

"Hey, Neptune." Vanhi smiles back, with apparent effort.

When Neptune turns to Kiana, his lips struggle to hold their Cheshire shape. After a long moment of appraisal, he shrugs. "Okay, I guess," he tells the bouncer droid. "Let her in, too."

Kiana knows she should feel insulted, but this shithead and his party, none of it matters.

Neptune leads them into a foyer of cracked marble floors

and peeling wallpaper. Ultraviolet blacklight tubes hang from a brassy chain. More burgundy drapes cover a trio of archways leading off the foyer. Muffled chatter echoes from somewhere in the house. The air reeks of mildew and animal urine.

"Good evening." A young woman in a white cocktail dress, luminous in the blacklight, steps forward to greet them. Clearly, Neptune has instructed the poor girl on how to smile.

"My hostess will assist you," Neptune tells Kiana. "While your friend and I conduct our business."

"I'll come find you," Vanhi says. Then she and Neptune disappear through one of the draped archways.

The hostess hands Kiana a black plastic bag, *Club Neptune* embossed in gold letters on its side. "VR glasses with earbuds are mandatory and included in the cover charge. Additional sensory stimulus devices are available for a small charge. All items are thoroughly sanitized after each use. What can I interest you in? Nasal? Lingual? Manual? Genital?"

Kiana shudders. But her mind tingles. Virtual smell, touch, taste. This is promising. "Nothing, thanks."

"You sure?" The hostess leans forward and whispers conspiratorially, "Not even nasal? They're only ten bucks a pair. I'm wearing mine right now!" She lifts her chin, revealing a pair of silvery inserts in her nostrils.

"So, how do those extra senses work here? I thought you needed a, you know, really high-speed internet connection for that."

It could also be that a programmer has engineered a basic sensory profile just for Club Neptune. The result would be a pale facsimile of the real thing: chemically scents, artificial tastes, a tactile experience even more rubbery than in the pre-regulated era of Level Up. And forget about the subtle perceptual flourishes—shifts in balance, changes in space—that once made the virtual realm so uncannily lifelike.

"Hm, I don't know how it all works." The hostess's pretty face scrunches helplessly. "Technology isn't really my thing."

"Sure, never mind." Kiana bluffs a light smile. "Just curious."

"Okay," the hostess says. "You'll need to log into your Level Up account using a personal device."

"Oh, sorry. I don't have a device on me."

The hostess tilts her head at Kiana. "Nothing?" The false smile creeps back into place. "Phone? Watch? Lens? Bracelet? Earpod? Implant?"

"Nothing." Kiana suspects the hostess of having a subdermal bluetooth chip attached to her cranium. Exchanging privacy and security for the sake of convenience seems crazy to Kiana. If her mother were alive, she would be appalled by this new tech. Alex certainly is.

"In that case," the hostess says, "you'll be limited to audio-visual input. You won't be able to verbally interact with other guests, and they'll see you only as a vague shape. To avoid collisions."

"Understood." Kiana slips on the VR glasses and inserts the attached earbuds. The foyer is instantly transformed into its former glory: marble floor shining like an ice-covered lake, neat lilac wallpaper filigreed with golden swirls. The blacklight now seems to emanate from a large crystal chandelier. Awful club music throbs through the walls.

The hostess pulls back one of the heavy drapes, and Kiana passes through an archway, into what must have been the ball-room. As with the foyer, the virtual decor is a hackneyed mix of Victorian elegance and night club glitz. The vaulted ceiling is mirrored, the ornate molding lined with pink and blue neon, the marble floor tackily aglow with glitter. And still more black-light chandeliers light the room.

Kiana stands at the edge of a dance floor crowded with

avatars of every sort: beautiful people sharply dressed, mythical hybrids of human and beast, comic book superheroes, sexy maids, hunky workmen, and other beings whose gender and species and apparel Kiana couldn't hope to identify. They step and sway to the shatter-pop music that's streamed into their ears. The generic beat is steady and relentless. The so-called melody is a synthesis of thousands of micro-samples of pop music's past, split apart and reassembled by an AI DJ.

Kiana pulls out the earbuds attached to her glasses. Now only faintly audible, the music is almost tolerable.

When she lifts her VR glasses, the ballroom is stripped bare—shabby and moldering away. And, of course, the dancers are reduced to ordinary humans, the majority of them either scrawnier or chubbier than their avatars, their clothing duller, their faces less symmetrical, their hair thinner, their complexions grayer.

Before someone catches her cheating, Kiana drops the glasses back in place. But who would notice? She reminds herself that, in the virtual eyes of everyone around her, she's nothing but a muted blob. And these dancing avatars are nothing to her. She's only here to search for Neptune's terminal.

Along the adjacent wall, Kiana spots yet another draped archway. After threading her way around the dance floor, she slips through the heavy fabric and into a high vestibule. Before her, a curved stairway climbs to the second floor. A neon sign hovers at the foot of the stairs: *No Guests Allowed*. An identical sign guards the archway to the right. The sign to her left reads: *See Hostess for Private Rooms*. Kiana lowers the glasses, resting the bridge on the tip of her nose. In reality, both the staircase and the hall to her right are barricaded by old furniture and splintered planks.

Most likely, Neptune would stash his network server on the

ground floor or in the basement, where temperatures are cooler. Kiana nudges the VR glasses back into place and heads left, her only option. She discovers that the doors are marked with virtual placards: *Private Room #1*, *Private Room #2*, and so on. Though it's relatively early at night for this kind of party, and the guests have yet to receive the doses of boost that Vanhi brought, Kiana has no interest in stumbling across any kind of sad Level Up orgy. As she hurries her pace down the hall, she realizes that the pain in her knee has subsided. A good sign, Kiana thinks.

At the end of the hall, she comes to a pair of doors marked *Staff Only*. When she opens the first, a cloud of dust billows forth. The particles catch in her throat, and she coughs her way inside, probing the dark space with the souvenir flashlight. Whatever its original purpose, the room has been gutted. Only the sour odor of mold remains.

Before trying the other room, Kiana buries her nose and mouth in the crook of her arm. Jimmy's work shirt, with its wonderful Javi smell of perfectly ordinary soap. Now she's glad she doesn't have the nasal inserts. Standing back, she opens the door. This time, she isn't subsumed in a smog of dust and spores. The room is an office, also apparently ransacked: filing cabinet drawers are open and empty, the bookshelves stand bookless.

An electrical hum draws Kiana into the room, toward a wooden desk. In a cubby at knee level sits a dark metal object the size of an upturned shoe box. An old tower server. Little colored lights pulse, its fan whirs inside. Kiana drops into a crouch and reaches behind the server. Her fingertips run down its sleek back, brushing over empty ports. There, a plastic connector. Crawling under the desk, she follows the ethernet cable to a terminal that sits on the floor. It looks cheap, newish, like her own. She turns the unit around, aims the flashlight at the words printed on the back. It is, in fact, the exact same model of terminal she has at home.

Worthless tech. How stupid she was, to get her hopes up.

An aching heaviness descends on Kiana. A numbness with weight, with heft. She crumples to the hard marble floor beneath the desk. If Javi were here, he would fold himself around her. No, that version of her husband lives in the past. In a time when, on groggy weekend mornings, their daughter would pad into their bedroom, burrow under the covers, and curl herself into Kiana. And Javi would curl himself around the both of them. They became a single organism then, huddled against the world. A pillbug in a garden of linens.

Kiana would give anything to feel that again. To have her daughter's body pressed tightly to her own. Actual or virtual, it wouldn't matter. Any semblance of her sweet Anza would sustain her right now, when she has so little to keep her going.

That goddamn music, leaking from the earbuds. How can she hold onto Javi and Anza with that awful music wheedling and skittering through her mind? Kiana swipes the VR glasses from her head. But they thud off the underside of the desk and land by her knee. The pointless sounds continue their assault, knifing right through her warm bundle of memories. A beautiful illusion, ruined by the ugly illusion that is Club Neptune.

Kiana reaches behind the terminal. She wraps her fingers around the power cord. Makes a fist. And yanks it from the wall.

The club music dies, and blissful silence follows.

Kiana shuts her eyes, but her pillbug family won't return to her.

CHAPTER FOURTEEN

DECEMBER, 2001

L indsay stood with her back to the living room wall. A crowd of faces swam before her, all of them happily aglow and gabbing away. New Year's Eve. A cheerful panic warmed the air. It was cold outside, by Los Angeles standards. Lindsay wore a long-sleeve shirt and tights under her skirt. She slurped her second gin and tonic. Piney and sweet, a burn against the chill.

Across the room, she spotted Judy D'Angelo, the party's host and Lindsay's former manager at AmbuRide. Judy stood talking to a vaguely familiar guy in a brown sweater. Maybe he'd once worked in the ER at Good Sam. Sweater Guy raised a hand in greeting to Lindsay. She smiled uncertainly, gave him a nod.

Was she supposed to mosey on over, reconnect with Sweater Guy? Lindsay had forgotten how to mingle. Anyway, she felt too buzzed to move, too wiped out to bother. She'd been awake all night with Taylor, who had a fever. Poor kid. By this morning, her temperature had simmered, only to rise again in the afternoon and plateau this evening. Now Lindsay had left her ex-husband to care for their daughter. She had to keep reminding herself that this constituted normal divorcée parenting. That Greg was six years into recovery. That he had a new wife, a shiny new moral compass.

Besides, Lindsay deserved some fun. Not just a New Year's Eve celebration, the party was also to welcome home Corey Ferber, her old EMT buddy. On the night Lindsay and Greg met, Corey was driving the ambulance. Two years later, he was a groomsman at their wedding. Around that time, Corey changed careers. He went to nursing school, joined Doctors Without Borders, and then departed for Western Africa. Or maybe Northern Africa? Lindsay had lost touch. And, so far tonight, she had yet to lay eyes on the guest of honor. Would she even recognize Corey? She still thought of him as he looked in the early nineties: pudgy and scraggily, with those mischievous eyes. Always joking around. An older brother kind of guy.

Shit, he must be in his forties now.

Lindsay, meanwhile, had turned thirty-two this year. Or had next year come already? No, even lost in her thoughts, she wouldn't have missed the group countdown, the drunken cheers. She turned her wrist to see what time it was, then remembered: she'd stopped wearing a watch months ago, after buying her first cell phone. The gray hunk of plastic filled her small purse, which she wore slung across her torso. Only 10:23, according to the phone's little green screen. And zero missed calls. No news was good news. She pictured Taylor, arms wrapped around her stuffed Pooh Bear, snug in bed. Then she remembered that the bed in question sat in the guest room at Greg and Courtney's new house. Another layer of tiredness wrapped itself around her.

"Did somebody glue you to the wall, Zelenko?"

Judy had sneaked up on her. Lindsay grinned, or maybe grimaced. She liked it that her old boss still referred to her by her old last name. As if Lindsay were an athlete or a soldier—someone other than a single mom doing freelance web graphic design. For the umpteenth time, Lindsay considered ditching her ex's surname. But remaining an Olsen provided continuity for Taylor at school. And the Zelenko name came with its own carousel-load of baggage.

"Just dipping my toes in the pool before I dive in," Lindsay said.

"The waters are warm, doll." Judy leaned her shoulder into Lindsay's. "Look at 'em. Everybody's got that nice pink-faced party glow."

Lindsay nodded. Some appeared almost feverish. Or maybe she was projecting. A jolt of worry rippled through her. She shouldn't have left Taylor. She should duck outside and call Greg, just to check in. No, no, no. Everything was fine.

"Actually, some folks are borderline sweaty," Judy said. "Maybe I'll crack open a window or two."

As she started to peel away, Lindsay grabbed Judy's elbow. "Hey, have you seen Corey yet?"

"Yeah, he just got here a little bit ago. You haven't even talked to Ferber?" Judy shook her head. She had a way of expressing disappointment that was somehow motivating. "Try the kitchen."

"You got it, boss."

Lindsay downed the last watery slosh of her G&T and disengaged from the wall. She swayed toward the kitchen. Bright granite countertops, shiny foreheads, cheery bottle of gin sitting on a granite island. She slalomed through the scrum of bodies, glancing at unfamiliar and half-forgotten faces. None of them were Corey's face. She might have briefly worked alongside this person here or that person there. She'd formed so few lasting bonds during her EMT years. The weight of realization knotted her shoulders. Her heels ached.

Lindsay pressed herself against the island, scooping cubes of fresh ice into her glass. Filled it halfway with flattening Schweppes and nearly to the brim with Tanqueray. Squeezed a wedge of lime and plopped it in. Maybe she should take up bartending. Any job would be livelier than sitting at home and writing HTML. She missed the adrenaline buzz of arriving at the scene of an emergency, of throwing herself into the tangle of life and death. The precariousness, the uncertainty. The verge.

Greg himself had materialized from the verge. Literally, from a balcony, he fell into her life. Lindsay had smelled the liquor on his breath, had glimpsed the pills in the pocket of his blazer. And yet, when he smiled, she'd felt the thrill of him in her fingers and toes. Lindsay knew he would be trouble—and her gut had gauged that trouble as just the right amount—like in high school, stealing tubes of drugstore lipstick.

Eleven years after that night, and Greg Olsen had become a stranger to her. Those first months of dating, while Greg recovered from his fractured vertebra, Lindsay had felt they knew one another completely. Maybe it had been the oxycontin that opened his heart and mind to her. A few years later, after he wrecked the car, it was God who'd closed Greg off. When he'd first started attending NA meetings, Lindsay had witnessed his attempts to surrender control to any number of higher powers—Buddhism, the Collective Unconscious, Gaia, the Universe—but none had stuck. It was when they moved from their West LA apartment to the house in Covina that Greg fell under the spell of Rick Nash, his latest NA sponsor. Christian Rick, as Lindsay referred to him. The sixty-ish, pot-bellied, and mustachioed owner of a lumber yard, Rick was an avuncular walrus of a man. And the destroyer of Lindsay's marriage. First came Christian Rick's born again hooey. Then Rick introduced Greg to his comely Christian daughter, Courtney Nash.

A woman's hand reached in front of Lindsay—tanned and lean, unpolished nails—and snatched a bottle of tequila.

"Oh, Lindsay. Hi!" Now it was Tamara Wardell who'd sneaked up on her. With her strong face, pale green eyes, and blonde mane of hair, she looked like a lioness. Tamara was a paramedic and, for two years, she and Lindsay had worked every Wednesday evening shift together. They'd also both gotten married the same year and pregnant the next. During their respective maternity leaves, they'd drifted apart.

"Hey, Tamara. How are you?"

"So good, Linds." She poured tequila into a pair of glasses. "Yourself?"

"Oh, you know." Lindsay stopped herself before adding, *Can't complain.* "So, you still with AmbuRide?"

"No, after having Brendan ... well, I just kind of settled into motherhood there for a while."

Lindsay nodded. "Same."

"Also, to be honest? We didn't need the extra paycheck. You remember my husband, Rob?" While dispensing margarita mix, Tamara jolted her head vaguely toward a cluster of interchangeable men who stood by the refrigerator.

"Mm-hm."

"So, he started this tech company a few years back. Well, the IPO went through the freakin' roof." Tamara's lioness gaze shot up to the kitchen ceiling, as if her stock certificates were stashed in Judy's crawl space. "We actually just bought some land up north. Near Costa Perdida? We're ditching this whole LA scene, Linds. Organic farming!" She smiled and slowly shook her head, as if stunned by her own news. "How about you and ... Craig, was it? You had a little girl, right? Are you guys still in that same apartment off Sepulveda?"

"It's Greg, actually." Lindsay shrugged. Maybe she should have married a Craig. "But we got divorced two years ago. And

I recently transitioned into the field of web graphic design." *Transitioned into the field of?* How pathetic, trying to impress Tamara. Lindsay drank deeply from her G&T. "Taylor's really excelling in second grade." She was doing fine. "Now it's just us two girls, in our cute little home." The house was small, boring, a rental.

"Well, hey. That sounds great." Tamara shrugged. "But if you ever need a break from the city, you should totally come visit, okay?" She handed Lindsay a business card: *Seabreeze Organic Farm.*

"As long as you don't put us to work out in the fields!"

"Ha-ha, we just might." Tamara squeezed Lindsay's arm. "So glad I ran into you, Linds. Take care, okay?" She scooped up her margaritas and spun away.

"You, too," Lindsay said, but Tamara had already disappeared. She crammed the business card into her purse and took another hard swallow.

She hated herself a little now, plumping up her mediocre existence for Tamara's sake. No, it was for her own sake. Of course, it was. When a person dreams of moving to Los Angeles, the vision dancing in their head is never of a single mom scraping by in the Eastern exurbs. For Lindsay, it had been the Santa Monica Pier, of all places, that had glowed sunnily in her young mind. The opening credits to *Three's Company*, for a couple of seasons, were set among the Pier's fairground attractions. As a kid in gray Seattle, the blue sky that backdropped Janet, Chrissy, and Jack had suggested a vivid future within her reach. She'd held onto that vision until the day she turned eighteen and left for California.

As Lindsay threaded her way back through the kitchen, a good warm fuzz spread through her. She used both hands to hold her third drink close to her chest. The room softly tilted and swished.

In the hallway, she found another blank patch of wall to lean against and shut her eyes.

It wasn't just the blue skies over Santa Monica that had beckoned her south. The greatest allure for Lindsay had been the carefree smiles of those insipid sitcom characters. Young, single, and open to possibilities. The opposite, in other words, of Lindsay's parents. Even in her earliest memories, her father, Harry Zelenko, had the slouched demeanor of a doomed man. Lindsay's mother, Beverly, had always seemed bitter, disappointed. Drab clothes, hair in a bun. Old. In actuality, she'd just turned twenty when she had Lindsay—five years younger than Lindsay was when she had Taylor. She wished she could find some sympathy for her mom, but the well of generosity in her heart ran low these days. Lindsay didn't admire that in herself.

She peeled her eyes back open. Framed photos of the D'Angelos lined the hallway. Judy, her husband, and two kids standing before the rim of the Grand Canyon. Judy and hubby in Vegas, sans kids. One of the kids in cap and gown, followed by the other. The wall marked a progression of a life together, a through line that would carry forth to gray hair and grandkids. Lindsay and Greg's line had stretched thin and snapped.

She chugged the rest of her drink, unmelted ice clinking against her teeth.

Through the door across the hall, she heard the whoosh of a toilet. A faucet ran. She sort of had to pee.

The door opened, and a handsome man emerged.

"Hey, Lindsay!"

His face presented a tricky puzzle: curves, lines, planes, creases, hues. In the split second that Lindsay spent baffled by that face, the way the hall light caught the ice-blue flecks in the man's eyes solved the puzzle for her.

"Corey?" She laughed, delighted and surprised, as if her old friend had performed a magic trick. Since the last time she saw him, he must have lost forty or fifty pounds. His hair was short, neat, and dappled with gray. And he'd shaved his scraggly beard, revealing a sturdy jawline and a really very nice pair of lips. Had he also grown an inch taller? "Oh my god. Um, wow." She blinked hard, and he was still there, smiling at her. "It's so great to see you."

His arms engulfed her in a hug. "Mmm," he hummed—like easing into a perfectly hot bath. When he broke away from the hug, Corey held onto her shoulders. He looked at Lindsay as if she were the one who had magically transformed. "Man, Linds. It's great to see you, too."

"Okay, remind me. Where did you go? And what was it like? And how is it being back? And what are you going to do now? And, jeez, dude." She batted his chest with the back of her hand, stumbled back, caught her balance. "You're fucking ripped."

He laughed, and the hue of his cheeks turned from well-tanned to pink. He stared at his shoes. Comfy dress shoes, in place of the ratty sneakers he used to wear to similar events.

In fact, Lindsay remembered now. A genuine déjà vu. One of Judy's previous New Year's Eve parties. She and Greg were engaged at the time, so '91 going into '92. They'd whispered snarkily about Corey's overly casual footwear that night. They'd been really drunk. Greg had also downed an oxy, or maybe two. How he'd managed to avoid wrapping them around a phone pole that night—well, Greg would earnestly call it a miracle. The actual car wreck had occurred a couple of years later, while he was driving solo, drunk and stoned, after a night out with Yosef. Lindsay had been asleep at home, a tiny Taylor in her belly, second trimester.

Corey patted his empty shirt pocket. "I was just going to head out to the backyard for a smoke. Care to join me?"

"Sure." Lindsay didn't smoke, but she liked knowing that

Corey had retained at least one bad habit. In general, she approved of bad habits. Until they went too far, that is. "Oh, but hey. Isn't it freezing out?"

He shrugged. "We'll grab our coats."

Lindsay followed Corey to the guest bedroom, where a pile of outer layers—jackets, shells, and overcoats in fleece, leather, Gore-Tex, tweed—lay fanned across a fluffy comforter. A pleasant wobble ran through Lindsay's blood. She turned and fell back onto the soft rolling hills of coats.

Corey stood above her, smiling a funny smile. "Enjoying yourself down there?"

"Mmm," she said, echoing his hot-bath hum. She saw what would happen next, as if she'd skipped ahead on a video tape. Corey would swing the door shut. He would lower himself upon her. Hands and lips and more warm hums against her ear. Her body needed reminding of how to be in that state. Lindsay stared into Corey's eyes and waited for him to reach for the door, for the press of his body, for that fucking phone to stop ringing. Who was the idiot who'd left their cell phone in their coat?

Corey pointed to the purse at Lindsay's hip. "Is that you?"

* * *

This would be the third time that Lindsay sat beside the hospital bed of a loved one. The second time was in 1995, after Greg totaled their car. The first time was in 1978, when Lindsay was nine years old.

On that awful day, she remembered looking for her father through the gaps in the wooden dugout, while awaiting her turn at bat. He'd disappeared two innings earlier. Her belly wriggled with worry. The feeling never reminded her of anything like butterflies. More like a tangle of snakes.

Lindsay batted seventh in the lineup and played right field. She was one of only three girls in her Little League district. Her dad, Harry Zelenko, had taught her to play in the small backyard of their house in Beacon Hill. He came to every game—his lone contribution to her upbringing. That, and his welfare checks. Her father had been laid off by Boeing, fired from a series of dockyard jobs, failed the bus driver's test, and simply not shown up for countless interviews. Meanwhile, her mother feared the outside world. Beverly cooked and cleaned and watched soap operas, rarely spoke, and avoided physical contact with everyone, Lindsay included. Her grandfather, Danylo, helped her with homework and joined her on the avocado-green living room couch every Saturday morning for Looney Tunes and Cap'n Crunch. Harry showed up for sports, be it a boxing match on TV or a soccer game at his daughter' school. But her father loved baseball most of all. Whenever Lindsay stood at the plate or out on the grass, she could always spot him in the bleachers, huddled in his beige overcoat, his mustache droopy from the springtime Seattle drizzle. Though he looked forlorn, Harry never failed to cheer her on.

It was only when Lindsay sat on the bench that her father would sneak back to their yellow pickup truck. He kept a metal flask in the glove compartment. Before she took the field again, he would be back in his spot, a fresh grin beneath his mustache.

Lindsay took one last peek between the slats of the dugout before grabbing her aluminum bat and stepping into the on-deck circle—a ring of trampled white chalk on damp dirt. After each practice swing, she turned and searched for her father. Harry wasn't sitting in the bleachers, wasn't walking across the patch of lawn between field and street. From where she stood, Lindsay couldn't see their pickup truck, parked down the block.

"Batter up!"

Her teammate Tommy had hit a triple, which she"d failed to even notice. Lindsay barely registered stepping up to the plate. She struck out swinging on three pitches. From third base, Tommy gave Lindsay a puzzled look, a "what gives?" shrug. (A few years later, in the back row of a mostly empty movie theater, with Poltergeist glaring from the big screen, Tommy would be her first kiss.)

Her father had missed the worst at-bat of Lindsay's life. Where could he be? The knot in her belly tightened and squirmed. She dropped her bat and ran off the field, into the surrounding park. Her cleats dug hard into the wet grass, but Lindsay didn't feel the tug of the turf. Only dread, which increased with every breath. Her coach yelled after her, the sound of his voice both faraway and near—like when Grandpa Danylo's night-terror shouts invaded her dreams with Ukrainian words of war.

She ran through the gap in the waist-high chainlink fence that surrounded the park. Her footfalls clacked against the concrete sidewalk as she blurred past parked cars. The cab of their yellow pickup truck rose above the roofs of sedans and station wagons, but she didn't see her father's face behind the windshield. Her legs grew heavy, slowed her to a stop. How could he not be there, in the truck?

She heard him then: a wheezing moan, like the sound their old house made in a windstorm. That frightening sound drew her slowly alongside the bed of the pickup. She had to stretch up onto her toes to peer inside. At the sight of her father, Lindsay's heart went cold. Harry lay on the wet and grimy metal, splayed like a discarded doll. The lower half of his left leg was bent away from his body at a horrible angle. Red scratch-marks streaked his face and blood ran from his nose, pooling in his mustache.

The echo of her coach's voice grew louder, nearer—out of

the waking world and into her nightmare. Then the day went black.

* * *

Lindsay sat in the hard plastic chair she'd scooted up to the hospital bed, smoothing her fingers across Taylor's scalding brow. The room smelled sickeningly of disinfectant, and Lindsay still hadn't caught her breath after sprinting through the hospital, ten minutes earlier.

From the passenger seat of Corey's Jeep, Lindsay had run into the chaotic lobby—a New Year's Eve anti-party, all misery and open wounds. She'd felt helpless, without a patient on a gurney to wheel through the madness. Heart galloping, she'd pounded up two flights of stairs. In Room 220, she'd found Greg and Courtney standing near a wall, while a nurse prepped Taylor for a spinal tap. A local anesthetic on her tender back, a mild sedative through an IV drip. The doctor had explained that a blood sample had revealed a viral infection. They needed to test for meningitis.

"Okay, let's go ahead," Lindsay had said. As if Greg hadn't already authorized the procedure before her arrival. But the false sense of authority had kept Lindsay from sobbing herself into a useless state, or screaming nonsensical accusations at Greg and Courtney. It was on their watch that Taylor had gotten worse, after all.

But, really, Lindsay didn't blame them. She blamed herself. She didn't know *how* she could have known that Taylor's symptoms would so quickly worsen, but she felt certain that, as a mother, she *should* have known. When Lindsay handed off her daughter and left for the party, she'd believed Taylor was on the mend.

Now her baby girl lay in a hospital bed, curled on her side,

Pooh Bear in her arms. Pink cheeks, the soft little domes of her sleeping eyelids, golden brown hair dark with sweat, lips parted. A war being fought inside her little body.

Now that Lindsay's adrenaline had settled, she realized she wasn't feeling so great, herself. A queasy gut, a pulsing in her skull, tightness in her lungs. She was anxious, exhausted, frightened, and still drunk from the party. But acknowledging her own miseries only made her feel more miserable. She shouldn't be thinking of herself right now. Didn't she think of herself far too often, as it was?

That very night, she had abandoned her ailing child so she could drink G&Ts and throw herself at her former coworker. How fucking humiliating. The look on Corey's face when her phone rang, interrupting her sad seduction. A look of relief, wasn't it? A moment earlier, she'd felt so warm and good. But the urgency in Greg's voice on the phone had turned Lindsay cold. He'd explained how Taylor had woken up crying, with a stiff neck and a pain in her left ear. Her temperature had spiked. Greg was driving to the hospital when he called.

Now Lindsay's ex-husband sat beside her. Courtney had arranged herself at an awkward angle, diagonal to the corner of the bed, like when an uninvited guest slides an extra chair up to the dinner table. All three of them were lined up facing Taylor. Lindsay wondered what the doctors and nurses who bustled in and out thought of their trio. Did they look like a team? Team Olsen. Maybe Lindsay should go back to her maiden name, after all.

From the corner of her eye, she watched Greg's hand as he gently squeezed Taylor's ankle, over and over—like a batter's hands on a bat, anxiously waiting for the pitch. Meanwhile, Courtney kept her pretty blonde head bowed, her fingers worrying the yellowy gold cross that draped from her neck. She and Greg both had their eyes closed. Not in a weary way, but in a prayerful way.

Feeling the heat-prickle of anger in her chest, Lindsay returned her to Taylor. Her daughter's face looked so serene, yet so violent with heat. But heat was good for fighting a virus. And better that Taylor should have viral meningitis than the bacterial variety, according to the doctor. But the pain in her ear was worrisome.

Burn that bad shit away, baby girl.

Twenty-four years earlier, when Lindsay sat by her father's hospital bed, she had beamed similarly positive thoughts into Harry's blacked-out head. Her mother had kept a silent vigil in a corner of the room, handbag clutched to her lap for three days straight. It was Grandpa Danylo, with his sad and sunken eyes, who'd explained to Lindsay what had occurred that afternoon, outside her Little League game. "Your father. My son." Thirty years after emigrating to America, his Ukrainian accent remained thick as honey—though his breath smelled of stale coffee. "He has gambling problem, you know? He throws away money, betting on horses, on boxing, on this baseball that you love. He bets more money than sits in bank." While her grandfather spoke, Lindsay had watched her mother's face harden, the grip on her purse tighten. Beverly's eyes had pleaded for her father-in-law's silence, but he'd barreled on: "You know what is bookie? This is man who takes people's throwaway money. When bookie, he is not paid, he send tough guys to collect. Your father, he cannot pay tough guys. So they beat him. Maybe with baseball bats, who knows." Grampa Danylo had shrugged and sighed his heavy sigh. Aside from breakfast cereal and cartoons, all of the miserable world made him sigh. Even after Harry Zelenko awoke from his coma and was released from the hospital, his head and leg in casts, her grandfather had sighed. Perhaps he'd known that Lindsay's father would never change his ways. Maybe he'd even foreseen that, in the summer of 2001, Harry would be diagnosed with cirrhosis of the liver. That was six months ago. The prognosis was poor. In another year or two, he would likely be dead. This knowledge weighed daily on Lindsay's mind. But her father's health was not her biggest concern at that moment.

As she stroked Taylor's cheek, a murmuring slipped through the cracks of Lindsay's thoughts. Her husband's voice, barely audible over the hum of the HVAC. Now Greg's head was bowed as well, his thinning bangs draped over eyes shut tight, his lips working some prayer or verse that he'd memorized.

Lindsay could recall when interesting words had tumbled from his mouth. On their honeymoon trip to New Orleans, during a hungover Sunday morning stroll, Greg had steered her away from a public drinking fountain and toward a corner bodega. As he plucked two bottles of water from the cooler, Greg had told Lindsay just how many toxic compounds had been discovered in the city's drinking water. "People who can't afford the good stuff?" He'd held up as exhibits the ice-cold bottles, already sweating in the swampy June air. "Those people are more likely to die from cancer. And most of the poor folks here are Black. So, it's a class issue *and* a race issue," he'd explained. Lindsay had no idea that her newlywed husband had read extracurricularly in his field, or that he thought much about the socioeconomic ramifications of water contamination. Her love for Greg had expanded that day.

Now his once-thoughtful brain was crammed full of Bible quotes that his sponsor, Rick Nash, emailed daily. Doubtless, Christian Rick had spoon-fed these same inspirational platitudes into his daughter's pretty little head since birth. No wonder Courtney and Greg had so closely bonded whenever they'd "run into" one another at Rick's house, during the final years of Lindsay's marriage.

She could accept that Greg had betrayed her, ideologically speaking, in order to escape into the easy succor of Christianity, into the church basement where he shared his addiction woes with others, into the Nash family living room. And Lindsay could accept that Greg had betrayed his mother. After the crash, Ilse had openly displayed grave disappointment in her son. In her mind, driving while stoned on opiates was murderously reckless. And placing one's faith in a supreme being, even worse. But worst of all, in Lindsay's mind, was Greg's betrayal of his father. Frank Olsen was such a lovely man. As was his partner, Jonathan. They'd been so supportive of Greg, so kind to Lindsay, so sweet with Taylor. And they practiced kindness and generosity in their community. Despite which, the Nash brand of Christianity had persuaded Greg to shut his father out. It appalled Lindsay that anyone would belong to any such institution.

"What?" Greg turned to her, smiling his innocent smile—a smile which had at some point had gained an edge of irony.

"Nothing." Lindsay realized she'd been glaring at her ex. She looked away, brushed her fingers through Taylor's damp bangs.

"It's just a little prayer," Courtney said.

Lindsay flinched. For a moment, she'd entirely forgotten the other woman in the room.

"It can't hurt," Greg said to Lindsay, his voice quiet and tender.

Lindsay very much wanted to disprove that claim. If Greg and Courtney were the type of fanatics who believed only in faith healing, then, yes, relying solely on their prayers could hurt Taylor. But they had been the ones to recognize her worsening symptoms, to call the doctor, to drive her to the hospital.

Lindsay recalled the mantra she'd adopted since the divorce: *be civil*. Every time she pulled up to the curb outside Greg's new house, she reminded herself: *be civil*. And, whenever she and Greg spoke on the phone to coordinate childcare, she kept the words running through her thoughts: *be civil*. Because all that mattered was that her baby girl feel loved and cared for. And that she get better right away. The rest of it— relationships, careers, all the trials of the adult world—were just slings and arrows. Lindsay could take the hits.

Even now, with sorrow and frustration quivering in her jaw, she forced her lips into a civil smile. "No, I guess it can't hurt."

CHAPTER FIFTEEN

FEBRUARY, 2057

Despite her newfound quietude beneath the desk at Club Neptune, Kiana can't make her way back to the comforting pillbug version of her family. That memory has slipped away. Instead, her thoughts are now mired in a different day. One of Kiana's last days with her daughter. The day they drove Anza to Point Nada. The day their dying child's mind was uploaded to Level Up.

On that day, Kiana had sat in the backseat of the Accord, with Anza's fevered head resting in her lap, while Javi drove the winding coastal highway just north of Costa Perdida. Alex was there, too, in the passenger seat. She'd come down from Santa Cruz, both to provide emotional support and to inspect the tech that would be used to sample and digitize Anza's brain.

As she'd watched the brown hills blur past, Kiana had felt disoriented. Powerless and lost, as if entangled in a bad dream. A quiet sort of nightmare. Even the unusual configuration of bodies in Kiana's car unsettled her. She should be driving, with Javi beside her, and Anza sitting upright in the back, the passing world mirrored in her big, curious eyes. The sky was all wrong, too. It looked unreal—deep blue, free of smog, and stretched forever across the clear Pacific. She couldn't remember the last time she'd seen the water sparkle like that. What a horrible trick for nature to play. To pretend at beauty, while Anza lay dying.

Kiana's fingers had combed through her daughter's hair— dark and sweaty at the temples, then softening into chestnut waves, which the deceitful sunshine turned golden. The true color of that day resided in Anza's face, in the charcoal gray that seemed to pass like a shadow just beneath the surface of her skin. A shadow, or a ghost.

Spectral fever. The name of the disease was another part of the awful, unshakable dream. Until a few months ago, Kiana had never even heard of spectral fever. No one had. It had orig-inated somewhere in the Submersion territories of Southeast Asia and spread quickly through the swamplands, decimating the population of children. Then the disease hit the flooded cities, or what remained of them: Bangkok, Singapore, Kuala Lampur, Ho Chi Minh. Containment efforts failed. Within days, spectral fever had encircled the globe. At first, scientists had believed it spread through touch. No, via mosquito bites. No, water. No, it was airborne. The world's epidemiologists remained uncertain. Just as they had in the early days of that pandemic from the year Kiana was born. Except, that virus had preyed most fiercely on older people and those too brainwashed to get a shot in the arm. But science hadn't yet developed a vaccine for spectral fever. It was killing children with impunity. It was killing her child.

When Anza first contracted the disease, Kiana had been certain her daughter would be among the infected few who somehow survived. In the overcrowded hospital, while sitting at Anza's bedside, she'd reminded herself that her own mother had once been infected with a potentially deadly disease and had fought through it. She'd lost some hearing in one ear, but she'd won. Surely those same strong genes would see Anza through. That's what Kiana had wanted desperately to believe.

Alex reached her long arm between the seats and clasped her hand around Kiana's knee. Kiana tried to focus on her aunt's slender face, blurred by tears. She hadn't realized she'd been crying.

In the rearview mirror, Javi's thick eyebrows were clenched with worry. His anxious hands ratcheted tight around the steering wheel, not relaxing their grip until the car stopped before an old ranch house on the outskirts of town. Out back, a moldering barn slumped into the tall, brown grass. Nothing about the property suggested an illegal tech operation. Javi shut off the engine, and they all put on their surgical masks. Anza stirred into a semi-wakeful state, her brown eyes fogged over and blinking stickily. Kiana had to help her with her mask. Officially, they should all be in quarantine, and Anza should be in the ICU. But the National Guard was overtaxed, and the hospitals were overflowing.

A man and a woman greeted them out front of the house. They both wore blue jeans, white shirts, white tennis shoes, and white N95s. They both had the same shade of blond hair, washed-out, the color of lemonade—another falsely sunny color. Were they twins? Kiana didn't trust them. They belonged to the unshakable dream.

Kiana wanted to call off the upload, to retreat to their home, to cancel the fever burning in Anza's brain. But Javi was already scooping their daughter into his arms, and Alex was following the twins up three wooden steps and onto a sun-bleached porch. As Kiana stepped out of the car, the imminent loss struck her: a blow to the knees that nearly crumpled her. Loss in advance of loss. Grief ahead of death. In the years to come, she would never understand how she managed to walk inside that house that afternoon. Each step had only carried her deeper into the nightmare.

Now, outside the office in Club Neptune, footfalls rumble down the marble hallway. Kiana is crawling out from under the desk when the door flings open. She stands abruptly, her body rigid.

Neptune stares at her from the doorway, his eyes wide, mouth slack. "What the fuck did you do?"

"I'm sorry." Kiana raises her hands. "It's the terminal. It got unplugged. I don't know why ... I just ...."

Neptune runs at her. Kiana leaps aside, sure he's going to tackle her, strangle her, who knows what. Instead, he ducks and scrambles under the desk. As he works at plugging the terminal back in, Kiana turns toward the door.

The bouncer droid stands there, arms folded across its chest. It fixes Kiana with a blank stare.

"Get her out of here," says Neptune's muffled voice. "The other one, too. Vanhi."

With a tilt of its blocky head, the bouncer motions Kiana toward the door.

Fine. She's failed anyway. As she walks past, the bouncer shoves her shoulder, and she stumbles into the hall. Why does everyone keep fucking shoving her? Kiana thinks of the box cutter in her pocket and entertains a brief fantasy of slicing the android's fake ugly face. Oh, the microsecond of satisfaction she would feel—right before her skull is crushed.

Vanhi stands at the end of the hall, by the ruined staircase. Even from that distance, the disdain etched into the lines of her face is clear. Kiana keeps her eyes lowered as she's marched along.

"Come on," the bouncer tells Vanhi. "Let's go."

As they're escorted through the lobby, the hostess's voice

comes through the drape: "We'll be back online in a moment, folks! We appreciate your patience!"

On the front porch, the bouncer android gives Kiana another shove. She bumps shoulders with Vanhi, who makes a disgusted sound, a growl crossed with a sigh, and stomps down the steps. Kiana follows, two paces behind, dread in her gut. As she reaches the bottom step, Vanhi turns on her.

"What the fuck, Kiana? I probably just lost a good client because of you! You know I need the money, right? I explained that to you, didn't I? For Cath. That I need it for ...." Vanhi chokes on her words. Her face trembles, as rage crumples into sadness. Tears dart from her eyes.

"I'm sorry, Vanhi." Kiana reaches out her hands, then pulls them back, fighting off the impulse to embrace her friend. "I was looking for an unregulated terminal."

Vanhi's lips part. She blinks at Kiana. "What?"

"For Javi. He's dying." Now Kiana's crying, too. "Lung cancer. I need that terminal." She shakes her head. She's so tired, she doesn't know what she's saying anymore. "To upload his mind, I mean. To Level Up, to be with Anza."

Vanhi's eyes go soft. Her hands rise to her mouth, as if in prayer, or maybe shame. She nods her head slowly, up and down, up and down. "That's why you asked me to drive you to work." Her voice is gentle now, like a breeze in the night. "For the terminal at the desal plant."

"Yeah."

"My god, Kiana." Vanhi's gaze falls to the ground. "This fucking world."

Kiana doesn't know what to say, what to add, what to ask, what to do. She wraps her arms around her chest. Is she cold? She isn't sure. She stares into the distance, at nothing. No, she's staring at the gate, at the end of the drive. How many miles is she from work? It doesn't matter. She'll walk until she gets there. Her first steps feel like floating.

"Kiana, wait."

She feels a tug at the back of Jimmy Driscoll's work shirt. She slows, stops, turns.

"Come on." Vanhi sighs. "I'll drive you."

* * *

"Costa Perdida Police Department is reporting that the bodies of murder suspect Walter Brogan and defense attorney Jane Hamamura have been discovered in the old mercantile tunnels, their deaths the apparent result of a murder-suicide. We'll have more on this story as it develops."

"Volume down," Vanhi says, and the broadcaster's voice becomes a murmur. "They didn't mention you. That's good, right?"

On the drive back through town, Kiana has explained everything: Javi's dire prognosis, the black-market ventilator, the arrest, her escape from the station house, Brogan and his gun.

"I guess it's good. I don't know." Kiana stares ahead, down Beachfront Drive, beyond the pier, at the white glow cast by the lights of the desalination plant. The night has turned quiet: no more piercing sirens, no more roaring helicopters. Maybe the police have forgotten about her. Or, they know she's harmless and assume she'll turn up eventually.

As they drive past the pier where Kiana was arrested just a few hours ago, she looks for her old silver Honda. The detectives had told her they'd be impounding her vehicle and, sure enough, the car is gone. Not that she would have been stupid enough to drive it. They could easily have put a tracking device on her car, followed her home. They were so insistent on getting that address. But all they have is her PO Box. And, of course, her work address.

"Before we get too close," Kiana says, "you should let me out, okay?"

Vanhi glances over, skepticism in her eyes. "Um, sure. Where do you want me to—?"

Kiana extends her arm over the dashboard, points into the darkness. "Just up ahead, at the scenic lookout."

Here, just north of the desalination plant, the road veers inland and gains just enough elevation to offer a view over the seawall. It's a popular picnic spot—one which Kiana, Javi, and Anza used to enjoy together.

Vanhi eases off the road, onto a make-shift lot of gravel, sand, and grass. She kills the headlights but keeps the motor running.

"You'll go in the back way?" Vanhi says. They're near enough to the desal plant now to distinguish its various lights: security floodlights on the massive water tanks, flashing red bulbs atop the tall cooling towers, streetlamps in the employee parking lot, and the few windows illuminated in the main building. During the day, around fifty people work at the plant. At this late hour, only a skeleton crew is on site.

"Yeah. I don't know if the police are, you know, staking out the entrance." Kiana feels embarrassed as she says this. She remembers, from her youth, how ridiculous—how completely paranoid—it sounded to her when her mother voiced similar concerns about exposing herself to the authorities.

Vanhi shrugs. "Better safe than sorry, I guess."

Kiana shrugs back.

"How will you get home?" Vanhi says.

"I'll figure out a way. Hop a train, try not to get tossed off."

"That's a terrible idea, Kiana. Let me give you my ...."

Vanhi roots around in her bag, withdraws a plastic card. "Public transport pass. It's got a few rides left on it."

"Thank you, Vanhi." Kiana tucks the card into the breast pocket of Jimmy's shirt. "For everything. And I really am sorry about Neptune. I'll pay you back someday. I mean it."

"Forget it. And fuck that guy. I'll find some other lowlife who wants to buy my drugs." Vanhi manages to smile ironically and frown sadly, all at once. "It'll work out. It has to, right? One way or another."

"Yeah." Kiana nods. "One way or another."

She takes a deep breath, opens the car door, and steps out into the night. A damp wind sweeps in off the ocean, chilling Kiana's hands and face. The Pacific Ocean spreads before her, its deepest of blues scarcely interrupted by yellow blotches of light: from the desal plant to her left and from downtown to her right. Dead ahead, a mile or so off the coast, a colossal wind turbine stands as a black cut-out shape against the indigo sky. A sad monument to a more optimistic generation. The turbine's submerged connection to the power grid failed a few years ago, and the state of California is too broke to fix it.

As she crosses the parking area, the soles of her sneakers softly crunch the wet, gritty earth. She pauses at the edge of the lot, which ends in an embankment. The desal plant is only a couple hundred meters away, its ambient glow almost bright enough to light Kiana's way. She steps and skids down the soft dirt, scrub, and dewy grass. The hill steepens. Her sneaker slips on a loose patch of sand, and, when she reaches out to break her fall, scrapes the heel of her hand. She swallows a curse and picks her way more carefully down the rest of the hill. As the terrain flattens, she hugs her arms across her chest. Now she really is cold.

In the near distance, waves break in sighs against the concrete wall. As Kiana's path brings her closer to the sea, the sighs grow into rasps. And, with each step, the desal plant looms larger before her. From this angle of approach, and at this time of night, the place looks completely unfamiliar. As if she hadn't spent the last fifteen years of her life working there. And to what end? To provide for her dwindling family. To build a career that will soon be over. Everything Kiana's worked for: blown away, like sand.

A chainlink fence topped with razor wire surrounds the plant. When she reaches the fence, Kiana heads west, away from the parking lot and toward the ocean. She walks quickly, trying to build heat inside her, desperate to keep the damp chill from invading her body. Near the seawall, the fence turns southward. She follows the turn, into a narrow corridor of hard-packed sand wedged between the concrete wall and the wire fence. Her knee is aching again. In the cold and dark, the walk seems interminable.

At last, Kiana comes to a gate. She punches a code into a keypad, which triggers a retinal scan. The security panel squawks once, like a pissed-off crow. Then the lock clanks and the gate swings open. Her presence on campus is now logged into the system. What if the police are in contact with the plant? They could be notified. They might be here already.

Kiana's breath balloons in her chest. This is it.

She heads across the asphalt yard, toward a plain brown metal door along the back wall of the main building. Her office is in there. So is the server room. When she reaches the door, she repeats the code-and-scan procedure. Her use of an entrance typically reserved for maintenance duties will also be logged by security. As will the fact that she didn't swipe her ID bracelet.

In the interior hallway, banks of fluorescent bulbs surge to life. The pale blue walls, the yellowing linoleum floor: she won't miss this place. Kiana lowers her head and walks quickly, the bill of the baseball cap shielding her from the brightness.

Farhan's cap. She forgot to give it back to Vanhi. Another small debt she owes.

"Hello, Kiana Olsen."

The voice shakes her to a halt. It's a Gektor unit, one of the desal plant's security androids. She didn't hear it coming from around the corner. Like Neptune's bouncer, Gektors are also antiquated skindroids. Of average size and build, they have realistic-looking silicone skin that covers their thermoplastic skeletons, their circuits and wires. Gektor units are manufactured in the Ukraine. Kiana looked up the address once: the factory is just twenty miles from the town where her great-great-grandfather Danylo Zelenko was born. There was a time when this coincidence had endeared them to her. But, confronted daily by their bland affects and emotionless eyes, she has since changed her mind. According to the badge affixed to its gray work suit, this particular unit is Gektor-4. Plant employees typically refer to them casually, by number.

"Four. Hey." Kiana steps around the android and keeps walking.

"The current time is 11:44 pm." Four falls in stride alongside her. "It's unusual for you to arrive at work at this time, Kiana Olsen. Is there a security problem I should be aware of?"

"Nope."

Kiana turns down a different hallway, toward her office. The quietness of the building at this hour is unnerving. She's become accustomed to the rumble of water being pumped through the various systems: reverse osmosis, nano-filtration, multi-stage flash distillation. What she's not accustomed to is being followed by a security droid.

"Listen, Four. It's no big deal. I was nearby when the blackout happened, and I thought I'd run a systems check, just to make sure everything's okay. No need for you to hang around."

"I understand. But why, Kiana Olsen, did you enter the facilities by means of entry code and retinal scan?"

"Oh, right. I ... left my ID bracelet at home." Kiana's office is just a few doors away. Her actual plan is to reroute the plant's network connections, and she doesn't need a nosy robot interfering. "Now, why don't you return to your section, in case an actual intruder wanders in?"

"Another question," Four says. "Why did you enter through Rear Gate 3 instead of the front entrance?"

"Yeah, so ...." Kiana stops outside her door. She wasn't prepared for yet another interrogation. She needs to get rid of this thing. "I was parked at the scenic overlook and decided it would be a nice night for a walk."

Four edges himself between Kiana and the door. "The current air temperature, wind velocity, and relative humidity outside the plant suggests a moderately high level of discomfort for humans. Statistically, Kiana Olsen, your decision was anomalous."

"Well, unlike synthetic humanoids, real people behave unpredictably sometimes."

Four points to her head. "That appears to be dried blood, Kiana Olsen. Are you injured?"

"I slipped on my ill-advised walk and banged my head. I'm fine."

"I understand," Four says. "Another anomaly is the logo on your headwear, Kiana Olsen. It represents the Rattlers Little League baseball team, which is sponsored by the Costa Perdida Desalination Plant. Many of the plant's employees have children who currently play, or have played for, that team. However, your child's name, Esperanza Gallegos-Olsen, is not on that list of players."

"Hey!" Kiana stamps her foot. "That is very offensive! You can't just casually refer to my deceased daughter like that." She scowls at the android. According to the specs Kiana's read, the Gektor model can register certain body language and vocal cues. "I'm going to report this behavior. Now, go away!"

Shouting feels good. Rage has burbled in her gut all night, underneath the exhaustion, the fear, the sorrow. Now the anger burns like fuel in her blood. She kicks Four hard in the shin. "I told you to go!"

"I must warn you, Kiana Olsen: Though I don't experience pain, I can de damaged. Any expense incurred by the plant to repair or replace me would be deducted from your earnings. And further acts of aggression could trigger a forceful response, along with an alert message sent to local law enforcement."

"Fuck!" She turns and jabs her finger at the keypad for her office. The lock clicks loose, and she flings open the door.

"Based on your actions since entering the facilities, Kiana Olsen, and—"

"Do not follow me, Four."

"—according to my security protocol—"

She hurries inside and swings the door shut—no, nearly shut. The soles of her shoes skid backward on the linoleum floor, as Four pushes open the door and steps into Kiana's office.

"—I am obliged to monitor and escort you until you depart the premises."

"Right." She inhales deeply, exhales shakily. "Okay."

Kiana is not okay with this. After what she's been through, a fucking android is going to ruin everything? No way.

She drops into her chair, swivels to face her console, and wakes up her computer. From a series of panels embedded in the desk, three hologram screens pulse into being. She logs in and waits for the system to load.

The damn security android. She can feel it lurking behind

her, its cycles of mechanical hums like breaths, its radiant heat almost human.

Eight years as Operations Manager. Kiana has spent a large portion of her working hours sitting at this console, checking gauges and meters, and making sure that the pressure exerted by thousands of liters of water coursing through their system of pipes, filters, and treatment tanks remains within the proper range. By Monday afternoon, she suspects, the plant will have promoted one of her assistants to take her place. They're all competent enough. Her absence will hardly be noticed. Why kid herself? These sorts of redundancies are key to operational continuity.

That same philosophy of redundancies holds true for the plant's communications network. Most of the time, the plant only utilizes a small percentage of the data throughput that its internet connection can provide. The backup system should be able to handle the same load. On the other end of the property is an old wifi tower that easily predates Kiana's tenure at the plant—and possibly even her birth. Twice a year, she and the IT manager stroll out there, run a few diagnostics, and make sure the tower itself isn't about to topple. As long as the plant maintains some kind of internet connection, none of Kiana's coworkers will be alerted when she removes the unregulated terminal.

Remotely rerouting the connection to the wifi tower is easy. What she doesn't know is whether Four possesses the knowledge required to catch Kiana in her act of subterfuge.

Now that the system is active, Kiana works quickly, performing a blustery show of activity by using multiple screens, opening and closing segments, pushing through views, scrolling virtual pages and menus. Meanwhile, she opens a tiny holographic cube, near to her chest—near enough, hopefully, to block the android's view. She can almost see Four's biomimetic eyes tracking her movements. With a quick swipe, she commands the plant's central server to reroute all network activity from the central server room to the wifi tower. Between confirmation prompts—*Are you sure? Yes.*—she focuses briefly on another screen, flipping from one process check— *Really sure? Yes.*—to another. Then she waves all the windows closed.

"Done." Kiana prepares a mild smile before swiveling her chair around to face Four. "All systems check out."

"Excellent news, Kiana Olsen. Now, since you have concluded this task, I'll escort you off the premises. As I'm obliged to inform you, I'll be filing a security report about this incident. The security manager will then evaluate that report and decide whether to notify your superior."

"Yeah, great." She doesn't know why she imagined Four might now leave her alone. As if he'd be impressed by her show of diligence, by her performed allegiance to the company. Fucking robot, with his blank expression and nothing eyes.

Just then, Kiana notices the ceiling tiles in her office, above the android's head. Those tiles look identical to the ones at the Costa Perdida Police Station—minus the mildew. That awful interview room, that awful holding cell. She can't allow herself to be taken back there. But she also can't fail her family—or whatever virtual facsimile of family she can hope to maintain. And she certainly won't allow herself be stopped by a machine.

Kiana rises from her chair. "Okay, lead the way."

Four turns toward the door.

As Kiana slips her hand into her rear pocket, she tries to recall the blueprints for the Gektor model security android.

He takes a step.

She can almost picture the particulars of the wiring that run between the power module in the android's chest and the CPU in his head.

Four reaches for the door handle.

Kiana pulls the box cutter from her pocket and flicks the blade into position. *Shick.* As her arms whips forward, the android's head is already pivoting back around.

The razor blade slashes into Four's neck, through his silicone skin, and slices a band of wiring. For the briefest moment, Kiana is transfixed by the damage she has created in this nearly human thing.

The shock of pain jolts her back to attention. Four has a crushing grip on her arm. That blah face—those false eyes—they betray nothing.

"Stop it, Four. You're hurting me!"

The android doesn't acknowledge her plea, her pain.

Kiana struggles to free her forearm from Four's grasp, but it's no use. And the pain is too much. She whimpers through clamped teeth. Her body trembles. The box cutter tumbles from her hand and clatters to the floor.

Four opens his mouth as if to speak, but only static comes out. And his right arm hangs limply from his sloping shoulder.

She injured the thing. She has a chance. Kiana takes one lunging step away from the android and tries to yank her arm free.

As Four works to maintain his hold, the left half of his body lurches forward awkwardly, while his right half sags. Stuck, paralyzed, useless.

Kiana grabs her office chair and shoves it at Four. It thuds against the android's knee. He gives a staticky bark, but his grip remains steadfast. She stretches her free arm toward her desk. The tool drawer is just inches away. Once more, she pulls hard at Four. His feet skid on the linoleum floor, and he leans over the back of the chair. His hand slips, just a bit, before twisting and tightening around her wrist. Even through the thick sleeve of Jimmy's work shirt, the pain is a circle of fire. But now she's just able to reach the drawer, to slide it open. She pushes items aside: measuring tape, voltmeter, screwdriver, wire strippers.

Hammer. The wooden handle feels clumsy in her left hand. She steps, turns, and swings.

The hammerhead glances off the side of Four's skull. With only one arm working, the android is forced to release Kiana's arm in order to grab the hammer. He wraps his fist around the handle, just above Kiana's own. She knows she'll quickly lose this wrestling match. When she reaches back for the screwdriver, she can barely squeeze her right hand around the rubberized handle. But at least it's her dominant hand. Kiana thrusts the screwdriver at Four's face, throwing her full torso into it.

The metal tip pierces the android's eye. She leans in, driving the metal shaft through Four's retina and deep into his CPU brain, until the handle's hilt catches on the rim of his eye socket.

His hand falls away from the hammer. Then Gektor-4 crumples to the ground.

Kiana stares at the inert humanoid lying before her. Another lifeless body. The faces of Jane Hamamura and Walter Brogan flash through her head. But the body on the floor is just a machine, neither dead nor alive. And yet another body awaits her at home. A still-living body. The body that holds her husband's mind. His body is breaking down, but his mind endures.

Kiana just needs to get to the server room, detach the terminal, and get out there. From her desk, she grabs a couple of screwdrivers. And a canvas tote bag—pointless swag from some conference or other—for carrying the terminal.

"Alert!"

The voice over the intercom startles the breath out of her. For an instant, she thinks the android has come back online.

"This is an automated security alert. All staff members please remain at your stations while the security team assesses the issue."

Four. He triggered the alert. Other Gektor units will be heading straight for the source: Kiana's office. She turns and runs for the door.

CHAPTER SIXTEEN

OCTOBER, 2048

Alex sat back in the old Adirondack, watching her family: Ellen, Kiana, Javier, and Esperanza. Not the family Alex was born into, but the family that came to her. Her true family. They were gathered in a semi-circle on the flagstone patio, next to the vegetable garden that Ellen had dug and planted and kept all these years. The garden between Alex's and Ellen's homes—the Big House and the Small House, as Kiana named them long ago. Ellen had designed the Small House and built much of it herself. The chicken coop, too. She'd transformed this underutilized portion of Alex's land into a sustainable source of nourishment for them.

Alex tilted her head back. A thick layer of yellowy gray throttled the evening sky. Wildfire smoke, woodlands burning, but miles away, on a different ridge. They were safe here for now, but rarely far from danger. They'd survived how many fires on this tinderbox land? The smell of ash hug in the air, mixing with the savory aroma of the stew that simmered in the slow cooker and wisped through the nearby kitchen window.

Alex sat at one end of the family semi-circle, followed by

Javier and Kiana in the folding chairs. At the other end, in the matching Adirondack, Ellen sat bent at the waist, arms held out before her, having just released Anza, who now tottered across the uneven terrain, from grandmother back to mother.

"With the extra money," Kiana was saying, "we're hoping to upgrade our gray water system. Maybe add another solar panel."

She'd just told them about her promotion at the desalination plant. Well deserved. She'd worked hard for it. Alex was proud of Kiana. Vainly proud, actually, believing that her own work ethic had rubbed off on Kiana. But, really, Alex didn't know how *not* to work. Though tech growth had turned sluggish in recent years, the demands on microchip functionality continued to evolve. Designing chips: it was the only skill Alex had mastered.

Kiana hoisted Anza up onto her knee and smiled wide at her daughter. "Of course, most of Mama's promotion will disappear right into this little belly." Her ticking fingers earned a bubbly giggle.

That little laugh, it zinged Alex in the heart, every time.

How old was Anza now? Fifteen, maybe sixteen months? Just a blip in time. Alex's own blip had stretched to fifty-eight years. The older she got, the more it seemed like time had been knocked unsteady, that it warped and whirred. How could it be that Kiana was now a mother? Her birth remained so vivid in Alex's mind. The sea-green birthing tub in the living room. Gloria Birch leaning on its rounded edge, chanting her words of midwifery encouragement through a surgical mask. Alex had sat on the other side of the tub, clenching Ellen's hand as she grunted and growled and puffed bursts of breath from pink, sweaty cheeks. Ellen Taylor, who, just eight months prior, had driven onto Alex's property as Taylor Ellen Olsen: fugitive from the law.

Twenty-eight years later, Ellen was still here. Still on this land and still wound into this mortal coil. Here for now. The signs of her deterioration—her disease—had only just begun to show. But Ellen still looked the model of a healthy middle-aged gal. Blonde hair going gray, wrinkles branching out. As beautiful as ever. She would have been beautiful in old age, too. But Ellen wouldn't get the chance to grow old.

Life, it wasn't fucking fair.

"You all right, Alex?"

Javier's voice pulled her from the mire of her mind. He was leaning toward her, his thick, dark eyebrows lifted in kind concern. Kiana had done well, choosing Javi.

"Mm, yeah, fine." Alex sniffled and blinked, worked a smile to her lips. "Just feeling sentimental about family, I guess."

Javi chuckled. "Oh, I get it." He turned to look at Anza. "Happens to me at least once a day, just from watching her do the simplest things."

Alex remembered the feeling. With Kiana, the "simplest things" had seemed astonishing. She crawled! She spoke! She ran! It was the greatest surprise of Alex's life, how completely enthralled she became with that child. She, who'd never before imagined having kids. Or, no. She'd imagined it and had wanted no part of it: the diapers, the tantrums, the constant interruptions, the lifetime of worry. With Kiana, she had lucked into getting the best of both worlds. In her role as "Aunt Alex," she'd received a disproportionate heaping of gratitude for relatively small contributions to the day-to-day tasks of raising a child.

But what a tricky beast, Ellen's gratitude. Alex has never *wanted* to want her friend's thanks, but she craved it, nonetheless. Gratitude was hardly the same as love, but Alex had learned to accept whatever parts of Ellen's heart she would share. Yes, Alex knew that Ellen loved her: as a best friend. Mostly, that permutation of love was enough.

She'd become mired in her thoughts again. Alex surveyed the faces around her, each person lost in their own world, it seemed. A lull in the atmosphere. And a scent that made her stomach gurgle.

"Okay." She clapped her palms together. "Who's ready for dinner?"

* * *

Alex rested her spoon in the golden-brown traces of stew at the bottom of her bowl. She raised her beer bottle to her lips. A dark ale, nicely bitter, and slightly warmish here at meal's end, just the way she liked it.

Ellen sat to Alex's right. Her bowl remained half-full. She chewed and chewed each bite, then swallowed with effort. An effort that Alex was attuned to, though she doubted anyone else would notice. Not yet. Over time, swallowing would grow more difficult for Ellen, her struggles more apparent.

"So." Ellen looked across the table at Kiana, who had finished her meal and was nursing Anza. "Have you made a profilll ...." Ellen covered her mouth, coughed lightly. "An avatar for Anza yet? I've read that more and more parents are doing that."

Watching Ellen struggle with her speech caused Alex's shoulders to hunch and clench. She looked from Kiana to Javier, but neither seemed to have noticed this symptom either. It had been a long day, and Ellen was on her second glass of wine. Both factors probably contributed to the slurring of her words. They also normalized it.

"A Level Up profile? Oh, no." Kiana shook her head for emphasis.

"Well, not yet, anyway." Javier shrugged and smiled, that boyish grin of his.

Kiana arched her eyebrows at him. "Okay, eventually. Maybe."

"But you wouldn't uplll ... ahem." Ellen brought her fingertips to her throat, sipped her white wine. "Her mind? You wouldn't ...?"

Knowing Ellen disapproved of this practice, Alex looked to Kiana, who turned from her mother to her husband.

"Upload Anza's mind?" Javier frowned. "No, I don't think that's something we ... I mean, that's a decision that, I feel ... that *we* feel, only adults can make for themselves."

"Responsible and conscientious adult citizens," Alex blurted out. She was parroting a sound bite from a recent presidential speech about the steady increase in suicides attributed to Level Up addiction. A *pandemic*, according to the president. Alex balked at that term. She'd lived through pandemics. No, this mass hopelessness was just another horrible symptom of humankind's comeuppance. Of the Anthropocene fading out.

Alex gulped her warm and bitter beer.

"Well, you're right to poke fun at the idea," Javier told her. "Clearly, plenty of adults can't actually be trusted to make responsible decisions. Personally, I don't get it. Even though, admittedly, I really like Level Up ... and even though this world, well, it's just getting harder ... but still, I can't imagine choosing a virtual life over real life." His face pinched, as if struck by a sudden headache. He turned to Kiana, who had transitioned Anza from breast to shoulder, and his pained expression spread into a smile. "Of course, I've got reasons to stick around."

Alex watched Ellen, to see what her reaction might be to this talk of mortality. That lovely face, it revealed nothing but contentment.

Good. That's what Alex wanted for her. Contentment and comfort and love, right through to the end. The looming end.

Alex tore off a hunk of seeded bread and smeared it along the bottom of her bowl, sponging up the last of the chicken and black bean stew. A rare treat anymore: real animal protein. And from a creature raised on her land, no less. Mostly she and Ellen ate a lot of legumes. And a lot of PastAlgae noodles, courtesy of Javier. Which was fine, it really was. An inveterate carnivore, Alex missed the bounty of her youth, before the livestock industry became unsustainable, before pork and beef became extravagancies. But it gutted her, how all the world's animals were disappearing.

"Did you hear?" Alex spoke these words into her empty bowl, then realized she was speaking aloud, that her family was listening. She looked up. "The news this morning. No more tigers in the wild. The few remaining are all in zoos. Just a dozen or so Bengal tigers, that's all that's left."

From around the table, three downcast faces stared back at her. Everyone made their weary sighs, their grunts of disappointment. Only Anza, cradled safe in Kiana's arms, remained in a state of ignorant bliss. Tigers, for her, would be relegated to history—like dodo birds, like dinosaurs.

"It's just that everything's dying," Alex mumbled. "Sorry." She shook her head, took a gulp of beer, turned away. Out the window, the purpling sky did its best to conceal the choking air.

"It's okay," Ellen said. Her hand fell like a blanket over Alex's wrist.

She searched Ellen's eyes. They were full of the comfort that Alex had meant to give, not receive. She'd have to do better.

Ellen turned to Kiana and Javier. "I need to tell you something." She breathed in sharply through her nose and sighed the air back out.

Alex's own breath gripped her lungs.

"I've been diagnosed with something called progressive bulbar palsy." Ellen spoke the words slowly, taking the time to annunciate, just as the doctor had recommended. Even still, Alex noticed the blurred speech, as they called it: the smearing of her L's in *called* and *palsy*.

"My god, Mom. What is that? Is it serious?" Kiana's face seemed to open and close at once, an expression of curiosity and fear that Alex remembered from Kiana's childhood, each time she encountered one of life's uncertainties: the depth of night, kindergarten, a black widow in the house, the trembling earth, blazes raging on nearby hills.

Ellen lowered her head. Ashamed of her affliction? Or suffering its weight? Alex rubbed her shoulder. As if that weight could be massaged away.

"Yeah, sweetie," Ellen said, looking up again. "It's serious. It attacks the brain stem. Affects speech and swallowing." This last word, she spoke with extra care. "Two or three years. That's the prognosis."

Tears spilled from Kiana's eyes. She stood, handed Anza to Javier, and rounded the table. In an awkward crouch, she threw her arms around Ellen and pressed her face to her mother's chest. "Oh, Mom. I'm so sorry."

"Shhh." Ellen stroked Kiana's head, her brown hair streaked with teal. A different color every year since high school. With her slender adult frame, she could still look like a teenager at times. Younger, even. An echo now of Kiana as a child, crying in her mother's embrace. Not that she'd cried often. And now she had Javier to hold her when she turned tearful. But everyone needed their mother, from time to time. And Kiana was far too young—not yet thirty—to lose another parent. Sam Mahi'ai, killed in a prison riot. Kiana had barely known her dad, but, as she'd confided to Alex, the loss endured.

Alex's own mom had died seven years ago, and the grief remained sharp in her heart. She wished she could protect Kiana from ever knowing the deeper pain that would come from losing the person who had raised her.

Nor did Alex want to know the ache of grief again, the ache of Ellen's absence from her life. No, it couldn't be possible. She was right here. The roundness of her shoulder, so very present against Alex's palm. Her beautiful face, right here. The love of her life: right here.

* * *

Alex carried her mug of morning tea into the guest room, where she found Kiana gazing out the window, a folded sweater in her hands. A duffel bag sat open on the bed. Soon, she, Javi, and Anza would be driving back to Costa Perdida.

Alex drew up alongside Kiana, joined her in watching.

Out on the patio, Ellen and Javi sat talking while Anza explored the yard. Rails of light slanted between the tall redwoods and landed in long bright rectangles on the furrowed garden. Ellen and Javi looked peaceful out there, their gestures loose and their smiles easy, as if they'd set aside the question of death.

And maybe they had, but Alex couldn't. She felt certain that Kiana couldn't either. Sadness and fear, they clung to her, tightening her shoulders, molding lines into her typically smooth face. Those cold emotions, they hovered in the guest room's air.

Alex slowly wandered the room, the room where her mother had stayed when visiting from Boise. The room where Ellen had slept for several years, before building the Small House. Slept in this very same bed, under this same blanket, with its tropical floral print. Apparently, Kiana's Hawaiian grandmother had a similar blanket—or maybe an identical one, who knew? Alex couldn't remember where she'd gotten hers. Some generic online store, most likely. Before Ellen came along, Alex hadn't really cared about the aesthetics of things: furniture, linens, even art. She'd lucked into the one painting that Ellen had approved of, simply because her friend Nathaniel had created it. Alex missed sweet Nathaniel. It was he who built a crib for Kiana—for the baby his wife then delivered. The crib had sat over there, along that wall.

"Oh, right," Kiana said. She was looking down at the sweater in her hands. Smiling self-consciously at Alex, she stuffed it into the duffel bag.

Alex sipped honey-sweetened tea from her old ceramic mug. An acquaintance of hers had made the mug, the honey came from a bee sanctuary two towns over, and Ellen had grown the tea plants in their very own garden. Every aspect of Alex's world, Ellen had transformed. Enriched it, enlivened it. All of that life inside her, how could it be that it would simply go away one day?

"I'll take care of her, you know," Alex said.

Kiana looked up from packing the duffel. Her eyes seemed so fragile, on the edge of shattering. She nodded quick little nods. "I know you will."

"All of you," Alex said. "Your mom, Javi, Anza, you. My family. Whatever I can do." She shrugged, her gesture too big, mug momentarily forgotten, tea sloshing over the brim and splatting on the wood floor.

In an instant, Kiana had a wet wipe in her hand and was kneeling to mop up the spill at Alex's feet.

"Motherhood." Kiana glanced up with a sweet, sad smile. "Always cleaning up messes. It's become automatic."

"Thanks." Alex remembered when Kiana had generated the messes in this house, and Ellen had cleaned them all.

Before long, Alex would be cleaning up after Ellen. Drooling, apparently, a common symptom. Alex wasn't a fan of messes. When designing microchip functionality, messes were errors, and errors infected entire systems. But errors occurred in even the most beautiful systems. Alex would have to learn to accept the fatal error in Ellen's nervous system, the wiring within the greater Ellen-system, the steady surge that kept her good heart beating.

Kiana stood and tossed the wet wipe into the wastebasket by the door. She turned back to the window. "Do you think Anza will remember Mom, after she's gone?"

The idea jolted Alex, a thud to the chest. It hadn't occurred to her. "I ... I really don't know."

"I can almost see why people do it," Kiana said. "Upload themselves to Level Up." Her eyes searched Alex's, as if answers could be found there. "Maybe it's not always just for self-preservation?"

Alex shrugged, a small shrug, both hands wrapped around her mug, the pottery going cool now. "Because they're preserving themselves for others, you mean?"

"Yeah, maybe sometimes."

"Hmm," Alex said. "Your mom and I, not too long ago, we talked about this. She said that uploading oneself to Level Up is just another example of selfish gene theory. When I pointed out that she'd already once succumbed to the selfishness of her genes ...." Alex smiled and gestured to Kiana. "As evidenced by ...."

Kiana half-grinned, sniffed a little laugh.

"When I pointed that out, your mother claimed she'd evolved since then. That she wouldn't succumb a second time. So, if you're on the fence about the whole uploading thing, you don't have to worry about finding your mom in Level Up. Once Ellen Taylor is gone, all we'll have left are the old-fashioned reminders of her life: some photos, a few videos, our memories."

Kiana shook her head. "It seems impossible. That Mom could be reduced to that."

"I know." Alex sighed. The impossibility weighed on her more and more each day. "But, yeah, I do hope Anza has some of her own memories of your mom. And, you know, we'll share our memories with her. That way, we'll keep Ellen alive. That's how it works. Right?"

CHAPTER SEVENTEEN

FEBRUARY, 2057

"This is an automated security alert. All staff members please remain at your stations while the security team assesses the issue."

During the umpteenth repetition of that message throughout the desalination plant, Kiana works on disconnecting the terminal in the server room, pulling out wires, cables. She unplugs the power cord and unscrews the unit itself from the server rack. The terminal is substantial, weighty—like the one Detective Bell tricked her with at the pier. Kiana packs the terminal in her canvas bag and pulls the straps over her shoulder.

"This is an automated security alert. All staff members please remain at your stations while the security team assesses the issue."

She wishes she could shut up that god damn voice. It seems intent on reminding her that everything she went through back in her office—rerouting the internet, nearly getting killed by Gektor-4—it was totally unnecessary. Now the entire facility is in an uproar.

"This is an automated security alert. All staff members please remain at your stations while the security team assesses the issue."

In the moment of silence between alerts, Kiana leans close to the door. She can't hear anything over the hum of the server room fans, the booming in her blood. Before opening the door, she forces herself to take a long, slow breath. She stands up straight. She reminds herself that she works here, that she belongs. Then she pulls the handle and steps out into the hall.

No one in sight.

She keeps the tote bag pinned to her hip as she makes quick strides toward the same back door that she entered not long ago. She's walked this route hundreds of times before, thought nothing of it. Now, each step lasts forever and seems to take her nowhere.

"This is an automated security alert. All staff members please remain at your stations while the security team assesses the issue."

She just needs to turn left here and—

A body lurches around the corner.

Kiana vibrates to a stop. She reaches for her back pocket, but the box cutter isn't there. She must have left it on the floor of her office.

"Oh, hey, Kiana! Sorry, didn't see you coming."

It takes her a moment to understand that a real human face is babbling these words at her. A familiar face. Alberto, the swing-shift chemist. "Alberto. Hi. I'm just here to—"

"Do you know what's—?"

"This is an automated security alert. All staff members please remain at your stations while the security team assesses the issue."

Kiana glances over her shoulder. No Gektor units. She makes to step around Alberto, turning sideways, and he does the same. The polite dance of passing bodies—it usually comes so naturally. Now, she reminds herself to maintain eye contact, to appear reasonable instead of frantic, all while clamping her elbow across the tote bag, in case Alberto tries to peek inside. She's so close to getting away.

"It's just an electrical malfunction," she says. "Maybe caused by a power surge after the blackout? I think the problem's at one of the back gates. I'm heading out there now."

"Oh, I'm glad it's nothing serious." Alberto laughs uneasily.

Kiana's nerves pulse with the urge to flee. This conversation is eating valuable seconds. And she can't fight off the fear that the terminal in her tote bag will start howling like a wounded animal. She drifts sideways, away, away. "So, I'm just gonna—"

"Hey, do you need a hand out there?"

She makes herself smile. "No, thanks, Alberto. I'm good."

"All right." He laughs again. "Probably for the best. Unless chemicals are involved, I'm basically hopeless." With a wave, he turns and walks away.

Kiana jogs down the corridor. The back door is just ahead of her now. Will it open? She can't remember which security measures are triggered during an alert. Throughout her years at the plant, they've experienced just a handful of break-ins. She's never heard of someone trying to break *out*.

As she reaches for the handle, she realizes her fingers are trembling. As if her hand belongs to someone else. That shaking hand manages to pull open the door. She sprints for the back fence, the soles of her sneakers thupping on asphalt. A cold, wet, salty wind pushes against her.

"Kiana Olsen. Halt!"

She glances back. One of the Gektors is chasing after her, cutting diagonally across the yard. She has a good lead on him, and she's nearing the gate. But the skindroid is fast. Kiana tells herself not to look again, to just keep running. With each pump of her arms, the tote slips down her shoulder and she has to tug it back into place.

The Gektor unit keeps commanding her to halt. It requires no breath to do so.

Meanwhile, Kiana's own breath burns acidic in her lungs as she runs toward the fence. Not far beyond, the dark seawall looms.

Closer ... closer ... now!

Kiana skids her sneakers on the asphalt. Her shoulder slams into the wire mesh, jostling her head. She gropes for the gate latch, grabs it tight and pulls. It doesn't budge. She glances back again. The security droid is closing fast. She jabs her code into the blurry keypad. It beeps three angry beeps at her.

Fuck.

Her mind scrambles with impulses: run, fight, climb, cry, try again. She can barely focus on the keypad as she pounds out the code once more. It dings a happy ding. Surprised by her success, Kiana almost forgets to position her face before the retinal scanner.

The android's strong, steady footfalls are booming behind her, his barking commands growing louder.

The instant the security panel squawks, she yanks on the gate's handle. Too soon. Damnit. He's right behind her now. The lock clicks. When she pulls again, the gate swings free. Kiana throws herself through the opening.

The gate bangs into her hip, and Kiana hits the ground hard. Farhan's baseball cap, knocked loose, lands by her elbow.

She looks back. The skindroid stands at the threshold of the open gate, staring down at her. Gektor-7, his tag reads. "Kiana Olsen, you are in violation of plant security protocols. I will be reporting this incident ...."

She stops listening. She's no longer on desal plant property, and the security androids are programmed not to breech the property line. She's free. A massive sigh drains from Kiana's chest.

Then she sees it: the tote bag. It fell from her shoulder and now lies half on the sand-dusted asphalt, near the black shoes that cover Seven's synthetic feet.

"…. deducted from your next paycheck. Furthermore …."

The android hasn't noticed the bag yet. Or, because it doesn't know the contents, sees it as irrelevant. But, Kiana assumes, once she reaches for the bag, Seven may react to her interest and snatch it from her. She has to be quick, but she also needs better positioning.

"Yes, of course," Kiana replies to whatever the android is telling her. She looks into his fake eyes as she shifts her weight. She pushes herself up into a kneeling position, as if supplicating herself before Seven and his nattering reprimands. "I understand."

Kiana lunges forth, grabs the side of the bag in her first, and yanks her arm back. Seven reacts with a swift downward movement. She watches as the android's fingers barely miss the retreating strap.

Seven straightens himself, standing as if at attention. "Kiana Olsen, I'm obliged to inform you that the removal of property from the premises may result in employee contract termination."

She almost replies, then remembers that Seven is just a computer.

Kiana tugs on the Rattlers cap, pushes herself upright, and hunches the tote back onto her shoulder. With her first steps along the dim path between the fence and the seawall, pain twinges in her hip.

Seven calls out some final reprimand, but the android's words are lost to the crashing surf.

* * *

On the lookout point, she stands beneath the cover of a stout old oak tree. The light rail tram stop is across the road. Kiana looks to the south, where the tram will be coming from. No sign of it yet. She doesn't know the schedule at this hour. Only that the transit system runs until two a.m. on weekends. A much younger version of herself occasionally rode the last train back home, after a night on the town. Or what passed for such an outing in one of Costa Perdida's two bars. Mostly fruitless quests for the cure to loneliness. Even her successes were short-lived, often regrettable. How could she have known that the secret to finding true love was to break down at the side of the road?

Javi, appearing on his motorcycle, the rain pearlescent on his beard. The kindness in his eyes. And that smile, that smile, that smile.

Javi, dying in a secondhand hospital bed.

From her spot at the oak tree, Kiana looks for the tram again. Where the fuck is it?

She considers walking, but her hip still hurts like hell from where the security gate banged into her and her knee continues to ache. She must be ten miles from home, as the crow flies. More like twelve, when following the roads. Which is the route she'd take. She isn't about to go hiking over the hills, through the burnt-out woods, by herself, at night. No, public transit is her only option. Take the tram downtown, then catch the commuter train home.

She can only hope the police aren't checking CCTV cameras. By stealing the terminal from work, she's committed another felony. If she's arrested again, she'll spend decades in prison. Maybe even die there, like her father.

Down the coast, a single light appears, just inland from the desal plant. The tram. She wants to time her approach just right. The less time spent lingering out in the open, the better.

As Kiana steps away from the tree, a car roars up the hill from downtown. She jumps back, flattens herself against the oak, watches it pass. A brown sedan. She couldn't make out its occupants, but she's certain who they are: Detectives Turley and Bell. She half-expects the car to screech to a halt, to reverse course and hunt her down. Before taking another step, she counts five Mississippis. The taillights grow dim.

But the tram is drawing nearer, its beam of light like a small sun rising over the hill.

Kiana moves as quickly as her stiffening leg will allow—a jostling gait, like a wagon with one square wheel. The terminal thumps against the side of her thigh. She crosses the turnout, where Vanhi left her just a short time ago. It already feels like ages.

The tram stop is across the street, maybe fifty meters away. The brightly lit concrete platform is empty, aside from a ticket machine and the security cameras mounted on lampposts. A safe haven for most passengers, but not for Kiana.

She's across the street and halfway to the platform when the nose of the tram passes her. The lead car goes by, then the rear. As the tram slows for its upcoming stop, Kiana hurries her stride, clenching her teeth against the aches in her joints. She catches up to the rear car just as the tram comes to rest. Its doors open in a chorus of whispers. She pulls Vanhi's pass card from her pocket, waves it at an infrared sensor, and steps aboard.

The only other passengers in the car are a young couple facing away from Kiana, huddled in their private cocoon. She drops into the nearest seat, making sure to keep her head lowered: the bill of the ball cap is her only defense against the CCTV cameras that are mounted above each doorway.

The overhead speakers plink out a digital melody, followed by a recorded voice that issues garbled warnings about imminent departures and closing doors. Then the tram hums into acceleration. Just two stops before the downtown transit center, where Kiana will need to transfer to the inland-bound commuter train. She gathers the tote to her body, wraps her arms around the contours of the terminal within. Out the window, she watches as the low-slung skyline of downtown Costa Perdida gradually takes shape.

* * *

As she disembarks the tram, Kiana glances left, right. Moving bodies in the transit center are few. None of them appear to belong to either Nick Turley or Olivia Bell—or to any uniformed cops. It's a quick walk across an open-air expanse of concrete to the train platform, but she feels as if her limping progress is being monitored, judged, ridiculed. She imagines the police lying in wait behind that information kiosk over there, or that half-wall that separates the café from the platform. No, she's being paranoid. They wouldn't waste their resources by setting some elaborate trap for her. It's only due to blind luck that the cops haven't nabbed her already. Correction: nabbed her again.

Kiana consults the train schedule near the ticket window, keeping as far back as possible from the little camera mounted there. She's inherited good eyesight, but fatigue leaves her straining to make out the departure times. Squinting, she edges closer. The next train bound for the inland community where she lives departs at 12:15. According to the clock, it's 12:11 now. Another dose of luck. She could almost believe that some minor deity is watching out for her. But maybe it's also true that a different minor deity is against her, and Kiana is the fraying rope in their Olympic tug-of-war.

No, she's being absurd again. Self-aggrandizing now, instead of paranoid. In either case, borderline delusional. She has to keep her shit together, think rationally. But her mind is bouncing. She feels jittery, unsteady. When was the last time she ate anything? She remembers asking herself this same question hours ago. Kiana was in jail then. Soon, she'll be back home. A twenty-five-minute train ride, and another ten or fifteen minutes on foot. She can push herself just a little more.

A low rumble vibrates the soles of her sneakers. From around a bend in the tracks, the train's headlight emerges.

CHAPTER EIGHTEEN

APRIL, 2054

Standing before the window of the food cart, Javi placed his order in Spanish: "Tres empanadas de queso, por favor." Speaking his mother tongue connected Javi to his Mexican roots. For the same reason, he and Kiana spoke bilingually at home, especially around Anza. Should the US continue its rapid decline, their daughter would be prepared to thrive elsewhere in the Americas.

So few people seemed to thrive anymore. The global suicide rate remained high despite the Government's neutering of Level Up. Why? Because the rate of suffering continued to steadily rise, like the ocean just a few blocks away. Right now, no one suffered more than the people living across that ocean. Every day, Javi read about the further spread of spectral fever across Southeast Asia. So far, quarantines and travel bans had kept the disease contained to that region. But for how long?

Meanwhile, despite the near-constant wildfires and the polluted air, life for Javi and his family was relatively good. He and Kiana were fortunate to have decent jobs. Though just a rental, they loved their home. They could afford to care for their child's needs. And, every now and again, they could splurge on an empanada picnic.

But the goddamn heat. 84 degrees in downtown Costa Perdida in April? Ridiculous. As they waited for their food, they moved to the shady side of the alley. Anza leaned against Javi's hip, her sweaty hand in his own. Javi watched her wide brown eyes roam the colorful figures painted on the brick walls of the alleyway that the food truck called home. At seven years old, she was still young enough to gain new pleasures each time she encountered the same old mural—a somewhat corny mish-mash of Costa Perdida history: Native tribes, Spanish explor-ers, Colonial pioneers, Chinese laborers, and Latin American immigrants like himself. At least the latter group wasn't portrayed as "illegals" picking fruit for white farmers. In fact, the guy in the mural who most closely resembled Javi rode his bicycle down a pleasant lane of cheery homes and lush, green lawns. He checked the date below the artist's signature on the mural: 2018. The year Javi was born. How could he have forgotten?

"Ancient history."

"What is, Papa?"

"Oh, the painting on the wall. I mean, does that look like Costa Perdida to you, hija?"

Anza looked to the wall, then back to her father. She answered with a shrug.

Javi smiled. He wished he could see the world through such innocent eyes. Maybe, thanks to his daughter, his vision remained slightly less jaded than it might otherwise have been.

Behind them, on First Street, traffic was backed up from the light at Beachfront Drive. Javi checked his phone. Just after five, which meant Kiana would have just left the desal plant, on her way to meet them at their little park, one block away from the alley.

Javi had worked at PastAlgae until three o'clock. After picking up Anza from school, they'd spent the last couple of hours at a playground. While the kids swung from monkey bars and sweated through games of tag, Javi had stood chatting with the other parents under a canopy where only the stump of a shade tree remained. One parent had been laid off from the electric company. Another had just returned from a family road trip down to San Diego. And another confided to having recently been in a recovery program for Level Up addiction.

On the topic, Javi felt mostly neutral. He enjoyed his escapes into Level Up as much as the next person, but he still preferred the fucked-up real world. From the edge of the playground, he'd watched Anza sitting shoulder-to-shoulder with another little pink-cheeked girl on the stilled merry-go-round. The particular intimacy of the moment had struck him as impossible to replicate in the glossy realm of Level Up.

"Javier!" From the window of the food truck, the owner held out a brown paper sack for him.

"Muchas gracias, Lucia."

Javi took the bag and towed Anza from the alley. They strode through the crosswalk at First and turned past the bank—an old brick building from who knows when. Well, probably his wife would know. They rounded the corner, and there was Kiana at the end of the block, stepping out of her old silver Honda. Something about the moment—the movement of her body, his angle of his approach—reminded Javi of the first time he saw her. On that drizzly morning, Kiana had been exiting the same car, only the hood was propped open ominously, and her beautiful face was hardened by a scowl. Was it her fierce expression or the loveliness underneath that had prompted him to turn his bike around? Probably both.

Now, Kiana spotted them and waved. Anza tramped ahead and was scooped up into her mother's arms. Javi caught up and kissed his wife on the head, right where a streak of violet splashed through her honey-colored hair.

As they made their way into the park, Anza recited the events of her day for Mama. Having heard all the stories once already, Javi listened only for the music of their voices, a familiar call and response that soaked his heart with a happy calm. What little grass remained in the urban park had already yellowed, as it once did only in the late depths of summer. The parched earth soaked up just enough moisture to keep a few oaks alive. Beneath one such tree, Javi and Kiana claimed a shady bench. They planted Anza between them.

Though barely past five o'clock, Javi was ravenous. Apparently, so was the rest of his family. They wasted no time tearing into their empanadas—the golden dough, the gooey cheese, the light zip of spices. Between bites, he and Kiana exchanged their own stories of their days: the tiny-yet-exhausting battles with coworkers, the tiny-yet-thrilling victories over managers, suppliers, computers, and, in Javi's case, a bathroom soap dispenser. He was relating how he'd repaired the malfunctioning nozzle when Kiana's watch vibrated.

She swallowed her last bite of empanada, then tapped to answer. In the small holoscreen, Alex sat in her home office.

Javi's chest went tight. She never called on a weekday unless something was wrong. For a split-second, he worried that something terrible had happened to Ellen. Then he remembered: his mother-in-law had died nearly three years ago.

"What's going on?" Javi blurted the question. Kiana shot him a look. But, given Alex's dire expression, he had no patience for pleasantries.

"It's here," Alex said. "In the US. Spectral fever." Her forehead pinched into a frown. "The news just broke. Child refugees from Thailand were smuggled here in a shipping container. By the time the authorities rounded them up, they'd been circulating in the general population for a week or more. The CDC has confirmed at least twenty cases. Some of the kids are in critical condition."

"Where?" The tightness constricted around Javi's chest. He could barely get out the words. "The shipping container. Where was it?"

"San Diego."

The mom at the playground. *We just got back from San Diego last night.* It was her sweaty kid who'd sat pressed up against his own child.

Javi looked away from the holoscreen. Anza was staring up at him, a worried look in her eyes. Javi's chest ratcheted tighter, tighter. His blood beat too hard, too hot. On the outside, he'd gone numb.

"Javi?" Kiana's voice arrived as a vague impression, almost a memory. Her hand seemed to be jostling his shoulder.

In the years to come, he would ask himself how he knew for sure. Sometimes, in the void of night, he would convince himself that his paralysis in that moment had allowed the fever to take hold. To take his little girl.

CHAPTER NINETEEN

FEBRUARY, 2057

Kiana pulls down her cap as she boards the train. She heads for a seat near the back, close to an exit. As she walks down the narrow aisle, she presses her hand against her aching hip joint. Glancing to the side, she catches her reflection in the window. Her movements are mirrored by the ghost of her future self: an old lady, hampered by arthritis. She passes someone applying lotion to their hands, and the scent of coconut follows Kiana to her seat. Memories are bound to the rich, sweet smell. The memories trail her, too. As the train pulls out of the station, she glances again at her thin reflection in the glass. Maybe it's a different Kiana she's seeing. Maybe she's being watched over by the spirit of her namesake, Grandma Kiana Mahi'ai.

* * *

Kiana had just graduated from college when she flew to Oahu to meet her paternal grandmother. She rode a different commuter train that afternoon, from the airport in Honolulu to

Waipahu, a neighborhood just west of Pearl Harbor. From the Waipahu transit center, Kiana hauled her duffel bag the final half-mile to her grandmother's one-bedroom house, which was painted the same reddish brown as the desiccated coconut husks that lay scattered across the neighborhood. As she walked up the concrete driveway, a mottled mutt had strolled out from under the shade of the carport to greet her with a series of barks and wags. A moment later, an aluminum screen door swung open, and Grandma Kiana emerged from the house, a wide smile on her oval face. She wore a yellow tank top, a magnolia print skirt, and flip-flops—which Kiana would learn to call "slippers." Her grandmother's wiry arms held Kiana in a surprisingly firm embrace. "Aloha, dear girl," she said, her voice deep and strong. "Oh, Aloha." They pulled apart, each woman's eyes searching the other's. And Kiana knew they were both thinking of Sam, the absent link between them, and how he should have been there. How he should have been alive.

Kiana remembers every moment of that afternoon, which they spent sitting on the lanai in her grandmother's backyard. The chickens babbling in their coop, the dizzy scent of mangos rotting on the patchy lawn, the old mutt's sun-warmed fur. And a white-noise rumble that sounded like ocean surf. "Nah, just highway traffic," her grandmother told her. From afternoon to evening, they drank rum-spiked guava juice and "talked story"—another local term Kiana added to her mental list.

"This whole neighborhood," her grandmother said, waving her glass in a wide arc. "It used to be a sugarcane plantation, you know. Oh, yeah. And when they bombed Pearl Harbor? Those planes also bombed the plantation. Someone died right here."

Kiana must have looked bewildered, because her grandmother threw her head back and laughed. "No, don't worry. Not *right* here. But, you know, nearby."

"When the war broke out," Kiana said, "had your parents—my great-grandparents—had they been born yet?" Kiana had, by then, mapped out her mother's side of the family, going back several generations. And, based on genetic testing results, she had information about her heritage on her father's side. She knew Sam's veins ran with Cajun blood, Scottish blood, Japanese blood, Hawaiian blood. But, when trying to find specific names and dates from the Mahi'ai half of the family tree, she'd mostly hit dead ends.

"Oh!" Her grandmother's eyes and mouth formed perfect circles of surprise. "You don't know a damned thing about my side of your family, do you? Well, hold on a sec." The old woman then pushed herself up from her wicker chair, tramped back into the house, and returned moments later with a photo album.

They spent that the rest of that evening leafing through old pictures, tattered diaries, and other artifacts of the past. Kiana learned that her grandmother was born in 1975 and was christened Amy Mahi'ai. Amy's parents were Tommy Mahi'ai and Patty Kaneshiro. Tommy's mother was Kiana 'Aukai. "The original Kiana," her grandmother said. "When I was a teenager, I realized I'd been given a haole name. So I adopted my grandma's name. And now you've got your grandma's name, too!"

She handed Kiana a photo, sepia-toned from its century of exposure to the world. A skinny girl, maybe eight or ten years old, stands on the beach, posing in her polka dot swimsuit, a blur of surf crashing behind her. Kiana flipped over the photo. *Patty, 1956.*

"That's my māmā when she was a kid," her grandmother said. "Patty's parents—that would be your—let's see, your great-great-grandparents—their families emigrated to Oahu from Okinawa. They were both around twenty or so when

Pearl Harbor happened. They met in the Japanese internment camp."

Kiana looked up from the photo. She felt a jab at her heart, a ripple of pain from across the decades.

Her grandmother sighed, nodded solemnly. "Oh, I know. It's shameful. Well, but that's America for you, isn't it? The camp was just over there a ways, out past the highway and the Walmart."

When the jet lag kicked in and Kiana started yawning, her grandmother led her to the guest room. "This used to be your dad's bedroom. Of course, I took down the bikini girl posters a long time ago. Gave the room a feminine makeover, you know."

Kiana looked around at the particle-board bookshelf, the scuffed antique desk in the corner, the framed prints of tropical foliage and crashing waves, the single bed with its lightweight floral print blanket. She'd grown up with a blanket just like it, which Alex had happened to own before she ever met Taylor Ellen Olsen. Kiana's mom had told her of this coincidence many times. Too many times, maybe. But, as she smoothed the blanket on her grandmother's bed, Kiana's heart got all mushy. She loved the lines of connection that ran across generations.

"When Sam brought your mom here to visit, that bed saw a lot of action. Squeak, squeak, squeak." Grandma Kiana chuckled. Then she gave Kiana a funny look. "Hey, how old are you again? Maybe you were conceived on that very trip!"

Kiana shuddered, then laughed despite herself. "No, unfortunately, I've heard the story of that event. Happened a couple of years later, at a Motel 6 in Bakersfield."

"Ooh, high class all the way, huh? That was Sam for you. Well, on the inside, he actually was. In the important ways, I mean." A moment later, her grandmother's smile faded. "Unlike his father."

"Oh?" Kiana was hungry for more names, more stories. But

she could see in her grandmother's eyes that the topic of Sam's father still brought her pain.

Grandma Kiana sat on the edge of the bed, and Kiana joined her. The mattress was firm, with some good bounce to it. Too new to be the same mattress, or so she convinced herself.

"Jake Doucet, that's your grandfather's name. We met summer of 1993, I think it was. Jake came out here from New Orleans to surf. I'd just turned eighteen, was still living at home. Jake was twenty-three. My parents didn't approve, which only made him shine that much brighter in my eyes. We snuck around a lot that summer. He told me he loved me, that we'd be together forever—all the usual empty promises, you know? Then my big brother, Tua, he spotted Jake up on the North Shore, making out with some other chick. A blonde haole tourist, no less. Well, Tua and his buddies, I guess they beat up Jake pretty bad." Grandma Kiana winced. "They told him to fly his pale ass back to the mainland and stay there. Meanwhile, I'd just found out I was pregnant. I tried to get in touch with Jake a few times, but I never heard from him again." She sighed. "Could be dead by now, for all I know. He's older than me, after all. And I'm older than dirt!" Grandma Kiana laughed again, like tropical sunshine through afternoon rainclouds.

Throughout the rest of the trip, her grandmother told an abundance of stories: the subsequent boyfriends that came and went, raising Sam mostly on her own, managing a Sunglass Hut in Waikiki and other dumb jobs. Kiana drank it all in. She took copious notes and photographed everything, including the photos. Including the lone, faded Polaroid of Jake Doucet. As soon as she returned to California, Kiana updated her family tree and started piecing together her Level Up simulation of Grandma Kiana's house and garden. That's how she spent her first summer after college: tinkering with Level Up and sending out job resumes. One of which brought her to a desalination plant in Costa Perdida.

* * *

"Attention passengers. We are experiencing technical difficulties. Please remain on board the train. Thank you for your patience during this brief interruption in service."

It's 12:52, according to the clock above the door. The train has already been stalled for sixteen minutes. The transit bureau's idea of "brief" feels like an eternity. The power is on inside the train, so the issue must be external: the overhead line that propels the train down the tracks. Electromagnetic interference? An overtaxed substation? A domino effect from the blackout earlier?

Kiana sighs at herself. Why is she trying to diagnose the problem when she has no power to solve it? She squirms in her seat, but no position feels comfortable. Instead, she concentrates on taking deep, even breaths. With each inhalation, her abdomen pushes against the terminal. Its bulky presence is a strange comfort.

None of her few fellow passengers seems bothered by the delay—or even to have noticed. They're all lost in holographic worlds projected from their devices.

Kiana turns and stares out the window, into the darkness. A frontage road borders the train tracks. Beyond, she can just make out a smattering of trees, smudges of black silhouettes. Farther away, porch lights dapple the valley. One of those lights could be shining beside her own front door. But which one? And how far away is she? Three, maybe four miles? The gravity of home tugs at her gut. And the longer she stays put, the more likely the police are to track her down.

She gets up from her seat. With a cautious amble to the

front of the train car, she tests her injured joints. Her knee is a little tender, but mostly better. The pain in her hip has lessened—persistent still, but its stab has dulled. She can push through it. No more waiting. With the touch of a button, Kiana opens the door and steps out into the night. She crosses the frontage road and heads off into the chaparral.

Beneath the overcast night sky, she can barely see. As she walks deeper in, the bumpy terrain keeps tripping her up. She crashes through sagebrush. Bushes and trees lurch in front of her, their brittle branches lashing out. When she crawls between the wires of someone's fence, a metal barb snags and tears Jimmy's work shirt. She walks and walks, each step a new opportunity for scratches and stumbles. Sticky sweat gathers on her forehead and back.

How much time has passed since she left the train? Twenty minutes? Forty-five? Part of her feels hopelessly lost. Another part believes that she's nearing home. With every step now, she cycles through the conflicting emotions: despair, hope, despair, hope.

Somewhere nearby, a twig snaps. Footfalls crunch.

Kiana breaks into a run. A rustling at her back. She turns her head, looks over her shoulder. But she can't see a damn—

The ground abandons the soles of her feet. Vegetation whips at her face. Cattails, she realizes. Pond. She twists her torso and lifts the tote bag up, away. Her body splashes into water. But the pond is shallow. She barley breaks the surface before landing in a bed of muck.

Kiana raises her head from the water, and liquid spews from her nose and mouth. She coughs and spits. What comes out is more mud than water. Algae, too. An awful taste, like death, coats her tongue. But she's managed to keep her right arm out of the pond, along with the terminal in its canvas bag.

With her free hand, she drags herself from the pond and crawls up its bank, spitting mud from her mouth.

The sound of footsteps returns—panting breaths, rustling weeds. It's growing nearer. She gropes among the puny cattails for a rock or a stick. She briefly considers using the tote bag as a sling.

An animal's snout appears before her. That golden fur. She knows and loves that friendly face.

"César."

The dog's tongue slathers Kiana's chin with licks.

"Good boy." She wraps her arms around her dog. The familiar body is such a relief. Tears threaten to overwhelm her.

For César to have picked up her scent, she must be close to home. The neighbors to the west, didn't they have a pond? They abandoned their land a couple of years ago. Soon, Kiana will join the northward migration so many others have undertaken in recent years. Millions flocking to Oregon, Washington, Montana. Her own brief migration will end in the Santa Cruz hills.

She stands, dripping scummy water. The tote bag is spattered in mud, but the terminal inside looks only dry.

Her clothes are another story. Once again that night, soaked denim clings to Kiana's legs. The chilly night air sinks quickly into her bones, and a putrid stench assaults her nostrils.

"Come on," she tells César. "Let's go home."

The dog trots off, and Kiana follows, trudging through a former garden, now fallow like her own. Its furrows have hardened into ruts, like a washboard carved into the depleted earth. Further along, the dog plows into a field of knee-high grass. Kiana trails him, through the dry blades. Shivering all over now, she wraps her arms across her chest. She walks faster, hurrying against the cold, hurrying back to Javi.

In the middle of the field, she stumbles over a metal wire

dangling between old wooden fenceposts. She knows this fence. It marks the western border of the former Seabreeze Organic Farm.

César has stopped and turned to check on her, his ears raised in expectation or concern.

"I'm okay," Kiana says, and the dog continues homeward. She doesn't need to follow him anymore. She knows every square foot of this land. She knows, for instance, to circumnavigate their own dried-up pond, where her teenaged mother used to sit and read apocalyptic tomes beneath this large oak tree, which is slowly dying of thirst. She passes the tangle of thorny vines that once produced juicy berries and the spooky, leafless grove that once grew fruit. Kiana remembers picking tangerines from these trees, but that was fifteen years ago, when she first arrived. Land once rich, all but worthless now.

A soft light from the bedroom window draws her toward her house. She thought she'd never see it again. Relief and sorrow get tangled in her gut, a clamp against her breath. But she can't set the sorrow free, not yet.

As she rounds the front of the house, Kiana remembers that the key to her front door remains in police custody. She marches back around to the kitchen door, where a rubber flap covers the cut-out doggie door. The rectangular hole looks to be around the same dimensions as the gable vent in the police station's crawl space. She lowers herself to the small brick patio that extends from their kitchen. When she pushes her head through the rubber flap, César's face is there beside her own, his eyebrows forming triangles of curiosity. Kiana slides her arm through. Shoulder, torso. Walking her palms along the cool linoleum, she drags the rest of her body inside.

A mindless part of her brain tells her to stay where she lies on the kitchen floor. To curl up and sleep. After all, she's finally home. What more could she want?

Kiana slowly stands. She walks down the hall, afraid of what she'll find in her bedroom. She's gotten used to frequently checking on Javi while away from home—texting him, or, if he's sleeping, texting Malia as she watches over him. When was the last time she went so many hours without knowing whether he's still alive?

She leans against the doorframe, dizzy with dread.

The bedside lamp casts a soft glow. Javi is lying in bed, just as Kiana left him. His chest gently rises and falls. Typically, a sure sign of life. Except for the fact that a ventilator is breathing for him, with its eerie mechanical sounds.

Kiana makes herself walk the final steps to Javi's bedside. As she presses her fingertips to her husband's wrist, the vacant eyes of Jane Hamamura flash into her mind. The bad omen terrifies her: a sick jolt to the heart. Then she feels Javi's pulse, and Kiana's own heart rate slows.

When she hears his voice—muffled and faint beneath the clear silicone mask strapped to his pallid face—she has no idea how much time has passed. Javi's eyes are open. Heavy-lidded and glassy, but open. Kiana loosens the mask and rests it on his collarbone.

"Hey." His voice is a soft rasp. He winces in pain, his eyes half-shut. Cancer has blanched his light brown face almost white. It's like viewing a negative image of Anza when spectral fever darkened her forehead and cheeks.

"Hi."

She props up his head with an extra pillow. From the nightstand, she grabs a water bottle and eases its straw between his lips. Javi leans his head forward and takes just a few small sips. Then he falls back into the pillow. Six months ago, those same slight movements would have seemed effortless to him. Now his presence, once so large in her eyes, has been almost infinitely reduced. Tears slide down her cheeks, cutting trails through the drying mud.

"You look." Javi pauses for a long, shallow breath. "Terrible."

Kiana coughs out a laugh. He's on his deathbed, and *she* looks terrible? It isn't funny, but it is. Then it's not again, and the laugh balls up in her throat. New tears stream from her eyes.

"What." He breathes. "Happened?"

For a moment, she considers telling Javi everything. But it doesn't matter now. Kiana holds open the tote bag and leans over so he can see what lies inside.

The corners of his mouth lift into the faintest of smiles.

* * *

Kiana walks back into the bedroom, shading her eyes against the morning sun crashing through the window. On Javi's bedside table, she lays out everything she'll need for the upload process: her tablet, his electromagnetic skull cap, and the unregulated terminal. She's waiting until the last moment to power up the terminal. Kiana recalls Alex's vague warning about how long it might take her internet provider to notify the police: "pretty quickly." On message boards, estimates range from minutes to hours. Kiana can't allow the police to haul her off to jail. Definitely not while Javi is uploading. Not afterward, either. Once his consciousness has been transferred to Level Up, Javi will be waiting for her to log in.

Another item she's laid out: a small case that contains a syringe and a bottled mixture of barbiturates used in assisted suicide. The dose has been prepared in advance by Gilberto Ferriera, the nurse who's been helping her care for Javi these past few months.

Kiana leans over the bed and kisses her sleeping husband on the forehead, his flesh pale and cool. When she straightens again, dizziness washes through her. Only eight hours have passed since she crawled through her own back door, and she's barely rested since. After a rare long shower last night, she disinfected and bandaged the cut on her head. Sometime after three in the morning, she collapsed into dreamless sleep. At dawn, she woke to Javi's labored breath, his tight grunts of pain.

"I'm ready," he'd told her.

Kiana's heart had cramped in her chest. She'd tried to say something in reply but choked on the words. All she could manage was to nod and cry and squeeze his hand. She thought she'd be stronger when the time came. They'd already made the decision weeks ago, so the only question was when. Kiana would have put off the moment forever. But it had to be now. Javi's mental functions would only deteriorate as he slid nearer to death, and his quality of life was diminishing by the day. Kiana had pulled herself together and called Gilberto. He'd promised to arrive by nine.

Kiana powers up the stolen terminal. Such a mundane act, and yet she's exposing herself to the police, once again. It will take them a while before they come after her, she tells herself. There's no need to panic. She can only hope the ISP doesn't notice the data surge and remotely shut her down. She eases the electromagnetic cap onto Javi's head and logs in to Level Up.

Thanks to a hack that Alex provided, Kiana's able to access the backdoor menu for user consciousness profiles. She clicks the *Initiate Upload* button, then steps back to watch as the electrodes on Javi's skull cap pulse gently with silvery light.

The process will take an hour or so, as trillions of synapses are digitized and shuttled off to the Level Up servers in Greenland or Switzerland or Iceland—once of the few foreign lands that hasn't yet overheated, flooded, gotten bombed into oblivion, collapsed into fiscal ruin. A land where servers are kept secure and cool. A land too cold for Javi. Kiana feels a jolt of remorse. Then she remembers: her husband will soon be nothing but data.

She starts packing.

* * *

One duffel bag crammed with clothes is all Kiana is taking with her, all she'll have room for at the Small House. Crouched by the dresser, she zips up the bag and rises stiffly. She allows herself a moment to sit at Javi's bedside and check her tablet. The upload is at 97%. She wonders what resides in the remaining 3% of his brain that isn't yet digitized. It might include an important memory, like the day they met. Or nothing but scenes from his favorite TV shows.

She moves the wheelchair from the corner of the room to the sides of the bed, for when it's time to bring Javi outside. Though Gilberto is in his early sixties, he's big and strong. He'll be able to lift Javi into the chair when the time comes. Then, at the grave, he will lift him out again.

No, she can't think about that now. When she's able to concentrate on each step of the process, she can forget, for small moments, the end goal. She tells herself she can get through this. She has to.

Three soft knocks, each a thump in Kiana's chest. She gasps, even though it must only be Gilberto at the front door. Detectives Turley and Bell would have pounded harder and shouted her name. César would've barked at the presence of mean-hearted strangers.

Kiana's legs and hips ache as she walks down the hall and pulls open the door. Gilberto stands on the front porch, looking funereal in black shirt and gray jeans. The harsh noon sun catches the gray flecks in his short brown hair, the creases around his sympathetic smile.

"Kiana," he sighs. The gravity in his voice, the sorrow in his inflection. There's nothing more he needs to say.

"It'll be a few more minutes," she says. She's told Gilberto about the upload to Level Up. If she can trust him to lethally inject her husband, she figures she can trust him with that incriminating information, as well.

"Leaving today?" Gilberto turns and points to Javi's Subaru wagon. Its hatchback is open, the rear of the car nearly filled with boxes, plastic bins, a favorite lamp, a bag of dog food.

"Yeah, after ... this afternoon."

Gilberto's head nods slowly then settles. He stares into the distance, or maybe his own thoughts. Kiana appreciates his quiet presence, his apparent ease at a time when she feels overwhelmed. It's the kind of strength she's always loved in Javi. He's been Kiana's rock in every storm that's befallen their lives. Now he's little more than a collection of memories. Actually, two sets of memories: Hers of him, and his own memories, now arrayed as zeroes and ones.

"Beautiful land out here," Gilberto says.

Kiana steps onto the porch, squints at the glaring earth. The air is quiet and mild, a windless day. Her gaze lands on the falling-down yurt where she first lived after moving to Costa Perdida, and where her mother and grandmother once lived, too. The structure will crumble one day soon, its lattice of wooden beams eroding and returning to the earth. Just as Javi's body will.

"Well, beautiful to me, anyway," Gilberto says. "Since escaping the flooding in Rio de Janeiro, I appreciate the desert."

"I'm tired of it. I'm ready to live in the woods again." *Even if they burn*, she thinks, but keeps the words inside.

A bell tone chimes from the back of the house. They turn in unison and walk in silence to the bedroom.

Javi looks frail, drained, as if the upload has actually tapped his essence. Then the truth hits Kiana all over again: cancer has been draining his essence for months now. His essence was already nearly gone.

She checks her tablet. *Upload Complete.* Below that, a second message: *Data Processing.* In this stage, Level Up integrates the uploaded information into the user's avatar profile. Javi's mind is stuck in a digital interregnum. This in-between state makes Kiana nervous, but she knows the program is extremely reliable. Javi's data is secure.

She turns to Gilberto.

"It's time?" he says.

While Gilberto prepares the injection, Kiana crawls into bed alongside Javi and nudges him awake. She tries to smile for him, and her jaw trembles. "Hey, baby," she says.

His eyes barely open, flicker shut, crack open again. "Upload worked?"

"Yeah." Kiana watches Gilberto as he holds the syringe up to the sunlight. The liquid barbiturate mixture looks clear as water. Tears fill her eyes. She clutches Javi's hand in both of hers.

He lightly squeezes back. "It's okay," he tells her. His voice is so thin, thinner than air. "I'm ready," he says again.

Kiana will never be ready. But it's time. She looks up at Gilberto, nods.

The nurse sits in the bedside chair, his eyes locking firmly onto Javi's. Gilberto swallows hard. "Javier, it is your wish to receive a lethal injection? Do I have your consent?"

"Yes, I. Consent." Every couple of syllables, Javi takes a slow, rasping breath. "Thank you. Gilberto."

Then Javi's head turns slowly back, his kind brown eyes finding Kiana's own.

For the last time, she thinks, and a sob bleats from her throat. Tears pour out of her. "I love you so much, baby."

Javi's cheeks flinch as the needle enters his vein. The plunger sinks into the barrel of the syringe, and Kiana watches the deadly liquid vanish.

"See you. Soon." Javi smiles at her, and his eyelids fall shut. His grip goes slack between her palms.

Kiana lays her cheek on his chest, on the thin jade green cotton shirt she bought for him a dozen years ago. A lifetime lay before them then. The tears course from her eyes. She cries and chokes and gulps for air and can't stop crying. She's certain that she'll die like this, and she wishes that she would.

CHAPTER TWENTY

SEPTEMBER, 2057

Kiana drives slowly through the streets of downtown Santa Cruz. As she draws nearer to the ocean, the neighborhood devolves into squatter dwellings. Semi-homeless people shamble down the sidewalks. The area is frequently flooded by high-tide waves that crest over the seawall, water rushing through the old Boardwalk fairground rides and into nearby homes. Electricity is sporadic. It's only eight o'clock at night, but darkness lies heavy on the decrepit bungalows and sporadic encampments. As Kiana turns onto the remains of West Cliff Drive, a creature limps out into the street. She hits her brakes. A gray cat is caught in her headlights. It crouches, pausing to stare into the Subaru's bright beams, then limps away.

She longs to go after the cat, to bring it home, to care for it. It's the same with every stray she's encountered over the past seven months. But César doesn't get along with cats. And the Small House is too small to divide into territories. Besides, Kiana knows that a cat won't fill the void inside her. Nothing will.

Only one thing comes close.

She pulls into the motel parking lot and cuts the engine. Further inland, the late-summer air is warm, but, as she steps out of the car, a cold breeze rolls in off the ocean. She zips up her hoodie and threads her arms through the straps of her backpack. Though the fiber hookup is nearby, Kiana never knows when she might need to run.

"Lock." She waits for the soft clunking sound from her car door, then heads toward the back of the motel. The business went under years ago, but that doesn't mean the rooms are empty, that no one is watching.

As she rounds the wreckage of a stripped-for-parts minivan, she nearly trips over a pair of legs. For a moment, she thinks they belong to a dead body. Then she hears something between a mutter and a moan. A person lies slouched against the motel wall. A young man's face, high cheekbones. In the dimness, Kiana can't tell whether his eyes are open a sliver or completely shut. The sleeve of his black jacket is rolled up past the elbow, where a needle dangles from a vein.

The needle in Javi's arm. The image returns to Kiana, as vivid as the night he died. She remembers Gilberto's hand on her back, his sonorous voice informing her that Javi's pulse had ceased. Kiana had asked Gilberto, beforehand, to make sure she didn't get lost in grief, and he'd pulled her through. He'd wheeled Javi's body to the grave she'd dug. They buried him with nothing but his light cotton pajamas between his body and the soil. Returned to the earth, just as Javi had wanted. Her voice quavering, she'd read the poem he'd chosen, "Dame la mano," by Gabriela Mistral. After reciting the final line—which she translated in her mind as, *We'll be a dance on the hill and nothing more*—Gilberto had wrapped his arm around her shoulders and guided her back to the front porch. She'd pushed a wad of bills into his hand and turned away, before he could protest. Less than an hour later, Kiana ushered César into the backseat of Javi's car and drove away from their faded yellow house for the final time.

Kiana's focus returns to the young man lying at her feet. He's checked out of the world—whether for an hour or forever, she doesn't know. Tonight, Kiana has no extra room in her heart. Living each day is hard enough. She leaves the junkie where he lies.

A chainlink fence stands between her and the rear of the motel, but she scales it easily using moves she's learned from previous excursions to this spot. She's glad the fence is here. It decreases the likelihood that someone will stumble across her while she's distracted in Level Up.

Only a short stretch of cracked asphalt stands between the back of the motel and the crumbling seawall. From beyond the concrete barricade come the ocean sounds: the gasping breaths, the whispers and rasping moans. She crouches by the motel wall and moves aside the warped planks that conceal the fiber optic junction box. Kiana put the planks there herself, months ago. It's one of a dozen or so discretely located hookups she's found across Santa Cruz County. The authorities have since discovered several of these—quite possibly due to Kiana's own usage—and have entombed the junctions in concrete. On one occasion, at a spot near the old Safeway, she managed to disconnect her terminal and dash around a corner only seconds before a police cruiser arrived, its siren yelping. As though a murder had taken place. No, not even a suicide.

Kiana isn't ready to abandon real life for Level Up. Not yet. She still has César to care for. And Alex. Though remarkably healthy for a sixty-seven-year-old at this late stage of the Anthropocene, Alex is beginning to decline. Her strawberry blonde hair has gone completely gray, her long stride has slowed, and she no longer keeps abreast of the latest technological advances—what few advances occur anymore. Alex will need Kiana more and more, and Kiana still needs her. Both for the comfort and company she provides, and for the memories of Ellen that she holds. For the time being, Kiana will make do with these clandestine visits to her virtual family.

From her backpack, she withdraws her special terminal, plugs it into its battery pack, and connects it to the junction with practiced efficiency. She pulls on her skull cap, sits as comfortably as she can on the lumpy terrain, and logs into Level Up.

An instant later, she stands in an empty virtual space, devoid of sound and smell. Unlike the chilly Santa Cruz night, the temperature in her Level Up entry portal is just right. The walls are really mere suggestions of walls: neutral hues that shift gradually over time. Before her is her menu of collected worlds, from *Germany 1945* to *Honolulu 2041*. Kiana reaches out, touches *Home*.

Even after seven months of the multi-sensory Level Up experience, Kiana is surprised every time by the rush of stimuli upon reentry. A warm breeze graces her cheek. The light from the front porch of their house falls across their front yard, where Anza stands in plush green grass, throwing a stick for César. From the field out back, the sound of crickets pulses through the night air. The cushions of the wicker loveseat are soft against Kiana butt and back. She melts into the comforting presence of a familiar arm around her shoulders. This barrage of sensations causes her to gasp.

Javi turns. He stares at her a moment, then smiles his wide, generous smile. "Welcome back."

Kiana spends a moment lost in his eyes. She tries to speak, but emotions lump together in her throat. She was just remembering his death, and now here is, so vivid with life—or what feels like life. She swallows. "You can always tell."

"When it's the real you?" His soft chuckle, it warms her from the chest on out. "Of course I can tell."

She leans into her husband, inhales deeply. His shirt smells like their actual laundry soap, but she misses Javi's true bodily scents: the salt and musk of him. They watch their daughter, laughing as she pulls at the stick in César's mouth, playing tug-of-war.

Javi raises a glass to his mouth. Lemonade, it looks like. There's a bandaid on his thumb. Last week, it was mummified in gauze. The wound must be healing. An accident with a hammer, he'd told her, while repairing the greenhouse. In Level Up's default settings, a building would never need repair, and an injured thumb would heal instantly. Kiana likes it that Javi has decided to make their little world less than perfect. It's more interesting that way. The longer Javi can avoid Level Up inertia, the longer Kiana can maintain the self-delusion that he's her real husband. She depends on that delusion to get her through the dreary tedium of the real world.

Kiana sighs, expelling the gloom from her lungs. If only she could stay like this forever. She has to remind herself *not* to stay, not to be lulled into believing this is real. Just a minute or two inside Level Up, and she's ready to cast aside her actual human body. The one that's crouching in the dark like a feral creature. The one that, should she linger too long, might rot in jail, where the internet would be highly regulated. Her family, reduced to ghostly holograms.

She sits up straight.

Javi grunts and unwraps his arm from around her shoulder. He calls out to Anza, "Okay, hija. Come give Mama a hug before bedtime."

Anza releases the stick and bounds across the yard. César has won the game, but that was never his objective, and he cocks his head in befuddlement at his departing playmate.

Kiana could almost feel sorry for the dog, except he's not the real César, just a very good imitation. The actual César is likely napping on a throw rug, waiting for Kiana to return home.

Anza is halfway up the front steps when she freezes. For a brief moment, Kiana thinks it's a game her child's playing. But everything is frozen: dog, husband, the mild breeze, her own avatar's ability to move or smell or feel the virtual world. The seconds in digital limbo tick by. The sensation of nothingness crawls under her skin, gnaws on her nerves. She should give up, quit the session. But there is Anza's beaming face, her eyes nearly meeting Kiana's. Any moment now, the program will unstick. Or it won't. And Kiana will have to try again some other—

Anza's avatar jerks into motion again. She hops up the last two steps, completely unaware of the interruption to her world. Kiana throws open her arms as her daughter crawls into her lap. At ten years old, she's mostly outgrown this habit. Or, according to Javi, Anza only does this when Kiana's logged into Level Up and inhabiting her avatar. Apparently, her daughter can also tell the difference: virtual Mama from real Mama.

Kiana hugs Anza tightly to her chest. The weight and bulk and warmth of her little girl is nearly perfectly real. The sensation is such a comfort that Kiana can mostly ignore the telltale signs that she's being manipulated by a digital system. The flesh of Anza's forearm is pliant and soft against Kiana's fingertips, but in a way that is generic, vague. It's the feeling of touching someone in a dream. She buries her nose in Anza's hair and inhales the clean, floral scent of her shampoo. It is a smell of home. A smell that makes Kiana's chest ache and brings her a moment of peace.

A buzzing whine zips past her ear. A mosquito? Kiana flaps her hand uselessly at the air.

"Ow!" Anza smacks herself on the neck. The bug lies smashed against her skin.

Kiana flicks it off her daughter. In horror, she turns to Javi.

He laughs. "Don't worry. There's no malaria in Level Up, remember? No disease of any kind."

"Right." Kiana exhales slowly. She shakes her head. Javi has added mosquitoes now? Okay, good. More friction. She'd worried before that Anza hadn't faced enough challenges over the last few years, since her upload. Now Javi is here, inhabiting his avatar full-time, tweaking the settings, guiding the process. To make the ideal world truer, better. Because life without friction is meaningless. And all Kiana wants for her daughter is a meaningful life.

Though Kiana can only visit periodically, and only briefly each time, she now treasures every minute in Level Up. Being with Javi, watching Anza grow. So what if her husband and daughter are nothing but zeroes and ones? Maybe the so-called real world is just a simulation, too. Her heart and mind and soul, mere digital constructs. All her loved ones, encoded.

These theories, they don't matter to Kiana right now. Because, in this simple moment, the people she loves the most are so very real. For the next few minutes, they are alive.

ACKNOWLEDGMENTS

The act of writing is often viewed as a solitary pursuit. The truth is that a great many people contribute to the writing and publishing of a book. I am grateful to everyone who helped me bring this novel into the world.

Thank you to Lisa Diane Kastner, the Founder and Executive Editor of Running Wild Press, for believing in my manuscript. It means the world to me. And to my editor, Rebecca Dimyan, for her inspiring observations, careful eye, and enthusiasm for the project. Thanks, as well, to Evangeline Estropia for guiding my book through the production process, Emir Orucevic for his wonderful cover, and everyone at Running Wild for all they do.

Thank you to Joseph Levens, editor of *The Summerset Review*, for publishing "One Breath, and Another," an excerpt from *All Her Loved Ones, Encoded*, in their Fall 2021 issue.

I owe an immense debt of gratitude to my writing group, The Guttery. The novel I began in late 2019 is very different to the final version. The emergence of the COVID-19 pandemic shifted my perspective on the world and on the kind of story that felt important to tell. For their tremendous guidance in the rewrite of this novel, thank you to the thoughtful and talented writers in The Guttery during that time: Anatoly Molotkov,

Brittney Corrigan, Shari MacDonald Strong, Cheyenne Montgomery, Jessie Glenn, and Tammy Lynne Stoner.

Thank you to Annie Bloom's Books for providing the wonderful literary atmosphere that is also my day job. I wrote portions of this novel during my lunch breaks in the employee loft, where I would thumb urgent words into my phone.

Thank you to John Jones for technical guidance and steadfast friendship. Thanks to Laura Stanfill for her valuable advice and great kindness. A huge cheer to the Portland literary community, who are so supportive of one another and whose very existence inspires me to write.

A massive thank you to my mother, Gaynl. Throughout my life, she has always encouraged my creativity.

Thank you most of all to my wife, Liz, for her support and love, and for always believing in me.

Running Wild Press publishes stories that cross genres with great stories and writing. RIZE publishes great genre stories written by people of color and by authors who identify with other marginalized groups. Our team consists of:

Lisa Diane Kastner, Founder and Executive Editor
Cody Sisco, Acquisitions Editor, RIZE
Benjamin White, Acquisition Editor, Running Wild
Peter A. Wright, Acquisition Editor, Running Wild
Resa Alboher, Editor
Angela Andrews, Editor
Sandra Bush, Editor
Ashley Crantas, Editor
Rebecca Dimyan, Editor
Abigail Efird, Editor
Aimee Hardy, Editor
Henry L. Herz, Editor
Cecilia Kennedy, Editor
Barbara Lockwood, Editor
Scott Schultz, Editor

Evangeline Estropia, Product Manager
Kimberly Ligutan, Product Manager
Lara Macaione, Marketing Director
Joelle Mitchell, Licensing and Strategy Lead
Pulp Art Studios, Cover Design
Standout Books, Interior Design
Polgarus Studios, Interior Design

Learn more about us and our stories at www. runningwildpress.com

Loved this story and want more? Follow us at www.runningwildpress.com, www.facebook.com/runningwildpress, on Twitter @lisadkastner @RunWildBooks